T0152340

The Rabbi
Finds Her Way

The Rabbi Finds Her Way

A Pearl Ross-Levy Novel

Robert Schoen
with Catherine deCuir

Stone Bridge Press • *Berkeley, California*

Published by
Stone Bridge Press
P. O. Box 8208, Berkeley, CA 94707
TEL 510-524-8732 • sbp@stonebridge.com • www.stonebridge.com

This is a work of fiction. Names, characters, businesses, places, events, locales, and incidents are either the products of the author's imagination or used in a fictitious manner. Any resemblance to actual persons, living or dead, or actual events is purely coincidental.

© 2019 Robert Schoen and Catherine deCuir.

Cover and author photographs by James & Pamela Au Photography.

All rights reserved.

No part of this book may be reproduced in any form without permission from the publisher.

Printed in the United States of America.

10 9 8 7 6 5 4 3 2 1   2023 2022 2021 2020 2019

p-ISBN: 978-1-61172-052-5
e-ISBN: 978-1-61172-937-5

For our mothers

ז״ל

Charm is deceptive, and beauty is fleeting;
But a woman who fears the Lord is to be praised.

Proverbs 31:30

After all, Ginger Rogers did everything that Fred Astaire did.
She just did it backwards and in high heels.

Bob Thaves, quoted by Ann Richards

CONTENTS

The Rabbi
Finds Her Way

Pearl

December 19, 2003

On Friday night the rabbi and her husband made love, and she conceived.

Eighteen months earlier

"Usually at this point in the service, I'd give you a few words of Jewish wisdom, display my brilliantly subtle sense of humor, and then we'd finish up with some closing prayers and songs. But I know that's not why many of you are here tonight."

Rabbi Craig Cohen flashed a smile as he paused, waiting for the remarkably large crowd of congregants to finish laughing at their senior rabbi and settle back in the pews. Even in this congregation of almost a thousand families, a normal Friday night service typically attracted, maybe, fifty or a hundred. Perhaps more if there was a special musical program. But tonight's service marked the official welcome of Lakeshore Temple's new associate rabbi.

Craig scanned the crowd. He looked up into the first balcony, which was packed. Typically, the balconies of the large sanctuary were only open during High Holiday services, but tonight they needed additional seating. He continued.

"As I'm sure you've noticed, the young woman sitting behind me on the *bima* appears to know all the prayers."

Sometimes it's okay to go for the easy laughs, he thought, as the congregants again broke into sustained laughter. Craig turned around and watched his new associate smile the smile that had helped win over not only him and the cantor, but the members of the rabbinical selection committee as well. He turned back to the congregation.

"You may have already read or heard about Rabbi Pearl Ross, and some of you have had the pleasure of meeting her. But for those of you who have not, let me tell you a little about her.

"Rabbi Ross grew up just a few miles from here. She was born in Oakland [he paused for applause], and spent her teenage years in Berkeley where she attended Berkeley High School [some scattered applause, probably from her fellow alumni]. I've been told that her best friend was a Catholic girl who dragged her to Mass every Sunday. [Laughter.] In retribution, Pearl dragged her friend, Mary, to Shabbat services on Saturday. [More laughter.]

"Instead of attending the University of California at Berkeley, where her father was—and still is—a professor, she instead went to Stanford. [Cheers and good-natured boos, acknowledging the long-standing rivalry between the two universities.] All those hours attending Mass must have affected her brain a little, since she decided to major in Comparative Religion. After that, where else was there for her to go but to rabbinical school? The Catholic priesthood was out."

He was having a good time, and the laughs were coming easily. But it was time to hand over the mic.

"Let me thank the selection committee for their hard work interviewing some incredibly talented candidates. After you've all had a chance to meet her, I know you'll agree with Cantor Sanders and me that the committee made a wise choice. And although we don't usually encourage applause on Shabbat, let's make an exception as we welcome Rabbi Pearl Ross!"

Wearing her best black pants suit, a new white blouse, and a colorful *kippah* pinned atop her black curls, Pearl stood and embraced Craig. She stepped to the lectern, looking out at her new congregation, whose members stood as they clapped enthusiastically.

Rabbi Cohen had warned her when they'd met earlier in the afternoon not to expect as large a crowd at future services. "They can't wait to see our new recruit. But don't worry. They'll love you. Just do what you know how to do. We've got your back."

And as promised, behind her on the bima stood Rabbi Cohen and Cantor Sanders, joining in the applause. While she thought she should be nervous, somehow she wasn't. It helped that her parents were sitting in the third row, and the members of the large rabbinical search committee were all in attendance. And smiling.

"Shabbat Shalom! And thank you!"

As Pearl waited, thoughts flickered through her mind.

She'd graduated from the rabbinical seminary in Cincinnati, had been ordained just a year before, and had then spent the next eight months at a congregation in a Philadelphia suburb filling in for a rabbi who was on sabbatical.

Pearl thought of that time as a stint with a minor-league team while she waited for a position to open in the majors. She'd always wanted to move back to California, hopefully Northern California, where she'd grown up and gone to college, but believed the chances of that happening were remote—the number of synagogues (and jobs) was limited.

Then came the heads-up phone call from Ari, a friend

from rabbinical school who'd graduated a few years before she did. He informed her that he was leaving his position as associate rabbi at the Reform temple in Oakland to join a congregation closer to where *he'd* grown up in New York.

Pearl jumped on it, applying for the position the moment it was posted. There were, she'd learned, a dozen qualified applicants for the job.

In private, the woman heading up the search committee confided in her. "Pearl, you have virtually all of the qualities we're looking for. You're a local and know the Bay Area. You have practical and academic experience in the interfaith arena—that's really important these days. It's a plus that you can speak some Spanish. You have a good sense of humor, and seem to sincerely like both children and seniors. Also, I'd be lying if I didn't mention—further off the record—that it would be nice to see a female clergy member sitting up there on the bima. *I* feel that way, anyway. Our time has come. It's not a done deal, but you're in the running—in the top three."

Pearl was ecstatic when she was offered the job the following week.

As she scanned the many faces in the Sanctuary, Pearl *knew* she was in the right place. And her time *had* come. The applause died down, and the congregation sat.

"Thank you! Thank you all for welcoming me to Lakeshore Temple. Your caring and generosity have been overwhelming. As Rabbi Cohen mentioned, even though I spent much of my childhood in Berkeley, I was born in Oakland, and lived here for several years before my father moved us closer to the UC campus where he still works. He likes to say he moved 'for business purposes.' The same reason my grandfather gave when he changed our family name."

She waited for the laughter to subside.

"And that business about my friend Mary and me going

to Mass? It's all true. If you haven't been to church recently, I recommend it. It might give you a greater appreciation for the Saturday *Kiddush* lunches we Jews often take for granted.

"And if all of you Cal grads out there want to give me a hard time for going to Stanford, hey, you're in good company—my father *and* my mother are still upset about it. Imagine going to the Big Game and sitting on the opposite side of the field from your parents." This brought the reaction she knew it would, mostly chants of *Go Bears!* She laughed along with them.

"The Torah portion tomorrow morning is *Bechukotai* from the Book of Leviticus. In this *parshah* God promises that if the people of Israel keep God's commandments they will enjoy material prosperity and dwell in security in their homeland. But God also delivers a harsh 'rebuke,' warning of the exile, persecution, and other evils that will befall them if they abandon their covenant with God.

"Nevertheless—and this is what I personally love about God—even when we are in the land of our enemies, God promises to not cast us away:

I will never break My covenant with the people, for I am the Lord their God.

"I know as well as anyone that it's not always easy to keep our covenant with God. We live in a crazy world. Where's Moses when we need him?" She paused and looked out at her new congregation. She felt peace, contentment, gratification. Tonight was the culmination of ten years of very hard work and study. Okay, and some luck, maybe.

"But I've found that if we try—if we do our best to follow God's most important lessons ..." she turned slightly and gestured with her right arm to a carving of the Ten Commandments "... there they are, listed right behind me above the Ark—we stand a good chance of not going too far astray.

Just *do these things* and *don't do those other things.* You know the drill."

She felt it was time to finish up. After all, she didn't want to push her luck.

"I want to thank everyone who made it possible for me to join Rabbi Cohen, Cantor Sanders, and this wonderful congregation. You can't imagine how happy I am to be here. I sincerely hope that I can live up to your hopes and my dreams.

"And in the tradition of Jewish children everywhere, let me add, Thank you, Mom and Dad. I love you." Pearl blew a kiss to her parents as the applause began again. She spoke into the microphone.

"Shabbat Shalom. Please turn to page ..."

Mary

One Sunday morning as fourteen-year-old Pearl Ross was sleeping, her mother came into her room and sat down next to her on the bed. Shayna gently woke her daughter.

"Mom?"

"Yes, honey. Good morning." She brushed Pearl's dark curls from her face. The girl was now a freshman in high school, and maturing, it seemed, more and more every day.

"I guess I was sleeping."

"I know, sweetie. I'm sorry to wake you, but I need to talk to you, and it can't wait."

"Okay." As she brushed sleep from her eyes, she sensed a quiet urgency in her mother's voice.

"I have some bad news about somebody you know from school."

"Who? What happened?" Pearl was awake now.

Shayna took her daughter's hand in hers and looked at her beautiful young face.

"Pearl, there's a girl in your class named Mary Frances O'Connell. She's new in the school system this year."

"Sure, I know Mary, a little bit. Not too well, but, yeah. Did something happen to her?"

"Yes. There was a serious car accident. Her father was driving. There was a drunk driver. Mary's been severely injured."

"Oh no! Poor Mary!"

Shayna could sense the empathy in her daughter's voice. "Yes. But that's not the worst of it. Her mother was killed in the accident."

"Her mom is dead?"

"Yes."

Pearl was silent. Shayna knew that her daughter hadn't been in this type of situation before. She watched Pearl closely to see how she was reacting. Mild shock, if nothing else.

"How … is Mary doing?" Pearl asked.

"Not well. She was badly injured. She's had surgery. She's lost one of her eyes."

"Oh no!" Pearl put her hands to her face.

"And she has serious internal injuries. This all happened late Friday night. Mary's father wasn't injured, and neither was Margaret, her younger sister. They're both okay."

"But her mom is dead?"

"Yes, honey."

"And she lost one of her eyes?"

"Yes, Pearl. She's also had major surgery for the internal injuries she sustained. She's in the hospital. It will be a long recovery."

"What can we do to help?"

"The school called me. I'll be one of the coordinators working with the counselors in your school. Whenever there's a tragedy, we do things like this. Lots of the kids will have, well, reactions, just like you did. And we need to be there to help them through such tragedies."

"Mom, does this mean you'll be at school tomorrow?"

"Yes, honey, I'll be working with the counseling department. But I wanted to talk to you now and let you know what was happening."

Pearl was silent. Shayna continued.

"It's important that the family have as much support as possible, and as soon as possible. And because Mary Frances is your classmate, I thought you might want to help."

"Sure, Mom. What can I do?"

"I'm going over to the hospital after breakfast. I thought you might like to visit Mary Frances. But only if you feel comfortable. We don't know what friends or family might be there, but her father is probably still in shock. He'll need all the support we can give him. I know Margaret is staying with a neighbor."

Pearl didn't say anything. She just got out of bed and went into the bathroom. Shayna smiled. Her daughter, she knew, would be a *mensch*.

After a quiet breakfast with her parents and Ruth, her younger sister, Pearl and her mother got into the car, drove to Alta Bates Hospital, and parked.

They checked in at the desk, held hands as they went up the elevator, and walked over to the nurses' station. Sitting in the small waiting area was a man with his head in his hands. "I believe that's Mary Frances' father," Shayna whispered.

As they walked over, he looked up.

"Mr. O'Connell?"

He nodded. Pearl could see the grief on his drawn face. His hair was messy, and he hadn't shaved. She saw that one of his shoelaces was untied, and a half-eaten sandwich was sitting on top of a pile of *People* magazines nearby. He seemed much older than her mother, but Pearl realized that might not be true.

Her mother continued. "My name is Shayna Ross. I'm a therapist, and I often work with the Berkeley High counselors. This is my daughter, Pearl. She goes to school with Mary Frances."

He was slow to react, but finally stood and reached to shake her outstretched hand.

"Dennis O'Connell," was all he said. Then he sat again and Shayna sat in the chair next to him.

She said, softly, "I want you to know that we're here to help as much as we can. In fact, I'll be coordinating with other counselors and talking to some of Mary's classmates tomorrow, helping them adjust to this tragedy. But today, we're here for you, Mr. O'Connell. My daughter has come with me to perhaps spend a few moments with Mary Frances. We know that sometimes teenagers like to be in the presence of people their own age. Do you think that would be okay?"

He looked at her and said, "Mrs. Ross, I can use all the help I can get." He turned to Pearl and attempted a smile. "Tell me again, please. What's your name?"

"Pearl."

"Pearl, thank you for being here. I imagine this isn't easy for you, but your mother is right. Mary Frances is going to need all the friends and all the help she can get. Please forgive my condition. Did your mom tell you what happened?"

"A little. Mom said Mary lost … an eye. And, and her mother was …"

"Yes." He sighed. "It's going to be hard for her, and for all of us. Mary was in surgery all day yesterday. She has internal injuries—serious injuries, they tell me," he said, looking at Pearl's mother. She nodded. He spoke directly to Pearl.

"Pearl, we can take a look and see if she's awake. Do you want to do that?"

"Yes." They stood up and Mr. O'Connell led Pearl to Mary's room, opened the door, and saw that his daughter was indeed awake but quite immobile. He sat in a chair next to the bed and touched his daughter's bright red hair, much of which was hidden by bandages. There were IV bags on a stand above her bed, with tubes leading to her arm.

"Hi, honey, how are you doing?"

"Hi, Dad. I'm okay. I just can't see very well." Mary was speaking slowly.

"I know, baby. It will get better."

"I miss Mom."

"I know. I miss her, too. We all do. She's in a good place, though."

"I know, Dad. But I still miss her."

"We're going to miss her for a very long time."

They were both silent for a moment, and then he said, "There's someone here to see you. Someone from your school."

Mary paused again. "Who?"

"It's Pearl. Pearl Ross."

"I know Pearl. She's in my Spanish class," Mary said. "And another class. English." Mary tilted her head so she could see better. Half of her upper face was bandaged. The other half revealed a scattering of freckles. Her leg was in traction.

Poor Mary, Pearl thought. "Hi, Mary Frances," Pearl said, putting as much of a smile in her voice as she could.

"Hi, Pearl. Thanks for coming to see me."

Mr. O'Connell said, "I'm going to leave you girls by yourselves. Is that okay, Mary?"

She nodded, and grimaced as she did so.

After the adults left the room, Pearl sat in the chair next to the bed. Without thinking about it, she took Mary's hand in hers.

"How are you doing, Mary?"

"How do I look?"

"You look like hell."

"That's how I feel."

Pearl wasn't sure what to say next. "I'm so sorry about your mom."

"Thank you. It hurts when I cry, so let's not talk about it now."

After some silence, Pearl asked, "Do you want something? A drink of water, maybe?"

"That sounds good. There's a cup somewhere with a straw in it."

Pearl found it and held the cup so that Mary could drink through the straw.

"I'm glad you didn't ask me to get you, like, a Big Mac or something."

Mary smiled weakly. "I'm too tired to talk. You talk. I'll listen. Tell me about yourself. I don't know anything about you."

And with that, Mary Frances O'Connell shut her unbandaged eye, and Pearl told her about herself, where she lived, what subjects and teachers she liked and didn't like, her favorite foods. Whatever came into her mind. After a few minutes, she could tell Mary was asleep. Pearl was still holding her hand.

Pearl and Jack

Pearl met Jack on the second Friday of June 2002. She was staying at her parents' home in Berkeley until she found her own place to live. She'd been the associate rabbi at Lakeshore Temple for just four weeks, barely enough time for the ink to dry on her new business cards:

RABBI PEARL ROSS
Associate Rabbi

That morning at breakfast, her parents chatted about the faculty recruitment luncheon they'd be attending later that morning at UC Berkeley.

"Why don't you join us?" her mother asked.

Pearl looked at her mother and listened between the lines. She realized it wasn't really a question. *I guess I've learned something from my mother, the shrink,* Pearl thought, looking into her mother's dark eyes.

"Sure. Come with us," said her father. David Ross was a serious-looking chemistry professor at Cal. He had curly salt-and-pepper hair and wore wire-rimmed glasses that he was constantly putting on and taking off. "It's a beautiful day, and lunch is on the governor." Although she'd never seen him wearing a tweed jacket with leather elbow patches, Pearl often wondered why he didn't own one.

"Well, I don't need to be at work until two," she said. "And I'm always up for a free lunch." *Hopefully there'll be a salad.* She was still trying to lose the five pounds she'd gained at Passover.

And now Pearl was sitting alone at a table in the peaceful

Faculty Glade, watching as her father schmoozed a couple of candidates and her mother chatted with a group of faculty and spouses. The day was indeed beautiful, a little on the warm side. Pearl wished she'd gone for that long, early-morning jog she'd promised herself; but now it was (as it often was) too late for that.

For the luncheon, she'd chosen to wear a summery white sundress, sandals, and a straw hat with a brim. Her long, dark curls and favorite oversized sunglasses framed her face.

One of the faculty candidates had already caught her eye. He was tall, dark, and—she couldn't help hoping—maybe even Jewish. As he wandered over toward her table, she sat quietly, sipping her iced tea. He seemed to be several inches taller than her five-foot-seven. And, she thought, he had a nice build.

"Mind if I join you?"

Yes!

"It depends on how long you're planning to stay."

He laughed and sat down facing her, as he extended his hand.

"Jack Levy."

Yes!

"I'm Pearl Ross." She looked at his face. He had strong features, dark brown eyes, a bright smile, and a slight bump on the bridge of his nose that suggested a sports injury. "So, tell me, what's your field of study?"

He smiled. "Get ready to be bored. I'm primarily an entomologist, but my research involves a lot of chemistry."

"The chemistry of bugs."

"You could look at it that way. If you want."

They sipped their drinks.

"And what do you do?" he asked.

"I'm a rabbi."

He smiled again. "No, really."

Pearl was taken by surprise, but tried not to show it. She looked at him for a moment and thought, *What's the best way to handle this?* She quickly decided.

"I'll tell you what I really do," she said in a serious tone. "But you have to promise to be discreet."

"I am one of the most discreet men you'll ever meet."

Pearl reached into her purse, took out one of her new business cards and a pen, and turned the card face down so she could write on the back.

She looked at him again. "I'm an exotic dancer at a members-only club in Oakland."

He said nothing.

She continued. "And I want you to come see me perform tomorrow morning. Let me just say that this is a very special performance. After the show there will be a lunch by invitation-only." On the back of the card, she wrote, *10:30 a.m. sharp!* and *Free Lunch.*

Pearl put her pen away and handed him the card so that he could see what she'd written. She watched his dark eyes as he turned the card over.

Again, he said nothing; but she watched him blink as he stared at the card. And then he looked up and spoke.

"I'm really sorry. I'm such a jerk."

"And for being such a jerk, you're going to take me out to dinner tomorrow night. When I see you at the temple kiddush lunch after the service, I'll tell you where and when."

He put the card in his shirt pocket. Then he said, "Anything else … Rabbi?"

She thought a moment. "Not really."

He paused. "Why don't I bring you a small gift to make up for my mistake."

She stood, smiled, and extended her hand. "It's not really necessary. Pleasure meeting you, Jack Levy."

He stood and took her hand. "May I assume you are related to David and Shayna Ross?"

"Yes, they're my parents."

"My mother's name is Shayna, too."

"You're joking."

"Actually, I'm not.

Pearl just smiled and walked away.

The Pirate

David Ross drove his young daughter to Alta Bates Hospital after school on Monday afternoon. Hand-in-hand, they rode the elevator up to the floor where Mary Frances was recovering.

Mary's father was once again in the waiting area, and Pearl introduced her father to Mr. O'Connell. She asked him if she could see Mary.

"Why don't you take a look in her room—I think the nurses just finished with her." He paused, then added, "Pearl, please remember that Mary's not in the best physical or emotional shape right now." He tried to smile as he said this, but Pearl could see concern and pain on his face. Pearl sensed he might have been crying.

"Sure. I understand." She entered the room and again sat in a chair next to the bed. Much of Mary's head and one eye were still bandaged, but she turned and looked over.

"Hi, Pearl." She extended her hand, and Pearl took it in hers.

"Hi. How do you feel today?"

"How do I look?"

"You still look like hell."

"And that's how I still feel." She adjusted herself a little in the bed. "If it weren't for all the dope they're giving me, I'd probably feel worse."

"Well, at least you haven't lost your sense of humor."

"Yeah. I'm going to need my sense of humor. Because now my mom's dead and I only have one eye."

"I'm so sorry, Mary." They sat in silence for a while. A few tears rolled down Mary's cheek. Pearl grabbed a tissue from a nearby box and reached over to wipe her face.

Mary spoke quietly. "The only people with one eye are pirates." More time passed. Then Mary snickered, "Look out! I'm Mary Frances O'Connell, the notorious Catholic pirate! My treasure chest is filled to the brim with rosary beads and scapulars. I wear a black eye patch, just like Blackbeard, or Bluebeard, or whoever he was."

"Nah. I'd say you look more like Redbeard."

Mary and Pearl started laughing.

Mary said, "Stop making me laugh—it hurts! My ribs are broken."

"Sorry."

Mary paused, then said, "You know, I have internal injuries." She closed her eye. "I heard the doctors whispering. I don't think I'll be able to have children."

"Mary, you're too young to have children!"

Mary said nothing.

Pearl continued, "Maybe *I'll* have some children and you can just visit them and bring toys and gifts and stuff."

Mary laughed. "That might work."

"Or maybe I'll have an *extra* one and you can have it." They laughed a little louder.

Their laughter could be heard through the door by their fathers, who exchanged a surprised glance.

"I never thought I'd hear my daughter laugh again," Dennis O'Connell said. "Pearl seems to be bringing her the best medicine."

"My guess is that your daughter is making Pearl laugh!" David Ross replied.

Pearl thought about Mary for the next two days. *Redbeard the Pirate. No way.*

After school on Wednesday, she walked to the main branch of the library and asked the reference librarian where the magazine back issues were located and whether there was a photocopy machine she could use.

The following afternoon she paid another visit to the hospital, this time taking the bus by herself.

"I have something for you." She handed Mary a thin, flat, gift-wrapped package.

"Flowers!" Mary unwrapped it and held up a picture frame. There, looking back at her, was a color photocopy of the 1967 *Time* magazine cover featuring Moshe Dayan sporting his black eye patch.

Pearl said, "Listen. If you're gonna wear an eye patch, you need a better role model than some pirate. This guy's an army general."

Mary looked at the photo and Pearl could see many changes going on in her still-bandaged face.

"You're right. Thank you. You are so damned right."

Mary would keep that framed photo with her for the rest of her life.

Saturday Morning, Saturday Evening

It was now 10:30 on Shabbat morning and gold light filtered into the sanctuary through the stained glass dome and windows. Rabbi Pearl Ross felt awed by the beauty of the room, on this bright morning especially. She admired the carved wooden doors of the ark, which contained several Torah scrolls. Tall Corinthian columns surrounded the ark. She thought about how well this space symbolized Judaism itself—a religion filled with ancient and timeless tradition.

Above each side of the *bima*—the platform on which Pearl sat—was a balcony, perfect for a production of *Romeo and Juliet*.

The noise level rose as the congregation began to fill the pews and the aisles of the main floor. As was the case for most Shabbat services, the balconies were closed and empty (save for the bat mitzvah photographer). People chatted, coughed, laughed, or just looked puzzled as they waited for the service to begin. While some present today were familiar to Pearl because they attended Shabbat services on a regular basis, most were guests of the bat mitzvah girl, Maya Mankowitz, and her family. Although some had probably never been in a synagogue before, many had, including Maya's Catholic classmates from Bishop O'Dowd High School. Maya's family knew a lot of people, and it looked like it would be a well-attended service—two hundred or more.

And Jack did not disappoint her. The service began, and she watched him as he sat with some of the regular Shabbat attendees. He wore a temple-supplied *kippah* and *tallit*. Occasionally she would glance over, and was pleased to see that he knew the standard prayers and songs.

Yes!

But Pearl still had her job to do.

Both she and the senior rabbi, Craig Cohen, were on the bima along with Cantor Shelley Sanders (his real name was Sheldon, but no one ever called him that), Maya Mankowitz, and Miriam Harris, a temple board member.

Pearl and Rabbi Cohen had been taking turns guiding Maya through the preliminary prayers and songs, even though the bat mitzvah girl, her prayer book filled with yellow Post-It notes, was the one ostensibly leading the service.

And now it was time for Maya to carry the Torah around the congregation. The organ music began and the cantor led the congregation in song.

Maya carried the scroll down several steps, followed by Craig, Pearl, Maya's parents, and then Miriam Harris. As they walked up and down the aisles, there was a lot of handshaking, hugging, and kissing. Pearl hugged Dan Horowitz, a long-time member of the congregation and a current board member. Then she shook Jack's hand. The handshake took its own time.

"Glad you could make it," she said, with a smile.

"I never miss Shabbat services," he replied with a straight face.

Unless there's a game on TV, he thought.

Maya did a fine job chanting both her Torah and haftarah portions. When her parents gave their brief remarks and blessings prior to the Torah reading, they managed to include what Pearl was coming to realize were the three obligatory references: the sport in which their child excelled (soccer); a musical instrument in which she also excelled (guitar); and a remarkable pet (a poodle named Kugel).

And Jack did, indeed, stay for the free lunch. He seemed very comfortable sitting at a table with six other congregants, including Dan Horowitz and Miriam Harris. Pearl stopped by their table for a few moments, commenting only, "Thank you for welcoming Professor Levy to our Shabbat service."

One of the women sitting at the table, Birdie Goldstein, responded, "Yes, I was just telling Jack about my daughter— you know the one who teaches English at Piedmont High School? But sadly, he says he already has a girlfriend."

When Pearl glanced over at him, he just smiled.

Twenty minutes later, Jack came over to where Pearl was sitting to say goodbye. She stood, shook his hand, and discreetly passed him a small piece of paper.

Jack got into his rental car and looked at what she'd written.

6 p.m., Los Cantaros, 336 Grand Avenue. Do not bring girlfriend. Gift okay.

He took a deep breath. There was a lot to do and not a lot of time in which to do it.

Solomon P. Solomon

"Look, Solomon, it's the rabbi."

Pearl looked up when she heard Mrs. Solomon's voice. The Shabbat kiddush lunch was over, and Pearl was on her way up to her office to get her things. Mr. and Mrs. Solomon P. Solomon walked toward her at a painfully slow pace, her arm linked in his. Mr. Solomon was wearing heavy black eyeglass frames on an oversized nose. Now that Pearl thought about it, she realized his ears were oversized as well, and did a good job of supporting his glasses. His hair was thin and gray, and fashioned in what she'd call a classic comb-over. He wore a white, button-down dress shirt and gray slacks. His blue necktie sported red polka dots and was fastened to his shirt with a tie bar that featured the three initials: *SPS*. She wondered once again what the "P" stood for.

Mrs. Solomon was a beauty parlor blonde, with bright red lipstick and bright blue eyes. She wore a cream colored blouse that just barely buttoned over her ample bosom, and a black mid-knee skirt. Her three bangle bracelets jangled like spurs as she walked. Her gaze was intelligent—even, Pearl thought, all-knowing.

"*That's* the rabbi?" asked Mr. Solomon.

"Hi, Mr. Solomon. Mrs. Solomon. *Shabbat Shalom!*"

"Yes, Solomon, she's the rabbi. Didn't you have something you wanted to tell her?" said Mrs. Solomon to her husband.

"Right, right. Hey, rabbi, I got a joke for you!"

"Terrific! You tell the best jokes. Let's hear it," said Pearl, who always held out hope that he would be able to remember at least half of the joke he was about to tell. Even a quarter.

"So there's these four rabbis who like to play golf. And they go out with their golf carts, and play a few holes, and then, uh …" Solomon hesitated and looked off into space.

"Uh-huh. So the four rabbis are playing golf. And after a few holes, what happens?"

Solomon continued to look at her blankly.

She prompted him. "Are the people playing in front of them holding things up, anything like that?"

"Oh, yeah, yeah. So there's these four rabbis, and they're playing golf and they get to one of the holes and their game is held up because of … something …" Solomon paused and smiled a bewildered smile.

Pearl also smiled and waited. But he didn't continue. So she asked, "And why can't they play through? Who's holding them up?"

"Well, you see, Rabbi, they can't play through to the next hole because ... something ... somebody ..."

Mrs. Solomon quietly said to Pearl, "Keep going, don't worry. It's okay."

Solomon was still struggling. "Yeah. The four rabbis, they're playing golf, and they have golf carts and everything, but they can't ... they're being held up, they can't play through ..."

Pearl suggested, "Maybe one of the rabbis walks to the next hole and talks to the people there?"

"... Walks to the next hole ... They can't play through ..."

She tried again. "And one of the rabbis walks to the next hole to talk to the people ..."

But Solomon P. Solomon had lost interest and was obviously tired.

Mrs. Solomon took her husband's arm and kissed his cheek. "Come, Solomon. Shall we go? *Gut Shabbes,* Rabbi."

Mrs. Solomon and Pearl exchanged sad smiles. Sad Shabbat smiles.

The Solomons turned and headed, slowly, to the exit.

At the Taqueria

Jack was waiting for Pearl at one of the tables along the window at the popular neighborhood taqueria. There were some small piñatas hanging from the ceiling and a variety of brightly-colored Mexican decorations on the walls. Large screen televisions displayed the same soccer game. The TV sound was off, and mariachi music played through several speakers.

He caught her eye as she entered. She smiled and walked towards him. He watched as her gaze went to the package on the table.

"Ooh! Is this for me?"

Jack immediately diverted her attention from the package, which was about the size of a shoebox, but a little taller. He'd wrapped it in blue and white Hanukkah gift wrap and tied it with a red Christmas bow.

She obviously didn't notice the small air holes punched in the side of the box.

They left their stuff and the box on the table and walked to the counter to order.

"Anything here I shouldn't eat?" he asked.

"Eat *treif*, go directly to hell. Do not pass *Go*."

"Got it. No *cerdo*. No *mariscos*."

"*¡Muy bien!*"

They ordered fish tacos and a salmon and veggie burrito to share, plus some Mexican sodas. The pleasant guy behind the counter (he had really big biceps, and a tattoo of the Virgin Mary on one arm) passed Jack the credit card receipt to sign, and then handed Pearl a white plastic card on which was printed their order number:

18

She picked up the card and stared at the number—*chai*—for a long moment. Without taking her eyes off the mystical number, she turned and carried it back to their table. And that was why she missed the private smiles and fist-bump that passed between Jack and Pablo, the guy with the biceps.

"*¿Es el número mágico?*" asked Pablo.

"Sí. Pero más místico que mágico."
"Claro."
"Gracias, amigo," said Jack.
"De nada!"

Jack joined Pearl at the table with their drinks. While they ate chips and salsa, drank Mexican sodas, and waited for their dinner, she looked at the box.

"That's a big gift."

"You have no idea."

"Shall I open it now?"

Jack looked around the crowded room before he responded. "Yes. But you have to promise to be discreet."

"I'm one of the most discreet women you'll ever meet," she said as she unwrapped the box.

Her scream was anything but discreet, though she recovered quickly. Other diners who had turned to look went back to their meals and the soccer game.

As Jack removed the clear plastic critter box from the gift-wrapping, she regained her rabbinical composure.

Amongst a couple of rocks and a little man in a deep-sea diving helmet, was the biggest tarantula she'd ever seen—about the size of a tennis ball. Well, it wasn't really that big. Okay. It was sort of small. Maybe the size of a golf ball. Maybe a little smaller.

"Whichever way I move, I feel like he's looking at me."

"Yeah," Jack replied. "They have a habit of doing that. Also, it's a 'she.'"

Glued to the side of the container was a small plaque that read *Delilah*. In Hebrew.

Pearl and her gift looked at each other for a few moments. Then Pearl looked at Jack. They both started to laugh.

Jack

The night after their first date, Pearl and Jack had their second date, dinner at a neighborhood Thai restaurant on Telegraph Avenue.

Jack took a sip of his Singha beer and looked at Pearl seriously. "I'm concerned about your being able to take care of Delilah."

"You should be," Pearl said.

"I can return her to the Vivarium if you want me to."

"You don't think I have the proper skills to be a mother to a spider?"

He took a folded piece of paper out of his jacket pocket and handed it to her. She opened it up.

The heading was: *Instructions for Tarantula Care.*

"Thanks," she said, scanning the page. "Hmmm. Live crickets ..."

"I'm thinking it would be nice to live here," Jack said. "Cal made me a very attractive offer."

"Is anything holding you back?" she asked, looking up from the page.

"Actually, no. The forces drawing me here are getting stronger all the time. But it's a big move."

"It would be nice to have you here."

Their hands met in the middle of the table.

Jack said, "I have to find a place to live. Between now and next week."

"Let me ask around," Pearl said. "I know people who know people."

The next morning she knocked on the office door of Duke Sniderman, Lakeshore Temple's executive director.

He had been hired around the same time as Pearl—just a month earlier. And, like the new rabbi, he was still learning how the synagogue operated. There was no question, however, that he was a fast learner. Everyone at the temple who'd met him agreed that he was competent and intelligent.

"Good morning, Rabbi. Please come in."

Pearl decided to shut the door behind her, and then took a seat. Once she was seated across from him, it wasn't as obvious that she was three inches taller than he. She probably also had ten pounds on him, which did not make her happy. But it wasn't his fault. He wasn't the one who'd eaten the breakfast burrito. *And* the bagel.

"Duke, I need a favor, and I think you might be able to help me."

"Absolutely. What can I do for you?"

"My father is a professor at Cal, and they've just hired a young man to teach there. He's coming from the East Coast, and because of the housing shortage in the Berkeley area, we're trying to help him get settled."

"Is this a friend of yours?"

"Let's say we've met a few times."

Duke sat back in his chair and tapped his pen against his goatee before he spoke.

"Let me get back to you."

She thanked him and left. She had a good feeling about Duke.

Twenty minutes later, he knocked on *her* door. After closing the door behind him he sat in one of the visitor's chairs. "I think I might have something for your friend."

"What took you so long?"

They both laughed.

"I know someone who owns a house up on Grizzly Peak. It's really big—like five or six bedrooms. He's looking for a tenant."

Pearl nodded. "Sounds good so far."

"The rent is reasonable. Your professor friend would have his own bedroom and bath, and there's actually a very nice view. Of course, he'd be sharing the kitchen and the living room." With that, Duke handed her an index card with a name and phone number on it.

Pearl looked at it and asked, "Anything else we should tell him?"

"I don't know if he's interested, but there's a weight and exercise room in the house."

She smiled and said, "That's good!"

"And one more thing." He hesitated.

"Tell me, Duke."

"I hope he doesn't have a problem living in a house full of gay men."

"It wouldn't bother me, so it better not bother him," Pearl said.

They shared a smile and Duke left her office.

Jack and Pearl met for dinner a couple days after their second date. This time it was at a restaurant overlooking the Berkeley Marina.

Pearl asked, "So, how are you doing?"

Jack said, "You know, I have to decide whether to take this gig at Berkeley."

She said nothing.

He paused for a long time. "Would you say, from a rabbinical point of view, that I should take the job?"

She put her wineglass down, and looked at him very seriously. "From a rabbinical point of view, I'd say you need to get your ass back here as soon as possible, or Delilah and I are going to be very, very pissed off."

"There's the problem of finding a place to live. I hear housing is tighter than ..."

As he spoke, she reached into her purse and then snapped the index card down on the table in front of him as if it were the Ace of Hearts.

"Here's where you'll be living. It's a 15-minute drive or a 25-minute bus ride to the campus. I'm told the bedroom has an incredible view of the bay. You'll have your own bathroom, and share the rest of the house with a few other guys. It's a great place, from what I hear."

The card read "Brent," followed by a phone number.

"That's it?"

"Yes. Duke—he's the executive director at Lakeshore Temple—knows the owner. I told him that you get along well with gay men."

He laughed. "Well, I do, actually."

"Good. Me too."

The next day, Jack's first and last month's rent checks were in the mail, and he was on a flight to Florida, where he'd left his car and all his belongings at his parents' house.

He had yet to see the house on Grizzly Peak.

Jack in the Hot Tub

Jack was just sitting. Reclining, actually. He was pondering his future; reflecting on recent decisions that were changing the course of his life.

The July night was cool, but he was warm, as well he

should be; he was soaking in an outdoor hot tub high in the hills of Berkeley, California.

The hot water soothed his aching muscles, particularly his back and neck. Driving across the country solo was a young man's game, he decided. And even though he was still under thirty, he wasn't as young as he used to be.

After his initial few dates with Pearl, he knew. They both knew. It was serious.

Pearl was unlike anyone he'd met. Although everybody said that when they fell in love, he was sure that few were thinking about a rabbi when they said it. She reminded Jack of several people he liked or admired in the straightforward way she spoke. He found her very attractive—long dark hair with a lot of curls, a great smile, and big, light brown eyes. And curvy.

Although several inches shorter than he, Pearl met him head-on in many ways: the direct way she looked at him, heard what he said, and came right back with ideas or jokes of her own. She was smart, quick, and funny, and seemed to think he was funny as well.

Right from the beginning she'd been honest with him. She'd told him that for her, at least, dating was different now. She apologized when she said that she could not enter into a relationship at this point in her life without a commitment. As a rabbi, she explained, she was a public figure; she was in many ways viewed through a microscope by her peers, her community, and society in general.

"Viewed through a microscope, maybe like one of your specimens," she'd joked.

"One of my more attractive specimens," he'd replied. And they'd both laughed. "Of course, none of the other specimens has ever turned me on as much as this one," he added.

So he'd made a commitment. He'd signed a three-year tenure-track contract with the university, and then flown back to Florida. He took a week to drive back with whatever stuff he could fit in his car. He now needed to register the car in California. And get a new driver's license. Auto insurance. Voter registration. A new state income tax return. A new primary care physician. Change-of-address forms. All of that. It took so much time and energy.

Yet, he knew it was worth it. She was worth it. He believed it. She was special.

He recalled how surprised Pearl was when he told her that his mother had the same name as her mother—Shayna. They even spelled it the same way. A strange coincidence?

Jack knew that Pearl had asked Duke Sniderman, the executive director at her temple, to help her find "her father's new colleague" a place to live. He thought, *That was a euphemism if I've ever heard one.* And from what she'd told him about Duke, it didn't take a wink and a smile for him to understand what the real story was.

Duke had made one phone call and given the information to Pearl. Jack spoke to Brent, the owner of the Grizzly Peak house, the next day, took the room sight-unseen, signed the document the owner had faxed over to him at the University, and dropped it and a couple of checks in the mail. It appeared that a personal recommendation from Duke Sniderman was all it took. At Jack's request, the front door key and a copy of the lease would be mailed overnight express, waiting for him in Florida.

That was it. Boom, boom, boom.

The room was fine; he'd lived in all kinds of rooms (and tents) during his many years as an undergraduate student, a grad student, and a postdoc. Two postdocs. This room had its own bathroom, which was a very nice feature—no sharing with people messier than he. And it had an incredible view of the Bay Area—he could see two bridges in the distance. Brent, the owner, no longer lived in the house. He'd explained that he'd moved in with his partner, who owned a large condo in the Pacific Heights section of San Francisco, and this home, which he'd inherited from his parents *(and was probably worth a fortune,* Jack thought), was now just an income property. Brent told him it had five bedrooms, four-and-a-half baths, and a couple of living room areas, one of which had been converted into a fitness room.

French doors led out to a deck that featured a large Jacuzzi.

In which he was now sitting. Reclining.

He'd driven all day, arriving at nine in the evening. No one was in the house, and it was dark except for the porch light and one lamp in the upper-floor living room. He opened the front door with the key Brent had express-mailed to his parents' home, and turned on some hall lights. Finding his way to his bedroom (a welcome note was taped to the door), he used the bathroom and then carried a few boxes and suitcases in from the car.

Jack had planned on just going to sleep when he remembered the Jacuzzi, so he'd dug out a robe and flip-flops, grabbed a towel, and made his way through the fitness room, which featured a treadmill, a StairMaster and a couple of other machines, free weights, a pull-up bar, yoga mats, mirrors, a big screen TV, and a music system.

He turned out the light in the workout room and stepped onto the deck, where he removed the spa cover, found the button that turned on the bubbles, and slipped, naked, into the hot water.

Jack gazed over the treetops into the distance and viewed the nearly full moon, some scattered clouds, and a few stars that were visible. He looked at the moon, just pondering his past, present, and future, letting his mind wander.

He was drifting off to sleep when he became aware of the presence of another person sliding into the water a few feet away. All he caught in the moonlight was a glimpse of a naked man with six-pack abs one sees only on the cover of magazines at the supermarket. Jack and the other guy made eye contact.

"You're the new guy." He extended his hand and they shook. "I'm Brian."

"Jack Levy. Just got in less than an hour ago. Drove straight through from Florida."

"Straight through from Florida. Straight through. Is that code?" He smiled as he said it.

Jack laughed. "Don't tell me I have to watch my language in this house."

"Nah. Everything's cool. So, you're the rabbi's boyfriend."

Jack sighed. "Oh, Lord. And so it begins."

"What do you mean?" Brian asked.

"It's just ironic. I bust my ass for God knows how many years, and finally I'm a professor at one of the most prestigious universities in the world. And the first guy I meet knows me as 'the rabbi's boyfriend.'"

Brian laughed.

Jack was too tired to get upset. "It's not *that* funny."

"No. I was just thinking about this other guy I know in L.A. who was also the rabbi's boyfriend. But the rabbi's wife found out about it and threatened to cause a scandal. So they had to break up. My friend had been ready to convert and everything."

"It's always something, isn't it?" said Jack.

"Yeah."

"To tell you the truth, I need to be careful about the reputation of my own rabbi—her name is Pearl. She's not married, but people are very sensitive about this kind of thing. She doesn't want her reputation, you know, besmirched."

"Yeah, I can imagine."

"And also, we've only known each other a few weeks."

"Wait a minute," Brian said as he looked at Jack in the semi-darkness. "You two have only known each other a few weeks, and you just moved across the country to be with her?"

"Yes."

"But you're up here on Grizzly Peak living in a house full of gay men?" He sounded incredulous.

"Yeah. As Pearl often says, 'God works in strange ways.'"

Brian was still shaking his head in disbelief as the French doors opened and two men walked to the side of the spa, dropped the towels that had been around their waists, and slipped into the tub. As Jack and Brian made room for them, Jack couldn't help noticing that both of these guys also had muscular bodies. And six-packs. He sighed to himself, thinking about what it took to maintain that kind of physique.

There were introductions all around as he met Reggie and Patrick. Now the whole gang was here, Jack thought, until two more guys with six-packs walked onto the deck, dropped a robe and a towel, and squeezed in with them. They were Harold and Curtis, neighbors who lived down the street.

Everyone shook his hand and welcomed him to the house and to the neighborhood. They all knew Duke, and everyone seemed to know that Jack was the rabbi's boyfriend. Word had spread fast.

The men were hip-to-hip in the Jacuzzi, but no one seemed to care. Just another night in the hot tub.

The conversation revolved around their jobs, their workouts, and their diets. Jack was amazed at what these guys did to maintain their fitness. Two were models working part time for a particular agency. The fact that Jack was the only man in the tub who *didn't* have six-pack abs was not lost on him. He knew it was all about strict diet, endless cardio, serious workouts and most of all, discipline. They certainly had his respect.

He was also the only one with hair on his chest. Or legs, for that matter.

They asked about the classes Jack would be teaching in the fall. No one had ever met an entomologist before. Someone asked if he was into any particular sports, and when they found out he played pretty much everything, he was invited to join a softball team and play tennis.

Then the talk switched to snakes. One of them, Reggie, had a four-foot milk snake, and Jack asked him where he got the mice to feed it.

"The East Bay Vivarium. You know it?"

"Oh, yeah. It's a really well-known place nationally. In fact I was just there a few weeks ago." As soon as he said it, he realized he'd made a mistake.

"Really? What brought you over there?" Reggie asked. "Just checking out the merchandise?"

Everyone laughed. Jack knew he had to make a decision as to whether to tell the truth, or evade the question. The hell with it. He'd tell the truth. He was too tired to lie, and it might come back to haunt him at some point.

"Actually, I was there buying a gift for Pearl."

"Your girlfriend, the rabbi."

"Well, she wasn't my girlfriend then. And as I was telling Brian, we haven't known each other very long. Some might say we're in the early stages of our relationship."

"Yeah, yeah, yeah," Patrick said. "We all know about that 'early stages' routine." Everyone nodded their heads.

"What'd you get her? They sell jewelry at the Vivarium?" More laughter.

"No," Jack said, not without some trepidation.

Everyone was quiet, waiting for his response.

"I bought her a tarantula."

If he'd wanted to find a conversation stopper, he couldn't have picked a better one. The pause was pretty pregnant.

"What the hell!" someone finally said.

Another said, "Are you serious?"

"Yeah," Jack said. "She's a really nice one."

"The tarantula or the rabbi?" That elicited laughs, and Jack laughed with them.

"Well, she *was* surprised," he admitted.

"Surprised. I'll *bet* she was surprised," Curtis said.

Reggie, the guy with the milk snake, said, "I bought one of my old boyfriends a snake once. He thought it was sexy. You know, all that Freudian serpentine symbolism."

Patrick said, "Sure, but you're crazy. Like Freud. And Jack, here."

Jack responded to the assault on his sanity. "Look, laugh all you want, but except for that first scream in the restaurant …"

"The first scream? In the restaurant?" someone interrupted.

"Yeah. I gave it to her at dinner. I told her I'd bring her a gift, and it was the coolest gift that …"

"You are absolutely, positively nuts, man! Just out of your mind!" someone remarked. "The man gets his new girlfriend a tarantula as a gift. Unbelievable."

"Her name is Delilah," said Jack.

"Wait," Brian said. "I thought you said her name was Pearl."

"No. The tarantula."

That elicited more head-shaking.

"Hey, just make sure that some night when you're in a fit of passion you don't call the rabbi 'Delilah,'" said Curtis, which brought laughter.

Harold, who'd said he worked in retail, piped up. "Actually, I can see this as a new gift idea for the holiday season." He went into a radio announcer voice:

"Gentlemen, this year, give your loved one something different. Something she'll just scream about!"

The guys were having a good time, but Jack was getting tired, and he was warm from sitting in the tub.

"Hey, listen, it's a pleasure meeting you guys. But I drove over 500 miles today, and I'm fading fast. So, thanks for the warm welcome, and I'll tell Pearl that you guys approved of my gift."

Everyone shook his hand again and offered a farewell comment.

"Delilah. Great name."

"Need to get her a Samson."

"Absolutely."

"Best gift I've ever heard of."

"You're crazy, man!"

"Take care of your rabbi."

And as the comments, welcomes, and goodbyes continued, he managed to lift himself out of the crowded tub, found his robe, flip-flops, and towel in the moonlight, and exited the deck through the French doors.

It had been a long day. And a different night.

As Jack drifted off to sleep between some sheets he'd managed to find in one of his cardboard boxes, he thought about Pearl. And Delilah. And six-packs.

Her Own Home

A few weeks after meeting Jack, Rabbi Pearl Ross moved from her childhood room into her parents' bedroom.

She laughed to herself about the logistics of this move, but it was simple, given the background.

When her parents first married and her father became a professor at Berkeley, they bought a nice home in the Rockridge section of Oakland. After the birth of their second daughter, Ruth, they moved to a larger home, closer to the campus, in North Berkeley. They'd considered selling the Oakland house, but decided to keep it as an income property. That turned out to be a wise choice, since the home and the neighborhood became more valuable each year. They'd always been able to rent it out to families of visiting scholars who were teaching at Cal during their Sabbaticals.

Since moving back to California, Pearl had been staying in her parents' home in Berkeley—in *her* old bedroom, with her high school books and paraphernalia still proudly displayed on the shelves. But that had gotten old. She needed her own place. Especially now that she had, well, a boyfriend.

At dinner one night, she asked her parents if they'd be willing to rent her the Rockridge house. She knew that the current tenants were leaving very soon to return to Norway. In fact, their belongings were already packed up and ready to ship. Maybe her timing was good.

It couldn't have been better.

When she asked, her mother shook her head.

"Absolutely not, Pearl. We think you should continue to live with us until you find a husband and get married. Then you can move in with him and he can support you."

Her mother was funny. Ha ha.

They'd cut a deal and in less than two weeks she'd moved into the Rockridge house. Fortunately, the house was furnished, and she could live with what was there for a while. Yes, the timing was right. Jack had accepted the position at Cal and signed a contract. Then he'd flown to Florida to pick up his car and some of his stuff and had driven back to California. They were back on the fast track and had been on several dates since his return.

Their relationship had been briefly stalled by logistics. But now she was settled in the house in Rockridge and he was living in the Berkeley Hills.

Not the perfect setup for a couple approaching thirty. But things would change soon.

Duke

Richard "Duke" Sniderman, the temple's new executive director, had been on the job only eight weeks when he caught a thief.

Duke, who had taken over the position of a man who'd worked at the temple for over twenty years before retiring to New Mexico, soon realized that he had his work cut out for him.

During his first month on the job, Duke assessed the physical plant and set about cleaning up the place. Most of the work was done by the custodian, Jesús H. Cruz, a twenty-three-year-old with a constant smile and a genuinely friendly disposition. Duke had already found him to be a dependable and hard-working young man. (When asked about his name, Jesús H. laughed and told him that every generation of the men in his family included a Jesús, differentiated only by their middle names. His was Hector. His father's was Pedro. His grandfather's had been Mateo. And yes, he was aware that he and Jesus Christ had the same middle initial.)

Decades' worth of bags and boxes of detritus were hauled to a variety of places to be donated, recycled, shredded, or just thrown out. Floors, walls, cabinets, and many secret places (one was called The Anne Frank Room) were cleaned and scrubbed. A local exterminator took care of the rodents living in the basement, prompting Duke to recall an old joke:

In a certain city there are three Jewish congregations—an Orthodox shul, a Conservative synagogue, and a Reform temple. All three are infested by mice.

When he is told about the problem, the Orthodox rabbi calls an exterminator. Two days later, the mice are gone.

The Board of Directors of the Conservative synagogue meets with their rabbi, and they decide to solve the problem in the most humane way possible. They hire a "green" company that captures the mice live and then takes them to a nearby park, where they are released. Two days later, the mice have all returned to the synagogue.

The rabbi and the board of the Reform temple meet, and after a lengthy meeting they decide to make the mice members of the congregation. After that, the mice only come to the temple twice a year.

Duke's second month on the job began with him going through the temple's financial statements. He spotted the problem almost immediately. The petty cash was obviously screwed up; the receipts in no way equaled the reimbursements to the petty cash account.

How long has this *been going on?* he wondered.

Marsha had been a temple employee for a very long time. Before her job title was changed to administrative assistant, she'd been the principal secretary. As far as Duke was concerned, she was now the principal suspect.

Marsha was a short, plump woman, with dyed brown hair and gray eyes. She was cheerful, friendly, helpful, courteous, kind, and almost everything else on the Boy Scout list. Unlike a Boy Scout, however, she was not very good at covering her tracks.

One late afternoon, Duke had filled the large copy machine with paper and placed the remaining reams neatly in two even stacks on a nearby shelf. When he arrived early the next morning, the piles were no longer even. One ream was missing. The photocopier tray was still full.

The petty cash envelope, which he'd replenished the previous afternoon, now contained ninety dollars instead of the one hundred he'd put there the day before. No purchase receipts, however, had been added to account for the departed ten dollars.

Marsha, Esther, John, and some other temple employees arrived a few minutes later, all smiles and "good mornings." As he greeted them, Duke thought about what he needed to do.

The following Tuesday, Rabbi Craig Cohen poked his head into the cantor's office, where Cantor Shelley Sanders and Pearl were chatting.

"I see we have an emergency clergy meeting scheduled at 11:45. Anyone know anything about this?"

Shelley said, "Duke called and asked if we could all meet here. That's all I know."

Craig looked puzzled. Pearl watched the senior rabbi as he went through a series of facial emotions. Every time she'd ever seen him, including during her series of job interviews, he always wore a suit, a tie, a button down dress shirt—either white or blue, and a small knitted kippah. He wore his clothes well, she thought, and seemed to have an extensive collection of Jewish-themed ties. Today's featured tiny menorahs. Pearl always thought he looked like a Jewish version of Gene Kelly, only taller. His dark hair, graying at the temples, was worthy of a stereotypical banker, and his nose was sort of noble, in her opinion anyway, considering she wasn't too sure what a noble nose actually looked like. He had the shiniest shoes she'd ever seen, short of patent leather.

Unlike the senior rabbi, the cantor, Shelley, was wearing a teal blue sports shirt, khaki slacks, and running shoes. He was a little taller than Pearl and a little shorter than Craig. Pearl sometimes wondered if the cantor's light brown hair color was natural. It looked good in any case. His kippah today had little red treble clefs in a field of navy blue.

"Very strange," Craig said. "Duke's been here two months and he's already calling an emergency clergy meeting?" There was a knock at the door.

"Well, we'll soon find out," Shelley said as he opened the door and Duke came in and sat down on an empty chair.

"Thanks for responding on such short notice. I wouldn't bother you if it weren't important."

"What's up?" asked Rabbi Cohen.

"I needed to let you know that Marsha has just submitted her resignation to me. She's cleaning out her desk now, and I'll be helping her take her stuff out to her car."

"Is she okay? Is something wrong?" The concern on Craig's face was genuine.

Duke took a deep breath. "I've discovered evidence—confirmed on a security video—that Marsha has been stealing temple property and funds. We chatted about it, and she thought it best to leave quietly."

The clergy remained silent for a long moment.

Craig broke the silence. "Marsha," he said gravely, looking stunned. "I've worked with her for almost ten years."

Duke looked directly at Craig Cohen. "Rabbi, I know this is hard for you. But I've checked through what little evidence my predecessor left, and I can tell you that this has been going on for a long time. Marsha has probably stolen thousands of dollars in cash and supplies over the last ten years. It's my responsibility to correct the situation. It's my job."

Pearl took in the scene. She liked Marsha, too. Marsha doted on her more than her own mother did, and it was easy to become not only attached to her, but dependent on her for all the things that a good assistant does. But she also realized that Duke was in charge of the office employees. Well, sort of. Craig, or the board, could conceivably override his decisions. But in this case, she felt that would be a bad idea.

"Severance pay?" asked Craig.

"No," replied Duke. "Whatever severance pay she might have received, she's already taken it. Today's Tuesday, and she'll be paid through the end of the week. Plus vacation pay that she's accrued. Period."

Craig looked defeated. "No way to give her a second chance?"

Duke spoke calmly. "Rabbi, this is not easy. It's a bad situation. Frankly, it sucks. It's the part of my job that I dislike the most. But the chances are that many—if not most—of the other employees in the temple office are aware of what's been going on. They haven't ratted Marsha out because she's the senior employee and they like their jobs. And she was tolerated by her previous boss, who may have looked the other way. He may have even known and ignored it for his own reasons." The implication of this last statement sent a chill through the small room.

Craig sighed, then rose. "Thank you, Duke. The three of us know what it's like having a job that has its dark side. I trust you'll do the right thing. Good luck." He paused for a moment, then said, "Please tell Marsha I wish her the best and I appreciate the work she's done for the temple."

As he walked out of the room, the sadness was virtually dripping from him.

Shelley followed Craig saying, "I've got a lunch date with Susan. Just close the door on your way out."

As Pearl got up to go, she asked Duke, "Is there anything I can do to help?"

"Thanks, but no. I've sent the other employees to lunch. I want to preserve Marsha's dignity. She's been here a long time. I'm sure Rabbi Cohen will find a way to help her."

Pearl got up and walked back to her office. Ten minutes later, she looked out her window, where she had a partial view of the parking lot. She watched as Duke put several boxes in Marsha's car. He waited until she'd driven away.

Pearl saw that his shoulders were slumped and he looked exhausted. Duke rubbed his face with his hands and then took a handkerchief from his pocket and blew his nose. She moved away from the window and sat down at her desk.

This rabbi gig. People have no idea what it's all about.

Mah Jongg

When Pearl was a student at Hebrew Union College in Cincinnati, her mentor, a female rabbi and professor, hosted a group of five to ten female students a couple times a month. She rotated these students in alphabetical order, and no one ever missed a session.

The women would have tea and discuss the many issues a female rabbi might have to deal with. Typically, these issues were gender-specific: first period, pregnancy complications, miscarriage, as well as personal finance concerns for divorced or widowed women, or other personal problems congregants might feel more comfortable discussing with a female rabbi—if they had a choice. They also discussed the sexism—or even misogyny—female rabbis might face in their job search, their congregations, or in their communities.

One night, the professor told her rabbinical students, "Ladies, tonight we're going to have some fun!" They set up two card tables and some folding chairs, and sat down to play Mah Jongg.

A few of the students were familiar with the game and helped teach the others. Their professor had eight Mah Jongg cards—each player required a card to play the American version of the game—and gave her students the address where they could order their own cards if they wanted to.

Virtually all of them did, and Mah Jongg soon became one of their favorite activities. Some of them formed a group that played regularly.

When Shayna Ross learned that her daughter was playing Mah Jongg, she shipped her a set of tiles that had been sitting in the back of her closet for 30 years. It had belonged to one of Shayna's long-dead aunts. Pearl loved to look at and handle the tiles, which were covered with a variety of brightly-colored circles, flowers, dragons, and other symbols. It was an almost atavistic experience.

One evening Pearl, now Rabbi Ross, sat at her desk with the door to her office open. A woman walking down the hallway waved hello to her.

"Hi, Rabbi. Working late?"

Pearl returned the greeting, happy to be interrupted from a writing task that was eluding her.

"What's up, Hannah?" It was Hannah Weissbratten, a long-time member of the congregation and current president of the Sisterhood. "Something going on tonight?"

"It's our Sisterhood Mah Jongg night and I'm looking for another person so we can play two tables. Sorry to bother you." The woman continued walking down the hall.

"Wait! I'm coming!"

Hannah returned to the office doorway. "You want to play?" She sounded a bit skeptical.

"Absolutely. But my card's at home," Pearl said as she walked around her desk and turned off the light. "It's too old, anyway."

"Rabbi, trust me. We have an extra card for you."

QueenEsther

After forcing Marsha's resignation, an emotionally exhausted Duke Sniderman took a long walk, winding up in a small restaurant in Oakland's Chinatown, where he ate one of the daily specials—a forgettable chicken and vegetable dish— and drank lots of tea. He contemplated the office situation, and by the time he returned to the temple he felt much better.

When he walked into the office, no one looked at him. They just worked, their eyes down, avoiding both him and Marsha's glaringly empty desk, the surface of which, once filled with *tchotchkes* and office supplies that she had not yet stolen, was now just shiny and empty.

"Esther, could you please come into my office when you get a chance."

"Sure." She put aside the folder she was working on and followed him in, closing the door behind her. Duke noticed that some of the beads in her hair clicked softly as she sat down. A few of the beads matched her emerald green dress, which was cinched around her thin waist by a black leather belt. Her dark eyes seemed to be smiling, even though her mouth was not.

"Thank you," he said as he picked up a paper on his desk.

"Should I start packing up my stuff?"

He looked up. "Is that what you think I want to talk to you about?"

"I figured you're cleaning house. You fired Marsha, and I'm next."

He sat back in his chair, pondering again how the rumor mill of an office could be so fast. And so wrong.

"I did not fire Marsha. She resigned."

"Same difference."

"Why would you be next? Is there something about you or your job performance that I should know about?"

"Well, when I look around the staff, I'm like the odd man out."

"Because … ?"

"Because I'm black, for one thing."

"And I should let you go because you're black?"

"It's happened before."

"You're suggesting I would discriminate against you because of your ethnicity."

"Like I said …"

He sighed. "Esther, this is not what I wanted to talk to

you about, but let me ask you a question. I'm not just your supervisor. I'm a person. Do you think I've never been discriminated against? Do you think I don't know how that feels?"

"I wouldn't know ... I don't know you."

"You probably know that I'm Jewish. Did you know that I'm gay?"

"I suspected, I guess."

"The same way I suspected you're African-American."

She laughed. "Sort of."

"You know that Sammy Davis, Jr. routine where he tells the Vegas audience, 'Yes, it's true—I'm a black Jew'?"

"No."

"Sammy says, 'I've been a Jew for about ten years now,' and a lot of people in the audience applaud. Then he pauses and adds, 'I've been black for about ...'"

Esther laughed.

"Then he goes on, 'I've been black for about eight years. Before that, I was colored.'"

"I wasn't expecting that. That's funny."

"Anyway, something like that." Duke paused, then said, "Esther, I've known I was gay for most of my life. Before I was gay, I was either a 'homo' or a 'fag.'"

"Ouch."

"Yeah. I've been beat up on several occasions—both in high school and since then."

Quietly, she asked, "Have you ever been called a whore?" She pronounced it *hoe.*

He looked at her and responded. "Actually, yes. And I've been called a bitch many times. How about you?"

"No one would ever dare say that to *me!*"

They smiled at each other and then both started laughing. Quietly at first. Then more loudly.

"So, am I fired, or what?"

"No, you're not fired. But I *am* promoting you. You're now the office manager and the clergy's assistant."

"No shit!"

"No shit," he assured her. "Of course, in your new position, you don't say 'No shit' in the office. You'll get a raise, and all that."

"Excellent. When do I start?"

"After I meet with each staff member and tell them what's going on."

"Okay. Thank you."

"Tomorrow morning, please get here early and move your stuff over to what was Marsha's location."

"Great. Next to the window."

They discussed her new position, salary, and other details. Then he asked her, "Anything else?"

She paused, then said, "I could have told you Marsha was stealing from the office. But I'm not a rat."

"I know that. Everyone who works here would have known. Except the clergy."

"Yeah."

"That's why they need people like you and me." He looked at the paper on his desk. "I see on your file here that your full name is QueenEsther Robinson."

She smiled. "My mom gave me the name QueenEsther. It was embarrassing when I was a kid, but really, she was the only one who ever called me that." She saddened for a moment. "Now no one calls me QueenEsther."

"Your mother passed?"

"When I was nine. She had cancer. And then my dad died of a stroke the next year."

"Sorry."

"My aunt raised me. I have a cousin who's like a sister. She works in the mayor's office a few blocks from here."

He filed that bit of information away in his memory.

"And how about you? How'd you get the name 'Duke?'"

"You know who Duke Snider was?"

She nodded her head. "Brooklyn Dodgers, right? That was Jackie Robinson's team."

"Right. But I was called 'Duke' because my name was Sniderman, not because I could play baseball. Actually, the only person who *didn't* call me 'Duke' was my mother. She called me 'Richard' until the day she died."

They stood up, shook hands, and then gave each other a hug.

Duke had a feeling she was the right person for the job. And she would prove him correct.

Are You My Girlfriend?

The temple clergy maintained a rotating schedule when it came to certain tasks, one of which was visiting elderly congregants living in retirement facilities. This morning it was Pearl's turn to visit Grand Lake Towers, which overlooked Lake Merritt. Before leaving the temple, she stopped by the office to pick up the names of the residents she'd be visiting.

Esther, who had seamlessly taken over the role of office manager and the clergy's assistant, handed her a sheet of paper on which three names were listed; there was a short note after each.

"Enjoy yourself!" Esther said with a smile.

"Thanks," said Pearl, forcing her own smile. These visits were often pleasant, but sometimes they were, well, trying. Or challenging. Or some other euphemism.

When Pearl arrived at Grand Lake Towers, a high-rise

upscale retirement, assisted living, and skilled nursing facility, she parked in a visitor space and then took a glance at the list.

First up was Rose Gratstein. The penciled remark was clear:

If you stay more than 15 minutes, you'll be there for over an hour. Plan your escape early and carefully.

After checking in at the front desk, she knocked on Rose's door. It was quickly opened by a round woman wearing cat-eye glasses and a blue-flowered old-lady dress. Rose, smelling strongly of White Shoulders, enveloped her in an enormous hug. The front desk had obviously called ahead.

"Rabbi, Rabbi, I've been waiting for you! Thank you so much for coming to see me." Her accent was a combination of Lower East Side, Yiddish, and your grandma from Minsk.

Rose took her by the hand and led her to the sofa in front of a series of photo albums. "So, how come a beautiful girl like you isn't married yet? Don't you want children? Do you have any nieces or nephews?"

Pearl barely managed to squeeze an answer in between the rapid-fire questions. "Not married yet. I hope to have children someday. I don't have any nieces or nephews."

"Wonderful, wonderful! Let me show you some pictures of my grandchildren." And that was that.

Ninety minutes later, Pearl staggered out.

She then made her way to the apartment of the second person on the list: Rhoda Garfinkel. She read the note.

Rhoda sleeps all day. Don't expect too much, if anything. There was no answer when she knocked several times.

So Pearl went to the next name on the list: Bert Standish. The underlined message said *Do not visit between 11 and noon.*

She looked at her watch. It was 10:44. *Good.* She smiled to herself. *A nice, short visit.*

Unfortunately, it took her seven or eight minutes to find the right apartment, which was on the other side of the facility. This appeared to be a more "upscale" part of the Towers. Even the front door, which was slightly ajar, seemed classy.

When she knocked and called hello, a woman's accented voice replied from inside, "Come in. We're almost ready."

Pearl walked into the well-appointed living room. She noticed that the bedroom door had been removed and replaced with a curtain made of translucent fabric. She could see the vague outline of a short woman helping someone—a man—into bed. He appeared to be tall and lean. And completely naked. As the woman fluffed up his pillows, he asked her questions.

"Did I hear somebody come in? Is that my girlfriend? Is she here yet?"

"Very soon, Mr. Standish. And I know the two of you will have a good time."

Pearl assumed the woman was a caregiver. When she came out through the curtain, she seemed totally shocked to see Pearl.

"Who are *you?*" she asked, with what seemed agitation.

"I'm Rabbi Ross from Lakeshore Temple, to visit Mr. Standish."

"Oh, no! This is not a good time for you to visit! He is expecting his … his girlfriend." She was flustered and upset as she looked at the clock on the wall. "Very soon! Oh, no!"

"He has a girlfriend?"

The aide took the rabbi by the hand and led her to the living room sofa—this was the second time that morning she'd been led by the hand to a sofa.

"Yes, he has a girlfriend. He has many girlfriends. But he doesn't remember … He has dementia, maybe the

Alzheimer's." She paused a moment to catch her breath. "But he knows what to do when they get here."

Pearl was a bit puzzled, and thought maybe she should leave. But the woman was holding her hand in a tight grip.

Regardless, it was now too late to escape because at that moment a blur came through the doorway. A woman of a certain age—about seventy-five—was moving fast toward the bedroom curtain.

She was tall and lithe and had beautiful red hair that, Pearl observed, had been professionally—*very* professionally—done. Her lipstick was scarlet. The woman was somehow managing to unbutton her blouse with one hand while holding an old-fashioned train case with the other. She looked at Pearl, and threw "Who the hell are you?" over her shoulder as she moved toward the bedroom. She didn't wait for an answer as she parted the curtain and closed it behind her.

Although the view through the curtain was hazy, Pearl could see the woman kick off her shoes and put the train case on the dresser as she unzipped her skirt, which quickly dropped to the floor. The blouse, bra, and panties followed. She then popped the train case open and withdrew a large bottle of something, after which she held a small object high in the air. "Mirasol?" the woman called.

"Thank you," responded the aide. Pearl now realized the *aide* was Mirasol, as opposed to the condom that was being held in the air.

Inside the room, a dialogue began.

"Good morning, Bert. I see you're ready for me. Good for you!"

Pearl could hear every word, as Bert responded with a question.

"Are you my girlfriend?"

"I am today."

"Good. I like what I see."

"Bert, that's what you say every time. I just wish you could remember who I am."

"Who *are* you?"

"It's not really that important, is it? Move over a little. I don't want to fall off the bed."

Pearl sat there as the silhouettes moved behind the curtain. Mirasol squeezed her hand and whispered, "Don't worry. That's Millie. She's fast. It only takes maybe ten minutes. You the new rabbi?"

But Pearl could not concentrate as she wondered about the market for senior porn. She knew Mirasol was asking her a question, but the moans coming from the bedroom were making it hard for her to think. It began to sound like that scene from *When Harry Met Sally.*

To give credit where it was certainly due, it soon was apparent that each of them had reached climaxes. In less than the predicted ten minutes. She saw the woman leave the bed, pick her clothing up off the floor, and move to a bathroom within the bedroom. Pearl heard water running and the flush of a toilet.

A few minutes later, Millie, fully dressed with train case in hand, headed past her on the way to the front door. She was still tall and lithe, but her lipstick was all but gone. Millie looked at Pearl with what appeared to be a self-satisfied expression.

"Hope you enjoyed the show." Then she looked at Mirasol and said, "I'll be back next week. If Bert and I are still alive." And out she went in a blur.

Mirasol looked at Pearl. "I told you it wouldn't take very long. I'll help him get cleaned and dressed and then you can talk with him."

As the young woman stood, Pearl couldn't help but ask, "Does this happen every week?"

Mirasol looked at her with surprise. "Oh, no! It happens almost every day. Always at eleven o'clock. But of course with different girlfriends."

"Really? Different ... girlfriends? Every day?"

"Oh, yes. But he doesn't care. He can't remember."

"Frankly, this is a little difficult for me to understand."

Mirasol looked at Pearl with a slight smile. "Rabbi, Mr. Bert is very healthy, and happy, too. He just can't remember things. He likes his girlfriends, and they like him. He is very popular here, with so many widows. What do they say, 'In the land of the blind, the man with one eye, he is king.'"

Mirasol reached into an end table drawer and took out a single sheet of paper in a plastic sleeve, which she handed to Pearl. "Here. You read this while I help Mr. Standish. It's from his son."

Judging by the letterhead, Bert's son was a senior partner at a large Los Angeles law firm.

> *To Whom It May Concern:*
> *This is to inform you that my father, Albert (Bert) Standish, is physically healthy, and by long-standing mutual consent, will continue to live as normal a life as possible.*
>
> *He has a diagnosis of dementia, and is under regular medical care. He has the financial means to live in his current retirement facility with round-the-clock caregiver service. Please be aware that Mr. Standish has been sexually active all his adult life, and his medical team and I see no reason why this should be curtailed at this time.*
>
> *If a woman wishes to have sexual relations with my father, she is required to make a prior appointment with the caregiver, who will maintain a strict schedule. Each*

prospective partner must submit a statement from her physician that she is capable of normal sexual activity and is free of STDs. At each encounter, she must provide and use a condom, which she is responsible for applying in the normal manner after visibly displaying it to the caregiver. Additional lubricant is recommended for both parties.

Care must be given to ensure that my father is both physically and mentally cared for during the encounter, which will be discreetly observed by the caregiver. Any instance of physical, sexual, or mental abuse will be reported to me; we will respond to the full extent of the law.

It is hoped that both partners enjoy their time together, and that the female partner, knowing the mental condition of Mr. Standish, will be generous in her care for and attention to him.

If any party, administrator, social worker, medical professional, or member of the clergy should have any questions, they should contact my office at the telephone number or email address listed above. Please note that Mr. Standish has been deemed not competent to make legal or financial decisions, and that I am his guardian for all financial and medical matters.

Sincerely,
Robert Standish

Pearl finished reading the letter as Mirasol led Bert Standish, fully washed and dressed and looking tall and handsome, into the room. He was well-groomed, cleanly shaved, and his thinning white hair was combed straight back. Bert smiled at her as he extended his hand.

"Mirasol tells me you're a rabbi. They didn't have such pretty rabbis when I was a boy!" Pearl was enveloped in his smile, his warmth, and his obvious charm.

They had a pleasant fifteen-minute conversation, during which Bert asked Pearl several times if she was his girlfriend. Each time, she smiled and said, "No, I'm your rabbi," after which he'd reply, "Really! They didn't have such pretty rabbis when I was a boy!"

More than once she wondered, *If I were a 75-year-old widow, would I want to be one of his girlfriends? Hell, yes!*

As she was leaving, she knew she would return. But next time she'd be sure to arrive earlier—before the fireworks started.

Sodom and Gomorrah

First, thanks to everybody for coming to help me celebrate my bar mitzvah. All of the special people I want to thank are listed in the little handout you all got. But I want to send out a special thank-you to my parents and my little brother and sister—you know who you are.

And thanks, of course, to Rabbi Cohen. He's the man! And Cantor Sanders. He's also the man!

And Rabbi Ross-Levy. She's not a man, but if she were a man, she'd be the man, too!

The Torah portion for my bar mitzvah today is about Sodom and Gomorrah. As you know if you read the English translation while I was chanting from the Torah, those two cities were filled with evil people—a lot of bad guys. So God decided to destroy them.

As we see in the Torah, Abraham tried to cut a deal with

God to save the cities. Abraham said, "If there are even just fifty righteous men there, the cities should be saved." And God agreed to that.

But Abraham, he was a wheeler-dealer, and he kept on reducing the number to see what God would really accept, so he bargained God down from forty to thirty to twenty and then to ten. If they could find just ten righteous men, the cities would be saved.

But—and this seems hard to believe—they couldn't even find ten! Can you believe that? So God went ahead with the plan to destroy the place. Abraham's nephew—his name was Lot—he was allowed to escape with his wife and family, as long as they didn't look back at the cities being destroyed.

If you paid attention in English class, you'd know that this business about "not looking back" is called "foreshadowing." But most of the time, you don't know something was foreshadowed until after it happens. That's the problem with foreshadowing. For me, anyway.

Well, they're all running away from Sodom and Gomorrah and Mrs. Lot's curiosity gets the better of her. She looks back and is turned into a pillar of salt. A pillar is like a tall column—I looked that up.

When I started talking to Rabbi Cohen about writing my drash, he asked me what lesson or message I took away from the Torah portion and this story, and what I'd like to talk about today. I told him I'd thought about it and was really curious about the business with the salt. I thought maybe I would talk about the salt industry, and how it's changed from the olden biblical days to the point now where you can go in and buy one of those round boxes of salt that has the picture of the little girl holding an umbrella.

But the rabbi said I should look for something more meaningful and maybe more Jewish, so I thought I could talk about the salt industry in Israel. Or maybe Kosher salt.

He didn't seem to like the subject of salt that much, I'm not sure why.

But then I came up with the idea that if Sodom and Gomorrah is all about destruction, I could talk about what could've been done to make those cities a better place. You know, build a better society, clean things up. I mean, they couldn't even find ten righteous men. Give me a break!

So Rabbi Cohen suggested I check out the concept of tikkun olam, *which has to do with the repair of the world and making it a better place to live in.*

I decided to ask some people I know what they would do to start making the world a better place.

The first person I asked was my dad. He said that when he was a student at Cal, he was very much interested in improving society, and he and his friends decided to organize a demonstration. First thing they did was they made 500 posters at Krishna Copy and stapled them to telephone poles all over Berkeley. But it turned out that it rained the day of the demonstration and not too many people showed up. He thinks some of those posters are still there on a few telephone poles.

I told my dad I'm not sure this would help me, so he said, "Ask your mother." He always says that.

When I asked my mom for her suggestions, she said that everyone should just be nicer and kinder to one another, and that would make the world a better place. But if you know my mom, that's just the way she is—like, really nice to everyone. Then she recommended that if I wanted to talk to someone who really knew about the peace movement, like from the 1960s and '70s, I should talk to her older brother, my uncle Jerry, who's here today.

I really like Uncle Jerry because he has long hair and drives an old VW van, and he was around Haight-Ashbury back in the days of the hippies.

My mom and dad say that Uncle Jerry is what's now called an aging hippy. When I asked him about that, he said, "I guess that's true!"

Anyway, my uncle told me that he and his friends helped to get President Nixon to end the Vietnam war and then resign, and it all started one night when a whole bunch of people were sitting around in a hot tub. Rabbi Cohen told me to say that everyone in the hot tub was wearing a bathing suit. Ha! Get real, Rabbi!

Getting back to tikkun olam, the concept of repairing the world is mentioned in our prayer book, and in the Talmud, and also in Kabbalah, *which is Jewish mysticism, which is like magic, but Jewish magic. Hey, did you guys know that Houdini was Jewish and his father was a rabbi? Anyway, all of us have a responsibility to help repair, heal, and transform the world and the societies we live in.*

The way I see it, there are many, many small problems everywhere you look—in your neighborhood, in your school, in your country—even in your own house. But not here in the temple. Except maybe for the paint that's peeling off the ceiling way up there.

And we all have to do whatever we can to try and make things better, including helping those who are less fortunate than us—maybe like tutor a student who's failing, or pick up litter around your neighborhood, contribute what you can to charity, clean up after you walk your dog, work for equal rights, don't put graffiti on any walls including the bathroom, and be good neighbors and representatives of the United States when we travel to other countries. Like when my family went to Italy, which is not as modern as America, I was on my best behavior and always said buongiorno *and* grazie *to everybody.*

For my mitzvah project, I joined a crew of other teenagers a few weeks ago. We walked around Lake Merritt on cleanup day, picking up trash that accidently got into the lake. You wouldn't believe some of the stuff we fished out of the water!

There were kids from my school and also our temple, plus some other temples, and also a bunch of churches. And then we went out for pizza so all the kids could bond and get to know everybody else. It was a sunny day and we did a good job cleaning up the lake. The pizza was pretty good, too.

Oh, I almost forgot. Uncle Jerry told me that for a few weeks his girlfriend was Janis Joplin. Maybe you've heard of her.

Shabbat Shalom!

Allen Throws a Flower

A few months after Zinnia Chin had begun her bat mitzvah training, she noticed that one of the girls in her cohort had started dressing as a boy. Zinnia didn't give it much thought, but she did observe the changes in clothes and haircut.

When Zinnia's mother asked her one night at dinner what was new, she reported that Allison had asked her and the other kids at Hebrew school to call her Allen.

Dr. Dana Kornfeld Chin glanced at her husband, Stuart, who was also a physician. "And what did you say?" she asked. This was new ground.

Dana looked closely at her daughter's face. She could see shadows of her own grandmother, a refugee from Poland, as well as her husband's grandmother, whose image was captured in a stark black-and-white photograph that sat on his desk. There it was—the blending of the Jewish and Chinese features in Zinnia's black hair, dark eyes, smooth olive skin, and erect posture. Like many Northern Chinese, Stuart was tall—over six feet, and it looked as if Zinnia might be tall as well. At five-foot-two, Dana felt she'd soon be left behind, vertically-speaking.

"Me?" Zinnia held her fork in mid-air for moment. "I said, 'Sure, Allen. No problem.'"

"Good," was all Dana said. Stuart nodded in agreement, and they all went back to their dinner and other topics of conversation.

One day at services, several months later, seven of the kids in Zinnia's cohort were sitting together near the back of the sanctuary. Garth Resnick, a big kid wearing a big suit and a big tallit, was up on the bima for his bar mitzvah.

As Garth finished his haftarah portion and began to recite the concluding blessing, a few of his young cousins picked up baskets of flowers and began to distribute the carnations that family and congregants would toss at him after he completed the blessing.

As usual, the kids with the baskets of flowers were slow getting to the back pews where Zinnia and her friends sat, but they did arrive just as Garth finished.

Cantor Sanders started singing *Siman Tov!* while the congregation joined in and clapped. That was the signal to toss the flowers at the bima.

One by one, Zinnia and the kids around her threw a carnation (or two, or three) as hard as they could. (Some weeks the carnations were large and especially throwable.) The goal, according to legend, was to try to hit the bar or bat mitzvah kid in the head. You got extra points if you managed to hit the cantor or rabbi.

Rabbi Ross seemed to be one of the toughest to hit. She often snatched the flowers in midair. Everyone knew the rabbi's fiancé was a jock, but she turned out to be pretty good herself.

On this particular day, after most of the flowers had been

tossed and *Siman Tov!* was coming to an end, Zinnia noticed that Allen, wearing a blue oxford button-down shirt, red tie, khakis, and a crew cut, still had a flower in his hand. She watched the motion of Allen's arm. The red carnation managed to go in a short, high arc, landing about five feet away.

"Allen! What the hell, man? You throw like a girl!"

The heads of Zinnia and the rest of their cohort swung around and focused their combined glare on Warren Drabner, a short, skinny boy whose ears stuck out through his long, dark hair.

"*Warren!*" one girl shouted.

"*What?*" was all he could manage to say. But no one answered.

It took him four or five seconds to realize his error, at which point he turned to Allen.

"Oh. Sorry, man. I forgot."

Allen looked at Warren and then at the other kids, and then just started laughing.

Allen's friends, one by one, joined in.

That night at dinner, Dana asked, "So, Zinnia, how was the service today?"

Zinnia looked up from her plate. "Oh, it was pretty good. Garth Resnick gave a great drash about Sodom and Gomorrah, and salt, and tikkun olam, and his Uncle Jerry."

Stuart looked at his daughter. "Sodom and Gomorrah. Salt. Uncle Jerry."

"Yeah. He talked about Uncle Jerry and his friends sitting in a hot tub and trying to make the world a better place to live in. One of the best drashes I ever heard." She went back to her dinner.

"Uh, Zinnia," said her mother, "this was one of the *best* drashes?"

"Oh, yeah. Garth is a really cool kid. Hey, have either one of you ever heard of Janis Joplin?"

"Yes, of course. What about her?" Dana had no idea where this was going.

"Well, according to Garth she was Uncle Jerry's girlfriend for a few weeks. Turns out she was pretty famous."

Dana and Stuart exchanged glances, as they often did when having a conversation with their daughter.

Stuart asked, "So, other than Uncle Jerry and Janis Joplin and the hot tub, did anything else interesting happen?"

Zinnia thought. "Actually, yes."

She then told them what Warren Drabner said after Allen threw the flower.

After she finished the story, her father spoke.

"So, Z." Stuart paused. "What's the takeaway here?"

"Yes," added her mother. "I'm curious, too."

Zinnia was thoughtful for a while as she chewed her food. She took a gulp of water and swallowed.

"The takeaway," she said, "is that you can change your name and your clothes easier than you can change your throw." Then she went back to her food.

Her parents just looked at each other, shook their heads, and smiled. As they often did.

Solomon's Protégé

Solomon P. Solomon and his wife, Mrs. Solomon, made their home for many years in one of the more fashionable sections of Brooklyn. His lighting business was also headquartered in Brooklyn, although the offices and large warehouse were located in a more industrial section of the borough.

Every summer, the Solomons liked to go to the Catskills for two weeks. And now it was June 1962, time to escape the heat of the city. So they traveled up to "the country," as it was still called by New York Jews of their generation.

Several years before, they'd discovered Butler Lodge, a moderate-sized resort that appealed to them. It featured what Mrs. Solomon referred to as a nice dining room, a nice pool, and a nice little lake where they would often take out a rowboat or a canoe. Other than the mosquitoes, which weren't so nice, it was a great place to unwind. Like many of the Catskill resorts of the era, there was no air conditioning, and you could hear the distant slamming of screen doors all day long.

The Solomons arrived early in the afternoon. They parked the car, checked in, settled into their cabin, and ate dinner in the resort dining room at six. They decided to have dessert "in town" at a restaurant recently purchased and renovated by one of Solomon's old high school friends.

They drove over, found the place, and parked under a hand-painted sign that said "Guest Parking." They could see the building was still being renovated, but was open for business. Seven or eight other cars were parked nearby.

The Solomons strolled into the modest restaurant, her arm through his, and immediately heard a voice coming from a room to their left. Above the entrance to this area was yet another sign, this one professionally painted: "The Lounge." They walked in.

Mrs. Solomon said, "This is a nice space." There were twenty or twenty-five little tables facing a small stage.

On that stage was a young man holding a microphone. He wore a white dinner jacket, a black bow tie, and an expression that Solomon thought looked somewhere between a forced smile and unforced terror. About a dozen people sat at the lounge tables. The Solomons sat down at a table near the back wall.

"I just flew in from Miami Beach, and boy, my arms are still tired."

Groans came from the audience, and two people got up and left even before the next joke was delivered.

"You know what you call a dead duck?" he asked the remaining guests.

"Yeah. *You!*" shouted someone else.

The young comic tried to ignore the heckler and answer his own question, but his response was drowned out by two more people exiting noisily.

"Let me tell you about my girlfriend. She's not that good-looking. But she's ..."

"Uglier than you!" offered another heckler, who was drinking beer from a tall glass bottle.

The show went on, if one could call it a show. One painful joke after another. The Solomons watched as the other patrons drank, talked to each other, and generally ignored what was happening onstage. The guy with the beer bottle left.

Finally, Solomon's old friend and the owner of the place, Manny Sondenheimer, jumped up on the little stage, took the mic, put his arm around the young comic, and said, "Let's have a big hand for Sandy Wintergreen! Wasn't he wonderful? Please put your hands together for Sandy!"

The Solomons clapped, but they were alone in doing so. Given the fact that people were getting up, scraping their chairs, talking loudly to one another, and getting the hell out of the place as fast as they could, their applause made barely more noise than the sound of one hand clapping.

When everyone else was gone, they heard Manny tell Sandy, "Go get some dinner. We'll talk later."

With his head slumped, Sandy dragged himself through a side door.

As he put the microphone back into the stand, Manny looked up and saw there was still a couple sitting in the back of the room.

"Show's over, folks. Maybe you'd like to go into the dining room for a late dinner."

"Who's buying, Manny?" asked Solomon.

Manny squinted across the room. Then he took a pair of glasses out of the breast pocket of his Madras sport jacket, put them on the crooked nose in the middle of his craggy face, and took a closer look at his guests.

"Whoa, look who's here! The lovely Mrs. Solomon. And who's this character you brung with you?"

Manny strode to where the Solomons were now standing and he embraced first Mrs. Solomon and then his old high school friend.

"Come on, let me buy you a drink, or a snack, or something. Have you eaten yet?"

"We're ready for dessert, Manny. We saved room. We just had dinner over at the Butler Lodge," said Solomon.

"Oy, the Butler, one of my biggest competitors. Especially when it comes to comedy shows. Did you see what I've got to offer?"

"We saw, we saw. What's the story?"

"He's my cousin Gertie's son. Calls himself Sandy Wintergreen; that's short for Steven Weingarten. He wants to break into comedy. I'm thinking he'd have better luck breaking into a bank. This was his first night."

"His first night?" asked Mrs. Solomon.

"Yeah. He may have been funny in high school—that's what his mother says. But they don't have drunk hecklers in high school. I'd promised he could stay here for two weeks, but if I don't send him home soon, I'm afraid he'll throw himself into the lake. Or just die on stage."

"He seems like a nice young man," offered Mrs. Solomon.

"Nice? Sure. But 'nice' doesn't bring people into The Lounge or pay my bills. I shoulda listened to my ex-wife."

The Solomons looked at each other, but were silent.

"Come on," Manny said. "Let's get you some dessert. You can check out the dining room."

Manny brought them into the dining room, seated them, and a young waitress came over. "Louise, this is Mr. and Mrs. Solomon, my personal friends. Whatever they want is on the house."

And then to his guests he added, "I gotta tend to business in the kitchen, guys. I'll see ya' later." And off he went through a swinging door.

The Solomons ordered apple pie and coffee, and sat quietly as they waited for their food. Then Mrs. Solomon spoke.

"Look, Solomon—there's Sandy over there in the corner, sitting by himself."

Solomon turned around and spied the young man, who looked like he was ready to cry. Or had already been crying.

His wife said, "What do you think?"

Solomon P. Solomon was very sensitive to the fact that his wife loved children. They'd lost their only child—a daughter—to a genetic disease when she was seven.

Their loss had brought the Solomons even closer to each other, and they had a good life together. His lighting supply business was quite successful. They lacked for nothing, owned their modest home, and did not live extravagantly. Just a trip a couple of times a year.

He was thinking about what he might be able to do for this young man.

"What do you *think*, Solomon?" his wife repeated. That was his signal to stop thinking and do something.

He got up, and walked over to the table where Sandy sat alone, looking down at his half-eaten plate of food.

"Sandy, how are you doing?"

Without looking up, Sandy replied, "I suck. That's how I'm doing." He realized what he'd said, and looked up. "Oh, I'm sorry. I'm really sorry. I didn't mean to …"

Solomon patted Sandy on the shoulder. "That's okay. We all have bad nights. Listen, why don't you come over and join me and the Mrs. for some dessert. Come on. Don't be shy."

Sandy got up and followed Solomon to their table, where he sat facing them. The waitress looked over and nodded when Solomon pointed at his pie plate and gave the signal for "one more." Then he looked at Sandy and offered his hand, which the young man shook.

"My name is Solomon P. Solomon, and this is Mrs. Solomon."

"It's a pleasure to meet you, Mr. Solomon. And Mrs. Solomon. That's really cool that you have the same first and last name."

"It is. No one has ever forgotten my name."

"Can I ask what the 'P' stands for?"

Solomon looked at his wife and nodded. Mrs. Solomon made sure she had the young man's attention as she delivered her line.

"It stands for Psolomon. The 'P' is silent." She said it straight; without a smile.

It took a fraction of a second for Sandy to react. Then he smiled and started to laugh. And he continued to laugh. He laughed as if he hadn't laughed in a long time.

"That," he gasped, "is funny. Geeze. I wish I could be as funny as you, Mrs. Solomon. Your delivery was perfect."

"It should be perfect," said Mrs. Solomon. "I've been delivering that line for 22 years."

"Wow!" was all Sandy could say. "I wasn't even born …"

"Please don't remind us," said Mrs. Solomon.

"Oh, sorry."

"She's just teasing you," said Solomon.

"Oh." But he didn't look like he was sure.

"Okay, Sandy. Let's talk business."

"Business?"

"Yes. Tell us why you're here? What are you doing here?"

"Here?"

"Yes. Here in the Catskills. Telling bad jokes and crying in your beer—or ginger ale, or whatever it is."

"Well," he sighed. "I've always wanted to be a comedian. I thought I was funny. I *was* funny in high school. But I'm definitely not funny here. I suck here. Sorry, Mrs. Solomon."

"It's okay, Sandy. You really did suck," she said, gazing at his hazel eyes, reddish-brown hair, and face that featured both freckles and acne.

"Mr. Solomon is going to give you some very good advice, aren't you, Solomon?"

It wasn't the first time he'd been put on the spot by his wife, but this time at least he'd seen it coming. What Mrs. Solomon knew but Steven/Sandy Weingarten/Wintergreen didn't, was that Solomon P. Solomon was a storehouse of jokes, including hundreds of off-color jokes.

Solomon looked at Sandy. In the young man's face he saw what appeared to be intelligence. Eagerness. He was nice-looking, although that could sometimes be a minus for a comic.

Solomon had begun to hone his skills in the late 1930s in the Catskills where he was a *tummler* at a large resort, responsible for entertaining guests in the dining room and at poolside, encouraging them to participate in a variety of "fun" events— from shuffleboard to bingo, and warming up the audience for the itinerant comics who worked the Borscht Belt circuit. On off-days, when no entertainers were scheduled, he'd get a chance to do some stand-up comedy of his own. All this was in addition to his job as a waiter at the resort. As he served the guests he'd kibbitz with them, clown around, and earn pretty good tips.

In the off-season, he worked as a traveling salesman for a lighting fixture company, where selling and entertaining clients went hand in hand. Within a short time, he was topping the sales charts and making a very good living. The Catskills and his summer job as a *tummler* were soon left behind. But his comedic skills remained in his heart and in his soul.

Solomon eventually became a partner and then took over the business when the senior partner had a sudden heart attack one day and dropped dead on the golf course. (The following day, Solomon gave up golf.)

Within a decade, Solomon had built the firm into one of the major forces in the commercial lighting industry. Mrs. Solomon, who was a teenager when he first saw her at the Catskills resort pool—he kept her parents laughing while he wooed her—was always at his side.

"Sandy."

"Yes, Mr. Solomon."

"Do you carry a notebook?"

Sandy pulled a notebook out of his jacket pocket, along with a Bic pen. "Yes, sir."

"Good. You've just passed the first of three tests."

"Three tests?"

"Yes. Second test. How's your memory?"

"Well, pretty good. Excellent, according to my mother. I did okay in school. I was able to memorize a lot of stuff when I had to."

"He has potential," said Solomon to his wife, who nodded.

"Last test, which is a question." He paused, then let it fly. "When you're telling a joke, what's the most important ...?"

"Timing!" Sandy blurted out, with a smile on his face.

Solomon sat back in his chair, pleased that the boy knew the old showbiz routine.

"All right, Mrs. Solomon. The *boychik* has a chance."

"I could tell," she responded.

"Sandy, not only have you passed the three tests, but you've got the Mrs. Solomon seal-of-approval, which is very difficult to get. I'm still working on it myself."

Sandy appeared to relax a bit.

"How much is Manny paying you?"

"Paying me?"

"Yes. Paying you."

"Well, he's feeding me and letting me stay on the couch in the room above the kitchen. And he said I could appear in his lounge for two weeks. I never expected any money, really."

"I'm not surprised."

"But after tonight, I'm not sure he's going to let me stay the whole time." Sandy started to look depressed again.

Solomon thought for a minute. Then, without a word, he got up and went through the swinging door into the kitchen. He was gone for five minutes. When he returned, he sat back down and put his hands on the table.

"Listen, boychik. Manny is now paying you fifty dollars a night for the next two weeks at The Lounge.

Sandy looked stunned. "Fifty dollars? A night? For two weeks?"

"Yes. And you're going to do two shows a night. The early show at seven, and the late show at ten."

"Two shows?" Sandy looked confused.

"Yes, two shows. And he's paying the money directly to me, because I am now your agent. And you are paying me an agent fee of fifteen percent, just like the pros do. You understand? So you'll be netting forty-two-fifty a night for the next two weeks. At this point it will be in cash, so let's not worry about taxes and the IRS and so on. Understand?"

"Well, sure. You're my agent?"

"Yes, unless you have another agent. Do you?"

"No. I never thought ..."

"Okay, I'm your agent. Let's not worry about the paperwork right now. Mrs. Solomon is a witness to our deal. I'm your agent, you get fifty dollars a night for the next two weeks at Manny's lounge, two shows a night. And I get my fifteen percent agent fee. Agreed?"

"Of course! Yes! Absolutely!"

Solomon stuck out his hand and Sandy grabbed it, and they shook.

Solomon then took out his wallet and withdrew a business card that said *Solomon P. Solomon* on it, but nothing else. From his own shirt pocket he took a slim gold pen and wrote 9 a.m. on the back of the card, as well as the name and cabin number of the resort where he and his wife were staying. He placed the card on the table in front of Sandy.

"I want you to have an early breakfast and then be at our cabin at nine o'clock tomorrow morning. It's about a mile from here. Nine sharp. Bring your notebook. We have a lot to go over.

"One last thing, Sandy. I'm now going to tell you a little story. Think about it tonight. Tomorrow morning, you're going to tell it back to me."

"Sure," said Sandy Wintergreen, the aspiring comedian. And Solomon P. Solomon began, "So there are these four rabbis who like to play golf …"

The Nightlight

Within a month after moving into her parents' rental house in Rockridge, Pearl and Jack were definitely on the fast track. He was now staying at her house almost as much as he was staying at his own place on Grizzly Peak. She'd wondered what the neighbors would think, seeing him coming and going late at night and early in the morning.

She felt conflicted. A few of these neighbors had known her when she was a little girl. But now she was an adult. What was she supposed to do—make believe she didn't have a boyfriend or a personal life? Make believe she was still six?

As a rabbi, she felt people would probably hold her to a higher standard. After mulling it over, she'd decided that "higher standard" would have to be defined by just *one* guy coming and going rather than a bunch of different guys. Life is full of little compromises.

Pearl, of course, could have visited Jack at his place. But then *she* would have been the one coming home late at night or early in the morning. And here was where all her stuff was—a helluva lot more stuff than Jack had.

In the end, Jack solved the problem as, Pearl would learn, he often did. He walked to each nearby house, knocked on the door, and introduced himself to the neighbors. He told them who he was, and put everyone's mind at ease. Some of the neighbors who'd known Pearl since she was in elementary school actually told him they were happy knowing that

someone was "taking care of Pearl and watching out for her."
He offered to help take in one couple's garbage cans from
the curb, and agreed to assist in the feeding of someone's cat
when the woman went on vacation. Leave it to Jack. He also
made sure Delilah was watered and fed. Live crickets, indeed.

The first night they'd made love, God said it was good.
And they both agreed.
It had also been the first time Jack spent the night at
Pearl's. When he awoke briefly at four o'clock in the morning, he watched her while she slept. A nightlight just inside
the open bathroom was on. He could see her face in the faint
illumination.
A few days later, he spent the night again. At one point
he thought about turning out the nightlight, but it was her
house, so he left it on.
On the third night he stayed, the moon was shining
through the bedroom window, and without thinking about
it very much, he turned the nightlight off after a quick trip
to the bathroom. After all, he thought, she'd probably left
it on for him, and he didn't need it to find his way around
anymore.
Big mistake. He hadn't planned on the moon setting. It
was the second time he'd heard Pearl scream. Between gasps,
she yelled for him to turn on the light.
With the room light on, he just held her. They didn't say
a word, and she fell asleep again in his arms.

The next morning, Pearl sat with her coffee cup, not speaking
and not really looking at him.
He finally broke the silence. "Do you want me to leave?
Do you want me to stay? Do you want me to tell you a funny
story? A rabbi and her parrot walk into Bloomingdale's …"

"It's my dark secret, Jack," she said, without humor. "Simply put, I'm afraid of the dark."

"Afraid of the dark," he repeated.

"It's actually got a name—nyctophobia."

He was silent, just listening.

"I've talked to psychologists about it, including my mother. Most people think it's weird, but it's actually the most common phobia. And a hard one to break. I've always had it, and I probably always will."

He looked at her curiously. "Is this a deal-breaker?"

She looked up at him. "Wait. I'm supposed to ask *you* that."

"You mean, because you have a condition that makes you afraid of the dark I'm supposed to what, leave you?"

"I don't want to lose you."

"Okay. What do you want me to do?"

"I … I just want you to love me."

He came over and held her tight and said, "I'm staying. Screw the dark. It's overrated anyway."

The following year they were married. Delilah, who had grown, was among the honored guests.

Samson and Delilah

Jack had been living in the Grizzly Peak house for a few months, enjoying the view, the workout room, and the cool San Francisco Bay late summer evenings—especially when he could slip into the hot tub and look at the moon, the stars, and the twinkling lights of the city.

Many nights he was joined in the tub by his housemates

and their friends. He liked these guys. Even when they lapsed into what he thought of as "gay-talk," he was comfortable. If you just changed a pronoun here and there, it was essentially the same as any discussion about relationships and dating.

To them, he was still the "the rabbi's boyfriend."

Jack had played tennis with a few of them and had filled in on a mostly gay softball team a couple of times. A jock is a jock, gay or not.

Tonight he was at Pearl's house. They were becoming very comfortable with one another, moving toward the inevitable. They'd begun discussing marriage.

They'd just made love, and she was lying comfortably in his arms, a couple of candles burning near a mirror on the dresser. The nightlight was just a glimmer from the adjoining bathroom. Jack now called it the *ner tamid*—the eternal light, a fixture in every synagogue.

Pearl said softly, "A shekel for your thoughts."

Jack held her close. Then he asked a question that had been on his mind recently.

"What do you think about me getting a six-pack?"

She smiled as she responded, "Well, I've never been much of a beer drinker, you know. It's generally wine, maybe some Kahlua or something like that. I'm not thirsty. Are you?"

"No, no. I'm not talking about beer. I'm asking if you'd like it if I had a six-pack, you know, really ripped abs, like the guys in the fitness magazines. Like my housemates."

He waited for what seemed to be a long time before she spoke.

"This is a very interesting dilemma. I'm actually glad you brought it up," she said in a serious tone of voice as the light of the candles flickered on the ceiling.

"You are?" He was surprised. "Why?"

"You know, in my fifth year I was in a study group with

some other female rabbinical students, and one time we were discussing this very topic—all about men's bodies." She said it matter-of-factly.

"Really?"

"Yes. One of the girls brought it up when we were reading through *The Book of Delilah.*"

"The Book of Delilah?"

"Yes. It's one of those Jewish Apocrypha books that's not included in the Tanakh. But when you're going to be a rabbi, you need to know about all this esoteric stuff. And men's bodies were a big topic in the book. And that Delilah—she really knew what she liked."

"How so?"

"Well, at the time the Philistines were looking for a woman to seduce Samson, who was decimating them."

"Yeah, with a jawbone."

"Right. As you probably know, there was a lot of gladiator activity going on in those days. People needed entertainment …"

"Like bread and circuses."

"Exactly. So they send this guy to scout out the Muscle Beach section of the Mediterranean. He was looking for a certain type of woman who hung out there—someone very beautiful and attracted to macho men. And he found her."

"Delilah."

"Yep. Here was a woman who would only partner up with the strongest man with the best body. These guys would fight over her and kill to get a chance with her."

"I never heard of this."

"Well, it doesn't really add a lot to the Samson and Delilah story. It's almost a frivolous distraction." She leaned over to take a sip of water.

"Anyway," she went on, "this guy, our scout, tells her

about Samson and guarantees she will just adore him, and that he puts her current Philistine boyfriend to shame. He says that if she agrees to help, well, she'd really be helping the Philistine nation, blah, blah, blah. And there might be a little something extra in it for her. In other words, she could have her cake and eat it too. He didn't mention that they actually planned to kill Samson. By the time they'd captured him, Delilah would just be collateral damage."

"Remarkable."

"Yeah. In any case, you can imagine how she just flipped when she first saw Samson. He was, like, Hercules. On steroids."

"Absolutely."

"There's actually some discussion of this in the Talmud. There's a famous Talmudic scholar—have you heard of Reish Lakish?"

"Actually, I have. Wasn't he the circus strongman?"

"Yes! Very good! He was not only a strongman, he was a gladiator. He actually mentions Samson several times in the Talmud."

Jack was skeptical, but he had to believe her. Why would she make this up?

"So yes, when we Future Female Rabbis of America would get together, especially after a morning workout at the Cincinnati YMCA, the conversation was always peppered with talk about six-packs, and pistols, delts, quads, traps, and so on."

"That's incredible."

"Yes, it *is* incredible. It's incredible that you would ask me what *I* must say is one of the most incredibly ridiculous questions that I've ever heard from an otherwise intelligent man."

"Ridiculous?"

She climbed up on top of him and grabbed his face in

her hands, then put her face close to his. "Look at me! And listen! Do you think, even once since I've known you, I've thought about how much more I'd love you if you had stupid six-pack abs?"

"Hey, they're not stupid. It takes a lot of work to ..."

"I *know* it takes a lot of work. And a lot of self-deprivation. I've seen women with six-packs at the gym. I actually heard one of them say to another that she would *never* have children because it would ruin her figure."

"Well, yeah, it probably ..."

"Jack! You have a beautiful body! I love it. And you. But you've been hanging out with too many bodybuilding model-types who wouldn't know Reish Lakish from Victor Mature."

"Isn't he the one who played Samson in ..."

"Jack! Stop it! There's no *Book of Delilah!* There's just a tarantula named Delilah. And she does not have a six-pack. She just has six legs."

"Eight, actually ..."

Pearl flopped over on her back next to him, shook her head, and said, "This is one for the books."

Jack waited, then put his arm under her shoulders and drew her close. He whispered.

"You really had me going with that *Book of Delilah* business. Did you just make that up?"

"Yes," she said softly, and moved closer to him.

"That was pretty good."

"Thanks."

"So I don't have to worry about getting a six-pack?"

"No, Jack."

"Good. One less thing to worry about."

He was asleep in less than a minute. She stayed up a lot longer, thinking about how complicated this relationship business could be. And how she needed to remember to tell a few of her girlfriends from rabbinical school about *The Book of Delilah.*

A Day at the Office

Friday morning the Rabbi hit the ground running, struggling through a Pilates class at the downtown Oakland YMCA. She yielded to temptation and weighed herself in the locker room. She wasn't happy with the number she saw, and sighed audibly.

The rest of the mid-July morning passed quickly as Pearl went through the tasks she realized took more of her time than she could have ever imagined.

Her to-do list included: looking over a draft of the upcoming Temple Bulletin; answering emails regarding an upcoming Shabbat hike and picnic in Roberts Park; meeting with a family that was considering becoming members; returning phone calls from the chairs of the Cemetery Committee and the Ritual Committee; chatting with a woman who was planning a bagel-baking competition (Pearl had been asked to be a member of the awards panel); settling a dispute that the LGBTQ group was having with its potluck dinner; working up notes for one of the temple book groups that she'd be leading (she made a note to herself to read the book); and writing a short drash for the upcoming bat mitzvah/Shabbat.

After eating lunch at her desk, she went out for a twenty-minute walk around part of Lake Merritt, taking in the sights and sounds of ducks, geese, and people. She calculated in her head that she'd burned off 64 calories. Maybe 65.

Her afternoon was much like the morning. She met with two b'nai mitzvah students who'd be celebrating their coming-of-age in the fall; emails regarding Tot Shabbat; a Temple-sponsored trip to Israel; and questions about the Scholar-in-Residence weekend coming up later in the year.

She deleted the link to a video of cute puppies and kittens that one of the congregants sent her just about every day. As she read an announcement in the Temple Bulletin about the Sisterhood's weekly Mah Jongg night, she smiled.

At least no one in the congregation had died in the past few days, and the news about Israeli/Palestinian conflicts was minimal.

The notes, the phone calls, the emails, the meetings, the students, the questions, and the answers were what she concentrated on as she went about her job. And although Jack was always in the background of her thoughts, she preferred it when he was in the foreground.

Surely God was looking over her—over them. Pearl got back to work.

A few minutes later the intercom buzzed and Pearl picked up the phone.

"What's up, Esther?"

"Rabbi, there's a woman on line two who says she's a friend of yours. Says her name is Mary Strawberry. Is that for real? Do you know her?"

Pearl laughed. "Yes, I know her. That's Mary Frances O'Connell. She's my closest friend. Whenever she calls, you can just put her through. Thanks, Esther."

Pearl picked up the phone. "Hello, Fresa!" she said, using Mary's childhood nickname. "How are things in Chicago?"

"Rainy. How're you doing? How's the rabbi gig?"

"It's great! I love it." She paused. "Except for the meetings. And the funerals."

"Don't talk to *me* about meetings! And death? I deal with it every day of my life. It's never easy, but most of the patients get better, thank God. Anyway that's not why I called."

"Let's have it," Pearl said, knowing what was coming.

"Okay. So, there's this horny old prospector who comes to town after being up in the hills for a year. And you know where he goes, first thing?"

"I can guess, but you tell me."

And so Mary Fresa told Pearl another in the seemingly endless list of jokes and stories she'd been collecting as long as they'd known each other.

Pearl closed her eyes and silently whispered, *Thank you again, Adonai, for saving the life of my dearest friend, Mary Fresa O'Connell.*

Craig and Grace

Each year, all Folsom Prison chaplains were required to attend a day-long meeting run by the director of the Chaplaincy Department.

That's where Rabbi Craig Cohen first saw Grace Haegerstrom.

He couldn't keep his eyes off her, as much as he tried. The wedding band on her left hand did not escape his attention. *Good*, he thought, *I'm safe. Just looking.*

Other than quick introductions at the start of the meeting, which included about twenty chaplains, they didn't speak.

When the group broke for lunch, some went out to a restaurant, and others wandered off alone. After some small talk with an administrator, Craig walked over to a small cafe nearby. He saw Grace sitting alone at a table, reading as she ate a sandwich. To his own surprise, he asked if he could join her. She smiled, closed her book, and invited him to sit.

After ordering a tuna sandwich and a Coke, they sat chatting for a few minutes. Grace asked him, "What would your wife say if she knew you were flirting with another woman?"

Craig sat back in his chair.

"Was I flirting with you?"

"Felt like it to me," she responded in a mock serious tone.

He felt embarrassed, and stood up. "I'm really sorry, Grace. I apologize." He started to get up from his chair, but she said, "Craig, please sit down."

He sat.

"Frankly, I could use some attention. I'm sure if you were flirting, it wasn't intentional."

Now he was flustered. He looked at her.

"Okay. I'm going to answer your question," he said.

"Which question?"

"You asked me what my wife would say if she knew I was flirting with another woman."

"Oh, yes," Grace said. "I did ask that."

The waitress delivered his order and he took a bite of his sandwich. After he'd swallowed, he spoke again.

"She would say that except for the fact that you're a married woman, I should go for it. She'd probably approve." He took a sip of his drink. "My wife passed away four years ago."

Grace looked closely at him.

"I guess I deserved that."

"What do you mean?"

"My husband died six years ago. And here we are, both still wearing our wedding rings."

"I'm so sorry."

"Don't be. His last years were a nightmare. He had ALS."

"Lou Gehrig's Disease."

"Yes. And as his condition progressed, at some point I just couldn't care for him at home anymore. I had to move him to the VA hospital."

"Grace, I ..."

"I hope you don't think badly of me for not keeping him at home."

Craig shook his head. "Of course not. Who am I to judge?"

"That's a very Christian way of looking at things. Not casting the first stone, and so on."

"Wait ... you're talking about Jesus. The famous Jew."

She laughed. "Yes. Same guy."

Grace paused, then said, "And your wife? I hope she didn't suffer."

"Fortunately, no. I was very unhappy at the time, and I certainly didn't want her to suffer. As your husband did."

"What does not destroy me ..." she started to say.

"... makes me stronger," Craig finished.

They sat quietly for a time. Then Craig spoke.

"I was thinking this morning at the meeting that you look sort of familiar, like I've seen you before."

"I get that a lot. You probably *have* seen me before. Do you watch TV at all, evening news programs?"

"Occasionally."

"Ever see one of those erectile dysfunction commercials where the couple is laughing and drinking wine or running along the beach?"

Craig laughed. "Sure, all the stuff they show people doing instead of the actual sex."

"Yes, exactly. Well, in some of the ads that's me, the loving, caring, sensitive wife of the guy with E.D. When they need a woman of 'a certain age' who has 'a certain look' for those drug commercials, sometimes I'm one of them. I've been doing commercials for years. My hair is silver now, but at some point it's been everything from strawberry blonde to lemon yellow."

"You're a very beautiful woman." He couldn't believe he was saying this to her, but he said it.

She smiled. "Thank you. I was told once by a Jewish director that I was a classic *shiksa* beauty. I took it as a compliment, but I wasn't sure at the time."

Craig looked at her face, framing it with both hands and moving from one side to the other—her small, even features and smooth, fair skin—as if he were setting the scene. "I'd agree. You *are* a classic shiksa beauty."

She smiled.

She looked at her watch. "Almost time for the meeting to start." But she just sat. Waiting. This did not escape Craig.

"Dinner? What do you think? Am I out of line? Just tell me."

"Let me think. Okay, I'm finished thinking. Yes."

That night they sat at a table in a small bistro a few miles from the prison. As they ate their dinner and sipped wine, their conversation became more comfortable. Both spoke about their deceased spouses.

"Forgive me for saying this," Craig said, "but everything I know about ALS I learned from watching Gary Cooper in *The Pride of the Yankees*. And that was a long time ago."

She smiled. "I know the film well. It's the only movie about ALS to win an Academy Award."

"Really?" Craig asked.

She laughed. "Nominated for eleven. Won the Oscar for film editing."

He watched her laugh and fell deeper.

It turned out each of them worked at the prison the first and third Mondays of the month. They made a date for dinner two weeks later.

And two weeks after that, he invited her to come up to his room at the Hilton. She did not hesitate.

They hadn't planned on the awkward moment when they needed to pass the front desk to get to the elevator.

"Hi, Rabbi Cohen. How are you tonight?" asked the young man at the desk.

"I'm just fine, Leonard. How are you doing?"

"Really good, thanks."

Without thinking too much about it, Craig said, "Leonard, I've got a special guest with me. She finally decided to join me here in Folsom. Same rate?"

"Oh, sure, Rabbi. Hi, Mrs. Cohen. Do you need an extra key card?"

"That's okay, Leonard. I'm good."

"Okay, just let me know."

Grace paused before moving on. She looked at the clean-shaven young man, dressed in his hotel-issued dark blazer, white shirt, and red Hilton tie. In another setting, he might have been taken for an enthusiastic missionary.

"Leonard, do you work here full time?"

He smiled. "Actually, I'm in my second year of college."

"What do you study?"

"Theology. I'm hoping to become a minister."

"Just like the rabbi here, except different, right?"

All three of them laughed.

Craig and Grace walked toward the elevator. As they rode up, he asked, "What was *that* all about?"

She stood close to him. "If I'm going to be playing Mrs. Cohen, I better start acting like Mrs. Cohen."

Rabbi Craig Cohen never thought in his wildest dreams that he'd ever love like this again. In the months that had passed since they first met, he'd fallen in love.

He glanced at the woman lying beside him and smiled to himself. *Classic shiksa beauty.* She'd said it herself. And it was true! Quite different from his wife, whom he'd always felt had *classic Jewish beauty.* Lorraine had dark hair with deep brown eyes. Grace had light skin, pale blue eyes, and blonde hair that she'd let turn gray on its own. His wife had been full-bodied, a wonderful armful. Grace was thin, willowy, tall.

This relationship was a jumble of conflicts. Love. Passion. Pleasure. A little guilt. Much laughter.

And she? Did she love him as well? She said so. She showed it in many ways. Her laugh. Her smile. Her cries of passion were nothing short of magnificent.

Grace had told him in no uncertain terms not to speak to her of marriage. She was a Christian, and that was not going to change. He was a rabbi, and that would not change either. They'd each had good marriages, followed by years of loneliness. Now was the time for them to enjoy their moments together.

He sighed for a second. Just a second, very quietly. Her eyes remained closed as she reached over to take his hand under the soft hotel sheet.

"You're driving yourself crazy again, aren't you?" she murmured, not opening her eyes.

"And you're mind-reading again." He reached over and held her breast.

She smiled. "Thank you. Less thought. More action. That's what we need around here."

He wrapped his arms around her, and their lovemaking recommenced. One thing for sure—they were both hungry.

And deprived. They held back absolutely nothing. And why should they?

He remembered something she had said more than once—"God has written us a prescription."

When she'd said that to him the first time, he was astounded by her ability to transform all his doubt into an act of God.

And so be it. He would live with the emotions he was experiencing, the guilt he was carrying, and the love, passion, and laughter they were sharing.

They'd each cried enough.

Ruth

Pearl's first Rosh Hashanah at the temple had gone smoothly. She'd delivered the Erev Rosh Hashanah sermon, and it had been well-received.

Now it was a week later, Saturday morning, September 14, 2002, and Pearl and Cantor Shelley Sanders were leading Shabbat services in the temple library, which also served as a small chapel and meeting room. There was no bar or bat mitzvah scheduled, and the service was attended by three dozen congregants. Rabbi Cohen had the day off.

The following night would be Pearl's first Yom Kippur service as a member of the clergy team. She was excited.

Midway through the Saturday morning service, as Pearl stood at the lectern leading the congregation in responsive prayer, she was surprised to see Duke Sniderman walk quietly into the room and approach the cantor. As the congregation responded aloud to the passage she'd just read, she saw

Duke whisper something to Shelley and hand him a pink phone message slip. Duke then put his hand on the cantor's shoulder, gave him an understanding smile, nodded to Pearl, and left.

Returning to her seat, Pearl observed the change in Shelley's demeanor as it went from Shabbat-cheerful to mild shock.

The cantor then took a deep breath and visibly pulled himself together in his "the show must go on" manner.

After the Kiddush potluck lunch, Pearl walked with Shelley back to his office.

There was no mistaking how upset he was. He barely held himself back from slamming the door, and then slumped into a chair.

"Shelley." Pearl sat down across the coffee table. "What's wrong?"

"We're screwed. That's what's wrong. Duke got a phone call early this morning from our Kol Nidre cellist. He slipped in the shower and broke his wrist. Obviously, he won't be playing tomorrow night." Shelley slumped even further.

"That's terrible," said Pearl, with true concern for the musician, whom she'd never met.

"Yeah," said Shelley. "I need to call him and wish him the best for a speedy recovery. I'll add his name to the *Mi Shebeirach* list so the congregation can pray for healing. Then you can add *my* name to the list."

He looked at Pearl. "We're going to have over two thousand people here tomorrow night, and most of them will be expecting to hear Kol Nidre on the cello. And I'm the one who's going to have to tell them, 'Sorry, folks—one slip and *poof*, no cello for you tonight.'"

Pearl did her best to calm him. "But you'll be *singing* the

Kol Nidre. And the organist can play it. All is not lost." She smiled one of her practiced rabbinical smiles.

Shelley was not to be so easily assuaged. "Yeah, yeah. I know. But Kol Nidre on the cello has been an important part of our Yom Kippur service forever. Sorry, Rabbi, but I'm not happy." He would have sunk even lower into his chair if it had been possible.

Pearl remained quiet for a few moments. She was thinking.

"Shelley, I might be able to help," she finally said.

He looked at her. "How?"

"Do you have a copy of the Kol Nidre cello music?"

"Of course." The cantor leaned over, took a folio off his desk, and handed it to her. "You don't play the cello, do you?"

Pearl rose as she said, "No. But don't do anything drastic for the next few hours. I'll let you know if I have any success." Without further explanation, she left his office, music in hand.

After a short telephone call from her own office, Pearl grabbed her jacket and bag and left the temple.

Fifteen minutes later she pulled up in front of a multi-colored Victorian in Oakland's Dimond district. Parked in the driveway was a black SUV. On the sides and back door were illustrations of a witch riding a broom. The witch was pointing a wand at a large cockroach, zapping it dead. Above the caricature was written *Samantha the Roach Witch*. A phone number and a contractor's license number were listed too.

Samantha Wyatt was the owner of a one-woman pest control company. She was also the domestic partner of Ruth Ross, Pearl's younger sister.

Ruth was a cellist. And her contact with Pearl over the last ten years had been limited.

Pearl walked up to the front door and rang the bell. It was answered by Samantha, whom Pearl had met only briefly at her parents' home six months before. Samantha was a solidly-built young woman about the same height as Pearl, but probably thirty pounds heavier. She wore her light brown hair fairly short, and had bright blue eyes that were not exuding much friendliness at the moment. She led Pearl into a comfortably furnished living room. The air was cool, just like Samantha's welcome.

"Have a seat. Ruth'll be here in a minute." And with that, she walked into the nearby kitchen and sat down. Pearl saw her pick up a newspaper in one hand and a cup of coffee in the other. Sentry duty.

Pearl sat and waited. She eyed the black and white cat sitting in a nearby chair, and the cat eyed her.

Ruth did arrive just a minute later, dressed in black. As always. Wearing black seemed to be one of the few things Pearl and her younger sister had in common. Ruth picked up the cat, set him on the rug, and sat down in the chair. The cat growled.

Ruth looked at him and said, "Be quiet, Trustworthy." The cat left the room without a backward glance.

Ruth turned her attention to Pearl. "I guess this is the first time you've been here."

"Yes. It's a really nice house."

"It's Samantha's. She's owned it for a long time. I moved in after we became a couple."

None of this was news to Pearl. She decided it was best to get to the point.

"Ruth, I need a favor."

"You need a favor? From *me?*"

"Yes. In fact, there's no one else I can turn to."

Ruth frowned. Her straight black hair, parted in the middle, was gathered at the back of her neck; a red lacquered chopstick held it together. Ruth's eyes were darker than Pearl's, and she had beautiful, slender hands, which moved through the air gracefully.

"What can I possibly do for *you?*"

"An emergency has come up at the temple. Tomorrow night is Erev Yom Kippur—the Day of Atonement, where people fast and ..."

"I remember, Pearl," she said with a look that said, *Do you think I'm stupid?*

Pearl was here on a mission, and wasn't going to get into it with her. She removed the music folio from her bag and handed it to Ruth.

"Our regular cellist was supposed to play this Kol Nidre music with our organist. It's a tradition in many congregations."

"I've heard it." Ruth opened the music folio.

Pearl quickly explained that the regular cellist had just broken his wrist and the cantor was very upset.

"And you need me to play. As a last-minute sub. Tomorrow night."

"Only if you can. Only if you want to. It would be a major favor for me, the cantor, and the congregation."

"A major favor ..." Ruth said to no one in particular. She was still looking at the music, paging through it as if it were a children's book.

"What time?" Ruth asked.

"The service starts at seven-thirty at the Lakeshore Temple."

Ruth stood. "Okay. I'll be there."

Pearl stood as well. "You can come through the side entrance. The security guard will show you where to park. Your name will be on his list." She reached into her bag. "Here are two passes for the service." She handed them over.

"Thank you, Ruth. I truly appreciate it. Mom and Dad will be there—just so you know."

"Okay. See you tomorrow night." She led Pearl to the front door and opened it for her.

Although they did not embrace or kiss, Pearl touched her younger sister on the arm, smiled, and again said, "Thank you."

Ruth stood at the door until Pearl got into her car and drove away.

As she closed the front door, she turned and saw Samantha standing next to her.

"What the hell was *that* all about? I thought you didn't want to have anything to do with your sister. And here you are, doing her this big favor? I don't get it."

"Samantha, it's complicated. I'll explain the situation to you later. Right now, I have to start preparing for tomorrow night."

As Ruth walked up the stairs to her practice room, she called down, "Are you interested in coming? I've got two passes."

"Absolutely. I'll drive."

"Great. Thanks."

And with that, the conversation was over.

Samantha returned to the kitchen table, her newspaper, and her coffee. Soon, the sound of the cello filled the house, as it did every day. This, however, was a new melody that Samantha had never heard before. *Not unpleasant. Sad. Maybe melancholy*, she thought, as Trustworthy jumped onto her lap. *But uplifting ... hopeful, even. Quite beautiful, in fact.*

Later that night, when they were in bed together, Samantha

said, "So what *is* the story between you and your sister? I was ready to hate her guts. But she seems to care for you, and respect you."

Samantha turned out the light as Trustworthy made himself comfortable at the foot of the bed.

Ruth sighed a long sigh. Samantha detected a small sob as well. She let Ruth settle down and calm herself. After a while, Ruth began speaking, softly.

"Ever since I was a little girl I treated my sister like crap."

"Why?"

Ruth exhaled heavily. "Why? I'm not sure. Jealousy. Envy. She was older. Smarter. Confident. Charming. Snappy. You name a quality, she had it. She's a natural leader."

"Any musical talent?"

"A little. She acted and sang in the school plays. But I was the musician in the family. It's the one thing I had that she didn't. I'm almost five years younger, though, and by the time I was any good, she was already at Stanford."

"What did you do to her that was so bad?"

"Oh, I was mean to her. I'd hide her stuff, steal it, break it. I was a complete bitch." Ruth cried softly. Samantha stroked her arm. Her hair.

"But that wasn't the worst thing. I knew my sister's secret. And I tortured her with it."

"Your sister's secret …"

"Yeah. She's afraid of the dark."

"Your sister the rabbi is afraid of the dark." She phrased it as a statement, not a question.

"Yes."

"Ruth, *children* are afraid of the dark. Rabbis, even teen-age future-rabbis, are not afraid of the dark."

"You'd think. But she has some kind of condition, a phobia. My mother once explained it to me. It's not uncommon among girls and women. She's deathly afraid of the dark; she can't help it. And I used to do all kinds of stuff to her."

"Like?"

"She always slept with a little nightlight on, and I'd turn it out. Things like that."

"What happened when you did this stuff?"

"She'd wake up screaming. She'd panic. She'd cry."

"You did that to her?"

"Yes. I was cruel. It gave me power. But now it just makes me sick to think about it." Ruth turned over and faced Samantha.

"And that wasn't the worst of it. Pearl was always kind to me. She protected me." Ruth paused, then said, "She even rescued me."

"Rescued?"

Ruth was quiet for a moment, then sighed again.

"I guess it's my own secret. When I was at Oberlin that one year, I was miserable. I was in over my head, the deep end of the pool. Because I was a pretty good cellist in high school, everyone expected me to go to the top. So I applied to Oberlin and got in. My parents were proud of me and money was not an issue. I realized right away I was out of my element.

"I wasn't motivated to excel the way the other students were. Many of them were headed to symphony orchestras all over the world. Some wanted to be professors. All I wanted to do was play my cello. I didn't give a damn about being at the top of the class."

"So?"

"So I screwed around, jammed with the jazz musicians, hung out with people I met in town, played little gigs here and there, cut classes. I started to drink. Took some drugs. Experimented."

"And …"

"And one winter night I was drunk. I was in a car with some other drunk people, and it was snowing. The guy driving was fooling around and the car skidded and we hit a pedestrian—she wasn't killed, but she was hurt pretty badly. Broken hip, concussion.

"When the cops came, they searched our car and found cocaine and speed. I had no idea that stuff was there. We were all arrested, and the next thing I knew I was in jail. I was scared out of my wits. My biggest fear was that my parents would find out."

Samantha squeezed Ruth's hand.

"And you know what I did?" Ruth asked. "I called my sister. My sister, the person I'd treated like crap my whole life. She was in Cincinnati at the rabbinical school—up to her ears in whatever you do there. That's who I called."

"What did she do?"

"What *didn't* she do?" Ruth reached over for some tissues and blew her nose. She drank some water. She breathed deeply.

"Pearl dropped everything. It was a Friday night—Shabbat. She made phone calls, got me the name of a lawyer in Cleveland."

"She got you a lawyer?"

"Not any lawyer. The *best* lawyer. The best *Jewish* lawyer. Then Pearl borrowed a car. She drove to Cleveland. It was dark. She hates the dark. It was snowing. She'd never driven in the snow before. She drove five hours in the dark. The next morning—Saturday morning—she and the lawyer got me out on bail. I found out later that she was supposed to be the student rabbi that morning at services and deliver a sermon. One of her friends had to bail *her* out!" Ruth laughed a sad laugh as she said this.

"And your parents?"

"They never found out. She never told them. She borrowed money to pay my bail. She stayed the whole week with me. The lawyer got me out of the mess somehow. She paid him with her credit card. I never paid her back."

"Geeze."

"I know. When I was a kid I resented her because she was better and smarter. After the jail thing, I avoided her because I was ashamed. I still am.

"I dropped out of Oberlin and came back to California with my tail between my legs. I told my parents I couldn't handle the competition and the stress. Their reaction wasn't as bad as I'd thought it would be, and it actually worked out for the best.

"My mother, the shrink, helped me through it. I enrolled at Cal State Hayward and worked with a wonderful cello teacher there. He played in the San Francisco Symphony— I've told you about him.

"I did great. The pressure was off. I got A's. I made new friends. I graduated. I got to play jazz, new music, weddings … all kinds of gigs."

"And now you're playing the Yom Kippur gig."

Ruth leaned over on her elbow and, in the semi-dark, looked at her partner. "Samantha, today was the first time my sister ever asked me for anything. Ever."

"And she asked you for the one thing only you could deliver."

"Funny, isn't it?"

Although Ruth didn't believe in God, as she fell asleep, she had a thought. *If there* is *a God, She sure works in strange ways.*

Do You Believe in God?

"So, Ruth said she'd play for Kol Nidre?"

"Yes. And Shelly was overjoyed. He hasn't stopped thanking me. He's acting like *I'm* the cellist."

"Well, sometimes things do work out."

The dark room was lit, as usual, by candles as well as by the Ner Tamid nightlight. Marriage plans were progressing, and they were both very happy. She'd never felt closer to anyone.

She spoke again, just above a whisper.

"Do you mind if I ask you a personal question?"

She waited for him to respond.

"You want to ask me a personal question."

"Yes."

He waited, then said, "All right. You can ask me a personal question. You can ask me about anything, except one thing."

"What's that?"

"You can't ask me about my prostate."

"*What?*"

"Yep. That's where I draw the line. No prostate-related questions."

She started giggling. She never knew what he would say at any given moment, and it was usually something that made her laugh. The only other person who made her laugh like this was Mary Fresa.

"Sure, go ahead and laugh," he said in a very serious tone.

"Jack," she replied, while trying to regain her composure. "I don't even know what a prostate *is!*"

"It's nothing but trouble. Just ask my father. You don't want to know."

How could she ask him a serious question when he did this to her. But she forged ahead.

"Okay, no prostate questions."

"Good."

"As a matter of fact, it's sort of a serious question."

"Pearl, there's nothing more serious than your prostate. If you have one, that is."

"Would you please stop already with the prostate! I have a serious, personal question to ask you."

"Shoot."

This wasn't going the way she thought it would. The hell with it. She just asked her question.

"Do you believe in God?"

He took a deep, audible, breath. "Wow, here I thought you were going to ask me something really difficult and personal. Instead you throw me a softball."

After a few moments of silence, he closed his eyes and started making snoring sounds.

"Jack! Stop it!"

"Oh. You're still here?"

"Jack!"

"Do I believe in God? Was that the question?"

"Yes. Do you believe in God. You heard me."

"Okay. I heard you."

She waited. He didn't answer. She decided to wait him out. Finally, he spoke.

"This is a trick question. I just know it."

She smiled in the semi-darkness. *Do you believe in God?* A trick question. She had to hand it to him.

"Why do you say that?"

"Because I can see where this might be headed, and I don't like what I see, Rabbi."

"Jack, don't call me 'Rabbi' when we're in bed together. Okay?"

He said, "All right. I changed my mind. You can ask me about my prostate."

She was getting exasperated.

"Why is this so hard for you to talk about? You're Jewish. You had a bar mitzvah. You come to services. I see you recite the prayers and read in Hebrew. Do you believe in God? Period."

Silence. Then he said, "Fine. I'll answer your question. I'll talk to you about God. But you just have to tell me something first."

"What?"

"Is this the deal-breaker? If I give you the wrong answer, or an inadequate explanation, or screw up the response in some way, is that it? I'm back on the street?"

"Back on the street?"

"Yeah. I have to go back up to Grizzly Peak with my gay buddies and start looking around for another girlfriend who tops you? Which will be impossible. So I'll just wind up going back to South America, living out the rest of my days with spiders and snakes in the rain forest?"

Pearl sighed. "You are beginning to piss me off. Just answer the damned question, will you? You're not leaving me and you're not going back to South America or any of that nonsense! I just want to know. Can we leave it at that?"

More silence. "Okay. I'll answer. But it's not a simple answer, because it's not a simple question." She waited what seemed like a long time. He leaned over on one elbow so he could face her. Then he held her hand and spoke.

"Pearl, I'm a scientist. I've always been a scientist. Scientists are skeptics; they have to be. We're always asking 'Why?'

"Why is the sky blue? Why do scorpions do their little mating dance? Why did the American chestnuts die? What happened to the dinosaurs?"

"That sounds like my father. He still wants to know where Jimmy Hoffa is buried."

"Exactly. And then there are all the medical questions, and the geological questions, and the logical questions. If the lady gets sawed in half, where's the blood?"

"I get it," she said. "I'm also hoping you're getting to the point."

"Okay, so let's talk about God. There I am, sitting in my temple in Florida. First I'm a little kid. Then I'm a bigger kid. And then a teenager. And the whole time I'm asking myself: Why wasn't the burning bush consumed? Did the sea really part? What's with the frogs? Did Elijah really go to heaven in a flaming chariot, and if so, where can I get one? Where's my jet pack? Don't even get me started with Noah.

"Miracle after miracle, they keep coming at me, and I'm sitting there with my little budding scientist mind questioning everything. I start asking the rabbi, my parents, the Hebrew school teacher, and all they do is give me stupid, nonsensical answers.

"So, I'm having to deal with all this by myself, and I'm not really equipped. Because in science, you question things until you find an answer. You know the answer may not be perfect, or even accurate, but it's an answer and it has to do until a better answer comes along, and maybe *you'll* be the one who finds it.

"Pearl, I've read about this process and I've seen it happen myself—and I'm still fairly young. Scientific 'truths' will often be found to be false. Hell, maybe I'll debunk some so-called facts myself.

"But with God and the Bible? That's not the way it works. You can come up with explanations for why something *could* have happened. Like, 'It wasn't really the *Red* Sea, it was the *Reed* Sea; and it was just some tides that moved water around so Moses and the gang could get through, and then the moon came up or went down and the waters flooded and drowned all the bad guys, and Miriam took out the old tambourine and sang her song. End of story.'"

Pearl moved closer to him and said softly, "I love you."

He kissed her hand. "But all of that is just a story. A myth. At some point I came to the conclusion that trying to 'scientize' biblical stories is worse than just believing them. Like, how come the unicorns didn't make it onto the ark? Did Noah screw up? People drive themselves and everyone else crazy with this kind of nonsense.

"Einstein once said, 'God does not play dice.' He had a God that *he* believed in. I read a story about him once where he said, 'Science without religion is lame; religion without science is blind.'"

Pearl whispered, "I didn't know that Einstein said ..." But Jack cut her off.

"Richard Feynman said that he doesn't believe that science can disprove the existence of God, it's just impossible. And if it's impossible to disprove, then isn't a belief in science *and* God a consistent possibility? He said something like that. He didn't say that he *believed* in God; just that you can't *disprove* God. Einstein. Feynman. These were smart guys."

Pearl said, "I read a book by Feynman one time, and ..."

"So you ask me, just an ordinary scientist, if I believe in God? Sure, why not? Because when you come right down to it, you gotta ask yourself, 'Who or what started the Big Bang? Who or what caused cells to evolve into organisms? Who or what caused animals to move from the sea to the land? Who put the ram in ..."

"... the rama lama ding dong?"

"Right. So sure, I believe in God. Why not? Can you think of something better to believe in?" Pearl waited for him to continue.

"My image of God is probably different, though. It seems a lot of people like the image of the old guy in the sky with the long white beard. But that's ridiculous. The God I believe in created some incredible things 'billions and billions' of years ago. And if that was just six days of 'God-time,' that's fine with me. Because *dust you are and to dust you will return.* No stoppin' it."

He was finished. She could tell. And all she could think was, *Wow.* He actually turned over in bed, facing away from her. She turned over next to him, and pressed her breasts against his back

"Thank you," she said softly to him, as she reached over and stroked the hair on his chest. "I guess that wasn't easy."

"No. Remind me to explain all about the prostate. It's much easier."

"Maybe it is. And you don't have to quote scripture."

A long silence. Then he spoke.

"And what about you? Do you believe in God? Is that part of the deal to be a rabbi? Why did you even ask me?"

She touched his arm. He had glorious triceps.

She spoke quietly. "My belief in God goes way back, and it had nothing to do with my being Jewish. I learned about God from Mary Fresa—after her mother had been killed and she lost her eye and suffered injuries that would prevent her from ever having children.

"Fresa taught me about faith, and belief, and courage, and so many other things. I'd watch her pray in church. Hell, she even prayed when we sat at Shabbat services in the temple. If she was in a House of God, boy, there was nothin' stopping her. It was like she had God all to herself, and God gave her courage, and strength, and fortitude. And I said to myself, *Hey, I want to feel that.* And after a while I did. And then I learned more about what God means to me, and that God is different for each person. And if a person doesn't want to believe, well, that's his or her own business."

She reached for a glass of water that was on the night table, took a sip, put it back down, and snuggled back into position.

"I've been a rabbi a very short time, but I'll tell you what happens when people come in to talk to me about something that's bothering them—I'm talking about adults, not kids. The first thing they say is, 'Well, Rabbi, my boyfriend and I want to get married, and we want to get married in the temple, and we want you to officiate, but I just have to let you know that I don't believe in God.'

"Or, 'It looks like my father's going to die any day now, he's got pancreatic cancer, and he told me he wants to be buried in the Jewish cemetery, and we'd like you to do the funeral service; but it's important for you to know, Rabbi, that my dad doesn't believe in God—never did. Neither do I, for that matter.'

"Craig warned me about this not-believing-in-God business. He said that probably most of the people in our congregation will tell you first thing that they don't believe in God."

Jack turned over, put his arm under her shoulders, and said, "What did Craig say you should tell these people?"

"He said you should just smile, be sincere, and explain that not believing in God isn't a barrier to being married. Or being buried in the cemetery. Or pretty much anything, including being a good Jew or a good human being. He also said that people often change their minds about God.

"Hell, lots of rabbis I've met have questioned their belief in God. I don't hold it against them. Or anyone. It's a very personal thing."

"Is that why you asked me?"

"No. I asked you because I want to know what I'm getting myself into."

"Now you know. I hope my answer was satisfactory."

"Considering that it was a trick question, you did just fine."

He grumbled a little. She fell asleep with a smile on her face.

Kol Nidre

As the last-minute substitute Kol Nidre cellist, Ruth was a sensation.

Many people were surprised when she, instead of the regular cellist, walked onto the Lakeshore Temple bima, sat in a chair in front of the choir, placed her music on the stand, and nodded to the organist.

The congregation, which filled the sanctuary and all its balconies, held its collective breath as she held the bow over her beautiful instrument for a long moment before playing the first mournful notes.

Ruth had insisted that the substitution not be announced beforehand; she wanted the music to speak for itself. In fact, there were fewer than a dozen people present who knew Ruth's identity. There had been no rehearsal. Ruth met briefly with Julian, the temple organist, and discussed form and tempo with him. Julian was somewhat alarmed when she said that at a particular moment in the piece she would be inserting a cadenza—an improvised solo section. He'd played the Kol Nidre for more than fifteen years and this was the first time a cellist had ever inserted a cadenza. It wasn't in the score. It wasn't suggested anywhere. It just wasn't *done!* But Ruth was obviously a pro. And, she was the rabbi's sister. If it didn't work out, hey, it wasn't *his* idea. Or fault. Frankly, he was curious to see what she would do, whether she could make it work.

She did make it work.

The piece began as always. The congregants settled in and many closed their eyes, moved by the familiar melody. Many had heard it once a year since they were children, and there were a fair number of people present who were over ninety.

When Ruth began her improvised cadenza, she closed her own eyes, and the music began to soar even higher.

Cantor Shelley Sanders, whose mind had been in a far-away place as he listened to the magnificent rendition of the melody, was brought sharply back to the present when he heard the unfamiliar improvised section. He at once looked for his wife. She was sitting in the fifth row with their children. Susan, who was an extremely accomplished musician, had a warm smile on her face. As she caught his gaze, she gave him a reassuring nod. It was okay, she was saying. So Shelley calmed down, sat back, and listened.

And as he listened, he could not help but like what he was hearing. It was ... genius. Simply genius. Ruth was incorporating sounds of the shofar ... a quote from the Shema ... a snippet of minor key notes from—was it George Gershwin or Irving Berlin? Maybe Harold Arlen.

Ruth's cadenza lasted less than a minute, and when she and the organist resumed the piece, somehow the congregants knew they had experienced something special. They just weren't sure what it was.

Because applause is not appropriate at Jewish services,

when Ruth and Julian completed the Kol Nidre music, the congregation of over twenty-five hundred remained silent. Pearl began to walk toward the podium, but made a detour and stood next to Ruth. She held her younger sister at arm's length, looked into her eyes, smiled, and then embraced her, kissing her on the cheek. The congregants watched and waited, many with tears in their eyes, as they began to put two and two together, realizing they were witnessing a special moment.

Pearl whispered something in her ear and Ruth smiled. She then took her cello and bow and exited stage right.

Samantha, whose cheeks were damp, met Ruth backstage.

Ruth said, "Let's go."

"I'd like to stay. Is that okay?"

Ruth was surprised. "Sure. I just thought you'd want to leave right away."

"No, I'd like to see what it's like. By the way, you sounded great."

So Ruth went back to the now-empty greenroom and put her cello in its case. Then they walked out through the side door, past the security guard, and around to the front entrance of the Temple. They showed their passes at the door, were given prayer books by a volunteer in the lobby, and then wandered up the stairs to the second balcony where they found two empty seats.

Ruth glanced at her partner. Samantha had asked someone the page number, and had begun following the service, reading along with a responsive prayer in English. She was now sitting and standing along with everyone else, and for some reason seemed to be enjoying herself. After a while, Ruth relaxed and stopped worrying about Samantha.

Ruth had never seen Pearl in her role as a rabbi, and

began to think about the past. The present. The future. She had declined her parent's offer to pursue bat mitzvah training—religious stuff was for Pearl. Ruth just wasn't interested.

Perhaps, she thought, it might be time to reassess her relationship with her older sister. It might be time.

At the conclusion of the service, Rabbi Craig Cohen read a long list of acknowledgements. Then he simply said, "And on behalf of the clergy and the entire congregation, we would like to extend a very special thank you to Ruth Ross, who filled in at the last minute for our regularly scheduled cellist who was not able to make it."

He waited for the murmurs to die down, and then added, "And yes, Ruth *is* related to Rabbi Ross."

He paused and smiled. "They share the same parents."

Laughter erupted, and he waited for it to end. "Have an easy fast!"

It was the first time he could remember seeing everyone leaving an Erev Yom Kippur service laughing and smiling.

Samantha shook hands and chatted with the people around her, and Ruth accepted congratulations in English, Yiddish, and Hebrew. She and Samantha waited until the Sanctuary had emptied, then made their way down the stairs, toward the bima, and finally backstage where they retrieved her cello in the green room. There they were greeted by Craig, Shelley, Susan, Pearl, Jack, Duke, Ruth and Pearl's parents, and some of the people who'd been sitting on the bima. Ruth wanted to leave, but Samantha maneuvered her from one person to another as each expressed their thanks and appreciation.

Craig shook Ruth's hand and would not let go. "Ruth,

you have done us an incredible *mitzvah*. Thank you so much!"

Shelley was equally effusive in his thanks, as well as in his praise for her unexpected cadenza. "I've never heard anything like *that* on Yom Kippur. Thank you!"

She kept a smile pasted on her face—as she did after all her performances.

An hour later they were home.

As they walked in the door Ruth said, "I'm starving!"

Samantha turned to her with a shocked look. "You're going to eat? I thought Jews fasted on Yom Kippur."

"Are you nuts? You know that after I play I'm always really hungry."

"I just thought …"

"Look, I'm famished, I haven't fasted on Yom Kippur since I was, like, fifteen. If you want to fast, be my guest." Ruth headed toward the kitchen.

"I think I will," said Samantha.

"You're kidding me."

"No. It seems like an … interesting idea. I've never fasted before. Maybe I'll lose a pound or two."

"Geeze! Are you going all Jewish on me?" They'd never discussed religion or attended any kind of service together.

Samantha ignored her and walked upstairs to their bedroom, calling over her shoulder, "Hey, are those passes your sister gave us good for tomorrow's service?"

Ruth sat down at the kitchen table, muttering to herself. "I can't believe this."

Later, when the lights were out and Trustworthy was purring loudly, Samantha asked, "Are you pleased with the way things went?"

"Actually, yes. It's always a thrill when you get to play solo in front of so many people who are listening to your every note."

"I can imagine," Samantha said. "And on Yom Kippur—the holiest night of the year."

Ruth couldn't resist. "Holier than Christmas?"

"Well, whether it's Santa or a Fiddler—somebody's always on your roof."

"You're right." They laughed. Trustworthy just meowed.

"Your sister was happy. Everyone seemed pleased."

"You know what she whispered to me when she kissed me on stage—on the bima? In front of over two thousand people?"

"What?"

"She said, 'Thank you. You saved our ass.'"

"No way."

"Yes. I saved their ass."

"Well, you did."

"Maybe. I guess I did."

"Mazel Tov, Ruth."

"Would you *please* stop with the Jewish *shtick* already!"

"But I *like* the Jewish shtick!"

Ruth groaned to herself. "*Oy!*"

At the French Cleaners

After a local dry cleaners ruined her best suit, Pearl took her mother's advice and began bringing her clothing to the French Cleaners in Berkeley.

Mrs. Kim, the Korean owner, looked up when Pearl came into the shop to pick up her clothes. Pearl estimated the well-dressed woman's age was somewhere between 50 and 70—there was no way to know for sure. Her jet black hair was curled and styled. Her nails were long, ruby red, and incredible. And her greeting was classic Mrs. Kim.

"Rabbi, Pearl. Pearl, Rabbi. You look so beautiful. Just like your mother. Let me see …" She pushed a button and the long circular rack started moving. Pearl hadn't even removed the pink receipt from her bag.

"Here we are, Rabbi Pearl." She went through the hangers. "One black pants suit. Two black pants suits. Three black pants suits. Four black pants … no, this is one black suit with skirt. And blouses, let me see—five white blouses, two cream color blouses. Very good. They make you wear the black suit and white blouse every day at your synagogue?"

"Well, no, but it's more professional, don't you think?"

"What *I* think? I think you are a beautiful young lady, a rabbi. That's like a priest, right?"

Pearl smiled. "Sort of."

"But a rabbi, she can get married, right?"

"Yes."

"Then you maybe need to wear something beside black. Or else maybe the handsome young men, they'll think you are an undertaker."

An undertaker.

"Yes, Rabbi Pearl, Rabbi. You are a very pretty young lady. Maybe a nice light-color suit. Or a dress. You would look good in red, I think." Mrs. Kim leaned over the counter. "You have nice legs, Rabbi. Maybe a *short* red dress."

Pearl paid, took hold of the giant bundle of plastic-wrapped black suits and white blouses, and lugged it out to her car.

An undertaker! Maybe I should *wear a short red dress on the bima.*

Revelation

One morning when she was in ninth grade, Pearl's home-room teacher passed her a note. It was from one of the school counselors, Mrs. Chapman, asking Pearl to drop in during her study hall period that morning.

When Pearl arrived at 10:08, Mrs. Chapman invited her in and closed the door behind them.

"Thanks for coming in."

"Sure," Pearl said. "I hope I'm not in trouble!"

Mrs. Chapman laughed. "Nothing like that." Then she became serious. "Pearl, as you probably know from your mother, we've been following Mary Frances O'Connell's progress since her terrible accident. I hear that you've been visiting her, and that you've become friends."

"Yes. I really like her a lot. It's just terrible what happened to her mom. And Mary was hurt …" Pearl started to tear up and reached for a tissue from the box on the desk. "We get along well. She's really funny. Did you know that?"

Mrs. Chapman smiled. "This is the first year that Mary Frances is in the public school system. She came from St. Agnes to attend high school. So we don't know her well at all. I just had one meeting with her before the accident. But I'll take your word for it. The fact that you're reporting that she has a good sense of humor is wonderful news."

Mrs. Chapman adjusted a file folder on her desk.

"Pearl, Mary Frances will need to be tutored for at least two or three months during her convalescence. From what I've been told, she'll be staying in the hospital for several weeks and then she'll be moved to a rehab center. Then back home after she recovers sufficiently."

Pearl nodded. "Yeah, she told me about that. It'll take a

long time, I guess. Her leg's broken, she has all those internal injuries. She said she's going to need physical therapy. Then she has to get a new eye."

Pearl was trying to hold herself together.

Mrs. Chapman said, "She's also going to need a study partner."

"A study partner?"

"Yes. The school district will be providing a tutor for her. But a tutor can only spend so much time with a student, and Mary Frances has an additional impediment because of her vision. It would be helpful if someone could read to her and help her with homework.

Mrs. Chapman picked up the folder and opened it. "Pearl, you and Mary are actually in most of the same classes. English. Spanish. Biology. Social Studies."

Pearl nodded. "Everything except Catechism."

Mrs. Chapman looked up sharply, and saw Pearl smiling. "You two might be better friends than I realized."

"Yeah, we have fun together."

"Would you be interested in being Mary's homework partner?"

"Sure. I want to help Mary all I can. You think I could do this?"

"Yes, I do. Your teachers will be made aware of the situation, and Mary will be tested when she comes back to school.

The counselor smiled. "Frankly, Pearl, I can't think of anyone who'd do a better job than you. As my own priest likes to say, it's a mitzvah.

Each morning, the school tutor visited Mary and went over what was being taught in class that day. And after school, Pearl would visit Mary for homework and study sessions.

At first, Pearl worked with Mary in the hospital. Then it

was the rehab center. And finally she went to Mary's home. Most of the time, she took the bus. Sometimes, her mother or father would pick her up. Mr. O'Connell often drove her home. He kept thanking her for all she was doing.

After the two girls had finished their science, social studies, and Spanish assignments, Pearl would read aloud to Mary. For English class, they read *The Color Purple, Slaughterhouse Five,* and *To Kill A Mockingbird.* She enjoyed reading aloud, especially when the book was good. She began to dramatize the dialogue, and Mary complimented her on her acting skills. They laughed together more and more.

One day Mary asked, "Would you be willing to read to me from the Bible?"

"You mean, like, *In the beginning … ?*" She hadn't spent a lot of time on religious studies since her bat mitzvah. No time, really.

"Sure. And maybe from the New Testament, too?"

Pearl paused. "I guess. I've never read it."

So the two girls worked their way through the Old *and* New Testaments, a little at a time. Months later they started on some books of the Bible that Mary said Catholics didn't normally read. Pearl had no idea most of these books even existed. But Mary was curious, and her curiosity sparked Pearl's curiosity. So the girls kept going.

After they'd finished reading *Revelation,* Mary said, "Wow, they should make that into a movie!"

While Mary's religious education had been an integral part of her academic studies at St. Agnes, Pearl's Jewish education had been tacked on, more or less, to her public school education. Hebrew school had been, for better or worse, preparation for her bat mitzvah. It wasn't a *bad* education. It just wasn't very deep. There was only so much you could cram into a couple of afternoons a week.

The more she discussed religion with Mary—especially when she was attempting to answer Mary's questions about "Why do Jews do this?" and "Why do Jews do that?" the more she realized how little she knew about her own religion. It was embarrassing.

Pearl was beginning to comprehend the differences between secular Judaism, Jewish learning, religious observance, and true scholarship.

When she talked to her parents about it one night at dinner, they told her that she was learning one of the most important lessons in life.

"The more you learn," her father, the university professor, told her, "the more you realize how much you don't know. It's a humbling experience."

Her mother nodded, adding, "Pearl, welcome to our world. Your father and I both have advanced degrees, and I can assure you that what we know *combined* is like a thimble-full of water thrown into the ocean."

Samantha

Several things had changed for Ruth and Samantha in the months that had passed since Ruth played Kol Nidre at Erev Yom Kippur.

Ruth began to get requests from temple congregants to perform at receptions, parties, and their children's wedding ceremonies. The word had spread that she and her chamber musicians could do it all. And Ruth had already been asked to play Kol Nidre the following year, replacing the previous cellist, who didn't seem to mind at all. It turned out that he'd been asked many times to play Kol Nidre at his own synagogue, which was much closer to where he lived. He had actually told Shelley he was relieved they'd found someone to replace him.

Samantha could also sense a change in her partner's feelings toward Pearl, and could see things between them improving.

The biggest change, as far as Samantha was concerned, was that she herself had begun studying with Pearl. Samantha Wyatt wanted to become a Jew and had taken the first steps toward conversion.

Ruth seemed surprised, and not particularly overjoyed.

Samantha was a bit surprised herself. She couldn't answer Ruth's questions as to where this desire had come from. Samantha, like her parents, had grown up in the Central Valley. She was an only child and her family never went to church services or talked about religion.

When she was in fifth grade Samantha said to her father, "Everybody believes in God except us! How come?"

Her father just shrugged. "Ask your mother."

When Samantha asked her mother, the reply was, "Ask your father."

By the time she reached high school, Samantha mostly hung out with the kids who didn't go to church.

In college at Fresno State, she attended exactly two religious services at the invitation of friends. One was a Mass at Newman House. She liked the music, but knew now that Ruth would have found it simplistic. Communion was small squares of what looked like very good bread, fished out of a basket and held by each communicant while the priest blessed it—consecrated it, her friend Gina had explained. Before she could put the bread in her mouth, Gina had taken it from her hand, whispering loudly to Samantha that she couldn't take communion because she wasn't Catholic. That aside, Samantha thought the ritual was interesting.

The second service was a prayer vigil held by a small charismatic sect. Samantha went with a couple of housemates, mostly out of curiosity. People had prayed aloud—shouted, really—in both English and a language she couldn't identify. When the bearded leader invited questions, Samantha raised her hand. But he didn't call on her. Rather, he invited several of the young men, whom he knew by name, to speak. That was the end of that.

She'd also attended a Buddhist meditation a couple times, but found she couldn't sit still for very long.

So when she first met with Rabbi Pearl Ross, Samantha was not sure about her own belief in God. In fact, an astronomy class she'd taken at Fresno State had gotten her thinking about God in a way that no church service ever had.

"Rabbi, have you ever seen the photographs taken by the Hubble telescope?"

"I have. They're amazing, aren't they?"

"The universe is huge, endless, really. And beautiful."

"And complicated," Pearl added, enjoying Samantha's enthusiasm.

"And awesome."

Pearl sat quietly as her new student composed her thoughts.

"It's hard for me to say this, but in my business I'm killing things all the time. And sometimes, I find this painful." Samantha was now looking out the window.

Pearl gave her time to think, then said, "Are these thoughts what prompted you to consider conversion?"

Samantha looked at her. "Yes, Rabbi. And there's nobody here telling me I can't ask questions."

"You know, you can call me Pearl. You are, after all, my sister-in-law."

Samantha laughed. "That's true!" She paused, then added,

"Is it okay if I call you Rabbi when we're here, and Pearl the rest of the time?"

"That sounds perfect," Pearl said. "Now, are you ready for a little homework?"

It didn't take long. Samantha had soon read everything the rabbi recommended. In addition to reading Genesis, she'd gone through the children's Hebrew coloring book, a thick handout containing excerpts from Buber, Telushkin, and Maimonides, and several books on conversion from the temple library. There was also fiction by Cynthia Ozick, Grace Paley, Philip Roth, and Nathan Englander on a reading list Pearl had given her.

"Oh, brother," Ruth said, when she came home one Friday night in January. Samantha and Trustworthy were sprawled on the sofa. Samantha was laughing to herself as she pored over *The Joys of Yiddish*. She had lit two Shabbat candles, and klezmer music swirled out of the stereo.

"So what clever term are you going to foist upon me tonight?" Ruth asked.

Samantha smiled at her partner. "Joy. I love Judaism. It really does give me joy."

"Joy?" Ruth said. "But what about all the stuff that's happened to Jews—the so-called Chosen People?"

"Trust me. I'm aware of all the bad stuff. Still, it gives me joy. I don't know why."

Ruth shook her head. "But you don't even believe in God. Do you?"

"Look. I'm not *sure* there's a God. I talked to the … your sister about it, and she told me not to worry about my belief in God at this point."

"That sounds weird to me. You sure you're not confusing

all this ... ethnic stuff ..." she swung her arm around the room, at the books, the stereo, the candles, "with Judaism?"

"I like it all," Samantha answered. "The food, the music, the holidays, the traditions. I like all of it. Why do I have to isolate the components of Judaism? No. I like everything."

"You like everything," Ruth said as she sat on the couch. "How the hell did this happen?"

"It must be *beshert!*"

"Samantha. That's what my grandmother used to say about meeting Grandpa."

Samantha moved next to her partner. "Well, that's how I feel about meeting you."

Ruth had no ready reply. The two women just sat there and looked at each other as Trustworthy licked his paw in the glow of the Shabbat candles.

Dying to Get on the List

A few weeks after her visit with Bert Standish, Pearl stopped by the temple office, where Esther handed her some phone messages.

"You got a call from Bert Standish's son. He asked if you could call him back when you get a chance."

Oh boy, Pearl thought. *Now it's gonna hit the fan.*

She closed her office door, sat down, and made the call. A pleasant woman answered the phone, "Thank you for call-ing the law offices of ..." followed by a long string of names ending with Standish.

"This is Rabbi Pearl Ross returning ..."

"Oh yes, Rabbi. Mr. Standish is waiting for your call. It's a perfect time. Hang on for a moment, please."

Pearl waited just fifteen seconds before he came on the line. A beautiful baritone voice said to her, "Rabbi, thank you so much for calling me back so quickly. I really appreciate it. I'm sorry I didn't call you sooner. I've been involved with a crazy case—a bicycle, a horse, and a wheelchair."

"No problem, Mr. Standish."

"Please call me Robbie. And thanks for visiting my father. It's unfortunate, but it seems we owe you a belated apology," he said.

She thought, *They owe* me *an apology?*

"I'm not sure what you mean. Why do you owe me an apology? If anything, I owe *you* an apology, stumbling in during your father's private, well, intimate …" How *could* she describe the sex scene?

"No, no, that doesn't bother me," he laughed. And from his tone of voice, it certainly didn't bother him. "The problem is, Mirasol tells me that Millie insulted you. She was really out of line."

The rabbi felt puzzled. "How do you mean? I would think it was *I* who was intruding on Millie's personal time with your father."

"No. Millie should not have said anything to you, especially a comment like 'Who the hell are you?' Not to mention her parting remark."

"Oh yes," Pearl laughed. "I think she said, 'I hope you enjoyed the performance!' But really, I shouldn't have been there."

"Okay, Rabbi, let me explain something, and please try to understand where we're coming from.

"This is a very unusual situation. My father has lost much of his memory. But he is still, as you found out during your visit, quite affable. And as you observed before that, he's still sexually capable."

"I would agree on both counts."

Robbie continued. "Millie has been warned in the past, and by me personally yesterday, that if she doesn't play by the rules, she will be taken off the preferred list. I can tell you that this upset her a lot, as well it should."

"The preferred list?"

"Yes. My father is quite the rarity. If we allowed it, he would wind up being no more than a stud at Grand Lake Towers, having a stream of women coming to his apartment day and night. Remember, after any encounter he has, he's soon forgotten all about it."

"I don't know what to say."

"The point is, I do not want him to get a reputation of being a whore. That's why we have to limit his sexual activity. Also, he's over eighty. I'm not sure what impact so much sex might have on his overall health."

Pearl couldn't believe this conversation.

"I understand." She paused for a moment. "Frankly, I was also impressed with Millie's ... let's say, performance."

Robbie laughed again. "Yes, I've heard about it. If it had been Rabbi Cohen who came to visit, I know Mirasol wouldn't have let him stay. I realize it was a judgment call on her part, and I trust her judgment. Mirasol also said you had a very nice chat with my father. I appreciate that."

"He's a wonderful man. I really liked him."

"He's a charmer, isn't he?"

Pearl had a feeling that Robbie Standish was a charmer as well.

"Yes. We did have a nice visit."

"Glad to hear it."

Pearl added, "I just—I hope I didn't spoil things for Millie."

Robbie Standish sighed. "Not to worry, Rabbi. I just told

her that you're part of his health and social care team, which you are."

Pearl was curious. "If I might ask, how many girlfriends does he have?"

"He usually has six guests per week. I decided to cap it at that. There were some women who were not happy about not being included, but we *are* talking about an 84-year-old man. To tell you the truth—and I hate to say this—but to get on the list someone has to die."

Pearl said, "I'm afraid to ask how long the waiting list is."

"You don't want to know. Well, I have to get back to work now, Rabbi. Any other questions?"

"I do have a question. Are you single yourself?"

Robbie laughed long and hard. "I am so happily married, with three children, that I could never see myself in my dad's shoes. As it were. My mother was his second wife, but I am his only child."

They said their goodbyes and ended the call. A waiting list. Someone has to die …

You can't make this stuff up, she thought. Pearl shook her head and got back to work.

Shabbat Candles

One Friday evening Shayna Ross watched as her daughter—now Rabbi Pearl Ross—got ready to serve dinner. Since the senior rabbi, Craig Cohen, was leading the service at the temple, Pearl had the night off and had invited her mother, father, and Jack for Shabbat dinner.

As Shayna watched her daughter put the final touches on the meal, she thought back to a Friday night fifteen years earlier when Pearl had asked her, "Mom, how come we never light candles on Shabbat?"

Shayna recalled how she had pondered that question. She herself had grown up in a thoroughly secular Jewish environment, and her husband, David, couldn't care less about what he called "the trappings of organized religion."

Yes, they were affiliated with the local temple in Berkeley. They paid their dues and attended High Holiday services and a few other events during the year—a poetry reading, a special musical event, a Shabbat service that observed the *yahrzeit* of one of their parents. But that was it, other than making sure their older daughter had a "traditional" Reform bat mitzvah. Their younger daughter, Ruth, had shown zero interest in pursuing the Jewish coming-of-age ritual.

"Is this something you'd like to do, Pearl? Light candles on Shabbat?" she'd asked.

"I think, maybe, yes."

"Do you know the prayer and what to do?"

Pearl nodded.

Shayna had gone to a cupboard, located the candlesticks she'd inherited from her own mother, grabbed two Shabbat candles from a box in the drawer where the birthday candles lived, found a book of matches that featured the logo of a long-defunct Berkeley head shop (*or maybe it* wasn't *defunct*, she thought), and put them all on the kitchen counter.

"Here. Be my guest."

Shayna Ross then watched and listened as her 15-year-old daughter slowly and carefully lit the candles, covered her eyes with her hands, and chanted the prayer. Shayna remembered smiling and wondering, *What's next?*

From that night on, Pearl rarely missed lighting the Friday night Shabbat candles. And years later, Shayna was not shocked when her daughter informed her she'd decided to enter the rabbinical seminary.

Mary Fresa

Every day after school, Pearl brought the homework assignments to Mary Frances O'Connell. Mary had progressed through her long recovery, first at the hospital and then at the rehab center. And now she was back at home. In some ways, this place was the most difficult—Mary's mother was absent.

Every day Pearl and Mary worked together. Math. Science. English. Social Studies. Spanish. And, of course, the Bible.

One afternoon as they did their Spanish homework, Mary looked at her friend with her un-patched eye. "Pearl, how the heck do you remember all these Spanish vocabulary words? You know, like, a zillion of them."

Pearl laughed. "My dad taught me a trick. He says that if you want to remember something, you just sort of associate it with something or somebody, and it'll trigger your memory to remember it. It works. Mostly."

"Really?"

"Sure. For example, when I think of the word *fresa*, I think of you!"

"Fresa? You think of me? Why?"

"Because you're just like a strawberry! You have beautiful red hair and freckles, and you're sweet! In fact, I never think of you as Mary Frances at all. To me, you're Mary Fresa."

Mary sat back, thought about it, and smiled. "That's a helluva lot better than Mary Frances."

"You think?"

"Yes. I *hate* 'Mary Frances.'"

"I didn't know that."

"Okay. From now on, my name is Mary Fresa."

"Fine with me ... Fresa."

"Yes. With a name like that, no one will ever forget me. I'll be famous! *Infamous!*"

They both started laughing, and it made Pearl happy to hear her friend laugh. She decided that the name fit her perfectly.

Shayna Explains the Joke

Mary's recovery continued, and she returned to school.

One evening, Pearl asked her mother if Mary could spend the next Friday night at the Ross home.

"Of course. Is it okay with Mr. O'Connell?"

"We asked him, and he said, 'Sounds like a good idea, Pearl. Tell your mother that I'll pay three months rent in advance.'"

Anticipating that Mary Frances might wind up being a regular guest, Shayna had an extra twin bed delivered, and set it up in Pearl's room. They also cleaned out a couple of drawers and some closet space. Mary did, indeed, become a regular guest at the Ross home.

During one of their Friday night sleepovers, the girls were still chatting quietly, even though it was close to midnight. As was her custom, Pearl kept her small nightlight on in a corner of the room. Once Pearl had revealed her secret fear of the dark to her friend, Mary never mentioned the light again.

Mary began speaking tentatively. "When I was in the hospital, I overheard these two nurses talking. One of them was telling the other one a joke. You want to hear it?"

"Sure."

"Okay. If you're a guy in the hospital and you're horny, who do you go see?"

Pearl thought, but couldn't guess. "Who?"

"The Head Nurse."

They both started laughing at the same time.

Then Pearl stopped and said, "Wait a minute. I don't get it."

"Yeah," said Mary. "Neither do I. But the nurses thought it was hilarious. What do you think?"

"Well, my mom's pretty cool. She'll explain it to us."

The next morning they strolled downstairs in their pajamas. Shayna Ross sat alone at the kitchen table drinking her second cup of coffee and reading the newspaper. Her husband, David, and younger daughter, Ruth, had gone out together for breakfast, as they often did when Mary stayed over.

"Hey Mom, Mary Fresa heard a joke in the hospital and we don't get it."

"Tell me."

So Mary told her. Unfortunately, when she delivered the punch line, Shayna had just taken a gulp of coffee, which she then projectiled out her mouth and nose. After she'd finished coughing and wiping up the mess, she looked at the girls and sighed.

"You have to do this to me, don't you?" She was suppressing a smile as she thought about how to handle it. The girls were sitting patiently, their hands folded in front of them like the good students they were. Mary was wearing her black eye patch, her bright red hair pulled back in a pony tail.

"Okay," she sighed. "I'll explain it to you. It's not what you might be expecting. But if I don't tell you, someone else will. You ready?"

And, starting at the beginning to determine what they knew and what they didn't, she explained. Mary's freckled face turned a shade of red, but she listened carefully. As did Pearl who did not blush. Her eyes, however, darted between her mother, Mary, and space.

After the explanation of oral sex and slang terminology was over, Shayna asked them if they had any questions.

Mary suppressed a giggle. "I don't have any questions. But that was certainly a lot to swallow."

The three started laughing and didn't stop until after lunch.

The Four Questions

Samantha was nervous. And she had every right to be.

Here she was at the home of Shayna and David Ross—the parents of both her partner and her rabbi—to celebrate the first night of Passover. That was bad enough, since she'd never been to a Passover seder before. But Ruth, sitting next to her, was in a pissy mood. She didn't want to be there, she didn't want Samantha to be there, and she couldn't understand why Samantha wanted to convert to Judaism.

"Why do you want to be a Jew? It's bad enough being *born* Jewish," she'd complained. "It's bad enough having a sister who's a rabbi. It's bad enough having to sit in the temple listening to the juvenile songs, composed using two—*maybe* three chords. And the constant requests to stand, pray, bow, sit, read, stand up again, sit down again. Then more camp songs. All they're missing is a bonfire and s'mores."

Ruth then went on about the bar mitzvahs and the bat mitzvahs, and the parents' speeches, which she loved to parody.

"Oh, Brittany," Ruth would whine, "You're so smart; you're such a good quarterback; you're such a good bagpipe player. Your great-grandma Becky from Transylvania would be so proud of you. Too bad about what happened when her cousin Bela bit her." Ruth never let up.

Samantha found Ruth's rants mildly annoying at worst and mildly amusing at best. But none of it bothered her. Because Samantha was happy.

She'd been working with Pearl toward her conversion to Judaism for almost six months now and had read every book recommended. She'd attended services, on either Friday night or Saturday morning (or both) pretty much every week, and had made new friends along the way.

At services, she sat with the regulars—including other lesbians—who answered all of her questions. She'd read through the Torah in English and was learning a little Hebrew as well, doing her best to follow the Hebrew words, not just the transliteration. And even though she often lost her place, more and more she didn't. No one ever minded pointing to the right spot on the page. It was all wonderfully enjoyable and intellectually stimulating. And if Ruth didn't like it, well, tough.

Occasionally Ruth would join her at a service; but mostly she didn't.

But this, the Passover seder, was different. Samantha felt like a stranger in a strange land. *Ger*, she'd learned, was the Hebrew word for stranger. She gazed around the table. Everyone was a born Jew except for her. But every-one appeared happy to have her there. Except, sadly, her own partner, who remained sullen and mostly silent.

Shayna and David Ross had told Samantha they were thrilled she was coming (and thanks for dragging Ruth along). And moreover, Samantha thought it was incredible to be celebrating Passover with her own rabbi at the table. How cool was that?

And Jack Levy, the rabbi's fiancé, he was really a nice guy—funny, smart, and obviously in love with Pearl. It was fun to watch him tease the rabbi and treat her like a woman. Samantha seemed to be the only one who noticed when the rabbi jumped a couple of inches off her chair after Jack goosed her.

There were two other couples at the table—a chemistry professor and her husband, who worked in technology, and some neighbors who were retired teachers and long-time friends of the Ross family.

But Samantha remained nervous because she knew something that was going to happen soon, and the only other person who knew was the rabbi. Sure, it was easy for the rabbi when she'd said, 'Don't worry, Samantha.' But she *was* worried. And nervous.

Jack had made everyone at the table laugh when, after being told by Shayna that he could grab a kippah from the top left drawer in the dining room cabinet, he pulled a pink one out of the jumble and put it on. Pearl said, "Jack, you're not going to wear *that*, are you?"

He took it off and read aloud from the printing inside. "Hmmm, 'The Bat Mitzvah of Pearl Ross.' Yep, this is the one I want," and he put it back on. He was that kind of guy. Samantha wanted to talk to him more about entomology. But not now. She'd learned years ago that people don't like it when you talk about insects at the dinner table. Even talking about a plague of locusts at the seder seemed risky.

The seder began with the lighting of candles, some prayers from the Haggadah, a few songs, kibbitzing, and wine. Then the description of the seder plate, the story of the Exodus, lots of business about being slaves in Egypt, and more wine.

Then, the moment of truth.

Shayna announced, "Well, now it's time for my favorite part of the seder, the Four Questions. Ruth, are you going to do us the honor? It's been many years since …"

That's all she got out. Ruth gave her a look that combined a tight smile and daggers, and replied, "Mom, thanks for offering me the honor. I'm going to pass."

"But … you're the …" Shayna was saying when Samantha got the nod from Pearl.

"It's okay, Mrs. Ross. Ruth's not the youngest at the table anyway. I am. So, it's really my responsibility—and honor—to ask the Four Questions, if that's okay with you."

When she'd said the word "honor," she'd cast a quick glance at Ruth, who still had her stage smile pasted on her face. Now that smile included a tinge of surprise; maybe shock.

"It's certainly okay with me, Samantha," Shayna replied. "And thank you very much. Go for it!"

And with that, Samantha chanted the Four Questions, just as she'd been practicing for the last eight weeks. She just looked at the page and did it as she'd memorized it from the recording, beginning with the opening line, which really *was* a question:

Mah nishtana ha-laila haze mikol ha-leilot?

This, she knew, meant "Why is this night different from

all other nights?" The last question—the last of four state-ments, really, was,

> *She-b'chol ha-leilot anu ochlin bein yoshvin u-vein m'subin. Ha-laila hazeh, kulanu m'subin.*

This meant "On all other nights we eat sitting or reclin-ing, and on this night we only recline." There they were. The Four Questions. Easier than the Gettysburg Address, which she also could have recited if asked.

Samantha looked up to see everyone at the table smiling at her, particularly Pearl and Shayna. When she looked to her right, she observed that Ruth's previous expression had changed to a more genuine smile. In addition, a couple of tears rolled down Ruth's cheeks, which she quickly wiped away with her dinner napkin.

Pearl ignored the drama and proceeded with the seder. She answered the Four Questions, added comments, back-ground, and trivia, and called on guests to read passages from the Haggadah. Quickly the evening was back on track, and the meal, thank God, was served.

Conversation moved to food, jobs, and the subject of Samantha's studies toward conversion. Samantha was happy to talk about what she'd recently been reading, and said that while most Jews take these things for granted, much of it was new to her. The chemistry professor assured Samantha that even though she herself had been Jewish her whole life, she was always surprised at how much about her religion she still did not know. Others agreed.

Then Jack jumped in. "Hey, if you really want to find out how little you know about Judaism, try planning a wedding to a rabbi." Everyone laughed.

Jack went on. "'We *should* do this, and we *can't* do that, and this person needs to say this, and we have to decide whether we're going to observe this new tradition or that old tradition, which is, you know, traditional.'

"Mostly I just say, 'Yes, dear,' the way my father taught me."

Samantha was enjoying the banter and the conversation. What made the evening even more pleasant was the hand that reached for hers under the tablecloth. Ruth was, hopefully, moving to a better space. Life seemed pretty good at the moment.

A few more songs, prayers, more discussion and wine, a half-hearted search for the *afikoman*—more talk than search, really. Everyone was too full, and a few guests maybe too tipsy, to put much effort into it. Then the goodbyes began.

Designated drivers had been agreed upon before the service, and more than one guest had been drinking kosher grape juice instead of wine. Samantha, who'd been drinking sips of wine instead of glasses of wine, drove home.

Later, Ruth confided that it was the best Passover seder she'd ever been to.

"This may sound ridiculous," Ruth said, "but I was really proud of you."

"Thanks."

"Yeah. Good job." Then Ruth added, "Mazel Tov!"

The Crying Room

Mary Frances O'Connell's remarkable recovery continued, although one month after returning to school she was still dealing with pain. She was now walking, slowly, without crutches, her broken femur fully healed and her physical therapy completed. Although it was no longer necessary, she and Pearl still did their homework together on a regular basis. They just made sure they had different answers once in a while. Typically, both answers were correct.

One afternoon, Mary asked Pearl if she'd be interested in attending Mass with her at church the following Sunday.

"Why would you want me to come with you? I know some Hebrew, but no Latin. Well, maybe *e pluribus unum.*"

Fresa laughed. "No Latin, silly! They stopped that before we were born. Anyway, I thought it would be neat if sometimes you came to Mass and maybe sometimes I went to a Shabbat service on Saturday with you. I always thought going to a service is like going to the theatre, except it doesn't cost anything. Well, my dad gives me two or three bucks to drop into the collection plate. Do you guys do that at the temple?"

"No. My dad just writes a check for two or three *thousand* bucks every year and drops it into the mailbox."

Fresa said, "And there are usually cookies after the church service."

"Wait a minute. Cookies? That's it? *Cookies?* Are you serious?"

"Yeah. What were you expecting?"

"At the temple they have bagels! Lox! Noodle kugel! Lunch. A *free* lunch. Every week!"

"You're joking. A free lunch?"

"Absolutely."

"Well, then count me in. Shabbat service on Saturday. Mass on Sunday."

"Cookies," Pearl muttered.

"Well … sometimes there are brownies."

They worked out the arrangements and decided to start with an early Sunday Mass first. Mary's father, with Mary in the back seat, had just pulled into the driveway.

Before she went out the door, Pearl's mother reminded her, "Remember. No kneeling. No eating wafers, and no drinking any wine. And as far as singing about Jesus Christ, well, just save that for Christmas."

Pearl couldn't stop looking around at the beautiful stained glass windows and the statues in Mary's church. At some point, Pearl sensed that her friend was in pain. She had her hand pressed to her side, near the site of her surgery. Maybe Mary hadn't really fully recovered yet, she thought.

Pearl whispered, "Fresa, let's take a break. Is there someplace you can lie down?"

Mary whispered back, "Good idea. Let's go to the crying room."

She winced as she got up and led Pearl to the left wing of the church, where they opened a heavy door and entered a cool, dark, leather-cushioned, glass-paneled, soundproofed chamber. It was early. Except for one woman nursing her baby and another stroking the hair of a sleeping toddler, the room was empty. Pearl could hear the service through a speaker mounted in a corner of the room.

She waited a few minutes while Mary stretched out on a leather bench. When she saw that she'd opened her eye, Pearl whispered, "This is so cool."

"What's so cool?" Mary whispered back.

"The crying room."

"What is so cool about a crying room?"

"I mean, your church is beautiful. It feels really holy. And then, if you're praying and you become so overwhelmed by the glory and magnificence of God that it brings you to tears, it's great that there's this special place where you can go to cry in private. We don't have anything like this in our temple."

Mary started to laugh, softly at first, then louder and louder, to the point where she was holding her side in pain but still couldn't stop laughing.

Pearl was puzzled. "What did I say that was so funny?"

"You idiot! The crying room is not for crying because you're overwhelmed by the glory and magnificence of God!"

"It's not?"

"No. It's where you take your little kids when they won't stop crying during the service!"

That's what Pearl learned when she attended Mass the first time. And for the rest of her life, whenever she passed one of the crying rooms that had become a fixture in many of the synagogues she attended or worked in, she'd smile and think of her best friend, Mary Fresa O'Connell.

The Wedding

Rabbi Craig Cohen stood under a white *chuppah* bedecked in flowers and greenery. Next to him was Cantor Shelley Sanders, and nearby were Mary Fresa O'Connell, the maid of honor, and Jack's brother, Josh, the best man.

The wedding day threatened to be absolutely beautiful, Craig thought.

Music for the pre-ceremony gathering, the processional, and the recessional was supplied by the Ruth Ross String Trio. The musicians sat nearby under a small canopy that, he'd been told, was needed to protect their valuable instruments from direct sunlight.

The bride, wearing a long white summer gown—quite a departure from her usual black wardrobe—and the groom, in a lightweight summer tuxedo, exchanged vows, and circled each other the traditional seven times, as the cantor chanted the traditional seven blessings. Craig then repeated the blessings in English for the benefit of the guests.

The *ketubah* was displayed on an easel near the chuppah for all to see. This traditional Jewish wedding contract had been signed by the bride, groom, clergy, and witnesses.

Craig reminded everyone present that Pearl and Jack were being married in the same place they'd first met, the UC Berkeley Faculty Glade.

He then explained that in classical Hebrew and rabbinic tradition, *kiddushin*, which means "sanctification" and comes from the word for "holy," was the first stage of marriage.

"Sometimes you will also hear the word *'erusin*,' which can mean 'betrothal.' In the Jewish tradition the couple was now considered married and a *get* would be required for divorce, even if they have not cohabited. In fact, a year or more could pass between this first stage and the second. Of course, in those days the bride might be under fourteen and would not yet have graduated from Stanford and the rabbinical seminary."

He waited until the laughter subsided.

"For the record, we are now in the second stage, *nisuin*, which includes this ceremony under the chuppah and the seven blessings—the *sheva brachot*, chanted so beautifully by Cantor Sanders.

"A few minutes ago, you watched as the bride and groom encircled one another. In this manner they declared that each will be the center of the other's existence and universe. Traditionally, only the bride would encircle the groom, which was believed to protect him from demons or enemies that might

try to harm him, particularly here on the Berkeley campus."
This brought a laugh, especially from a group of his academic
colleagues.

"While many of you are waiting for the bride and groom
to kiss, an equally significant part of the Jewish wedding ceremony is the breaking of the glass.

"There are many thoughts as to the significance of this
act. Some say it reminds us of the destruction of the Temple
in Jerusalem. Others say that the fragile nature of the glass
may be compared with the equally fragile nature of relationships, reminding us that we should treat each other with love
and care.

"Parents of the wedding couple have often told me that
to them it signifies that the bride and groom can finally move
all of their stuff out of their old bedrooms and into their
own place." Craig once again paused for laughter, and looked
at his rabbinical colleague and her groom with warmth and
affection.

He finished his remarks, placed the glass in a cloth napkin, and Jack stomped the hell out of it, drawing cries of
"Mazel Tov!" from the guests.

The string trio struck up the traditional *Siman Tov* melody. The couple kissed and then walked back up the aisle as
guests clapped, sang, laughed, and cried.

Craig and Shelley shook hands as they followed the wedding party, congratulating each other on a job well done.

Following the ceremony, the guests went inside for the luncheon reception while the bride and groom were secluded
in a nearby room, as per the Jewish custom of *yichud*. While
this was the time in past centuries where newlyweds might
"consummate" their marriage, Pearl and Jack took the opportunity to relax and enjoy some of the appetizers the caterer

had waiting for them. They would have plenty of time to consummate on their honeymoon.

Ruth Ross put away her cello and resumed the role of sister of the bride, joining Samantha at the reception. She listened with a professional ear to the band, a trio of first-rate musicians that Shelley Sanders had recommended. The trio was playing cocktail jazz and standards, as well as some Jewish selections. Ruth knew the bass player, Aaron, who'd graduated from Cal State a year after she did. They smiled and nodded hello to one another.

Soon after they joined their guests, Pearl and Jack had their first dance as newlyweds and then invited everyone else to join them on the dance floor.

Pearl loved the music and was very happy with the meal suggested by the caterer—poached salmon, wild rice, and sautéed vegetables. The vegetarian option was stuffed portabella mushroom.

She and Jack wandered around between courses, posing for pictures with their guests, including a few Grizzly Peak roommates, several Cal faculty, and three rabbinical school classmates who flew in for the occasion.

The wedding couple's parents sat at a table for four on the side of the room opposite to where the band was set up. Pearl noticed that Jack's father, Mort Levy, a Florida CPA, was wearing white shoes with his green pastel pants and cream sport jacket. Jack's mother, Shayna, wore a daisy yellow pantsuit, with matching bag and shoes. Her own parents, David and Shayna, were attired in less-colorful garb—he in a navy blue suit and she in a pink summer dress—rather conservative in comparison to the Levys.

After more eating and dancing, the toasts began. People took their seats, and the room became quiet.

The first to speak was the maid of honor. Mary Fresa was wearing a light blue summer dress that matched her eyes. Her hair was as red as ever. Around her neck on a gold chain was a small Star of David.

Taking the microphone one of the musicians handed her, she stood and addressed the gathered guests. Pearl, holding hands with Jack, looked at her old friend and thought of how they'd both changed over the years.

"Some of you know me, but for those who do not, please don't be fooled by my jewelry. To quote Lennie Bruce, 'I'm not really Jewish.'" She waited until the laughter died down.

"When I told my priest that I was going to be the maid of honor at my best friend's Jewish wedding, he said, 'Okay, Mary. You know the drill at Jewish events. You don't kneel and you don't thank Jesus for the meal you are about to receive.'

"But today I get to take part in the wedding of my oldest and dearest friend." She paused. "Let me tell you a little story.

"My name is Mary Fresa O'Connell. When I was fourteen, I was involved in a car accident that took the life of my mother and almost took my own. I was in the hospital following surgery, and as I lay in bed I was praying to God to help me, to redeem me, to save me.

"When I opened my eye a little while later—my one remaining eye—I looked up into the face of a girl my own age; she was smiling at me. I recognized her as a girl from school, but not someone I knew very well.

"She said, 'Hi, Mary,' and I said, 'Hi, Pearl.' And that was the beginning of my lifelong friendship with Rabbi Pearl Ross, now Ross-Levy, who, in many ways, helped save my life. Pearl was the one who gave me the name Fresa, which means 'strawberry.'

"She, along with my surrogate mother, Shayna Ross, helped me heal and become as normal as I could ever be, which, Pearl will tell you, is not *very*. Especially now that I'm the head nurse at my hospital in Chicago." Pearl and her mother looked at each other and shared a private laugh.

"I could have easily become embittered following that accident, but she brought sweetness, light, and fun into my life." Mary paused, and then looked at the groom.

"Jack, you are a fortunate man. In your hands you certainly hold a very, very valuable pearl. Please handle it with care."

With that, she sat down, pleased by the fact that there was not a dry eye in the house.

Jack's younger brother, Josh, stood, picked up the mic, and looked at the guests. He looked sharp in his tux, which while showing off a lean athletic physique not unlike his older brother's, did mask the six-pack abs that Jack quietly envied whenever they were at a pool together. Like many men of his generation, Josh seemed to always have a three-day growth of beard.

"The lesson I learned today is, when you're giving a toast, *never* follow the Catholic maid of honor who's wearing a Star of David." When the laughter subsided, he continued.

"My name is Josh, and I'm Jack's little brother, and here's what I can tell you about him.

"Listen, any older brother—pretty much anybody, for that matter—can teach a kid to ride a bike. That's a given and takes maybe an hour or two. But when you go beyond that, you find the love, the dedication, the patience, and the devotion of someone who truly cares.

"My brother Jack taught me to catch a baseball on the

short hop, so you don't take it in the chops."There was laughter, particularly from the men.

"He taught me to fake right and move left. He taught me to shoot a three-pointer when you're under pressure from two opponents. He taught me to try not to be at the bottom of a football pileup. He taught me that it's important to laugh at the other guy's joke even when it's not funny.

"He taught me how to not be a complete jerk when it comes to girls. He taught me that it's just as important to say 'no' as it is to say 'yes,' especially in business and professional settings. He taught me how to get an A in a class that sucks.

"And Pearl, you may be surprised to hear this, but Jack always reminded me that I was, indeed, a Levy, and that it was important to maintain my Jewish identity even when the odds were against me or when it wasn't convenient.

"And look—it worked for him!"Then he took a long sip from his wine glass.

"I continue to learn from my brother. Let me tell you something." He walked over to a little table nearby and pointed to the plastic box sitting there. "The next time I meet a woman I'm really interested in, she gets a tarantula on our first date!"

With that, he sat down, pleased by the fact that everyone was laughing. Not as good as tears, he thought, but still good.

Pearl stood, took the microphone, and looked at her friends and family, including her new family. She began, speaking in the present tense.

"I'm a little girl, maybe six years old. I'm sitting with my parents in a Chinese restaurant. My first fortune cookie is on a small plate in front of me. I'm puzzled. My dad tells me it's a cookie. But it's not like any cookie *I've* ever seen, that's for sure.

"My mother explains what a fortune cookie is, and I carefully break it open. I pull out the little strip of paper, and slowly read it to myself." Pearl held up an imaginary fortune.

"Mom, what does this mean: 'You will meet a tall, dark stranger'?"

"My mother tells me, 'It just means that at some point in your life you will meet a tall man who has dark hair.'

"I ponder this for a little while, and then ask my mother, 'Will I marry him?'"

"I remember my mother taking a sip of tea, putting the cup down, looking at me, and saying very seriously, 'Yes … if he's Jewish.'"

After the laughter died down, Pearl continued.

"Well, I've met my tall, dark stranger. And he's Jewish. And so much more."

She sat down and kissed Jack as the guests tapped their water and wine glasses with their silverware.

Jack stood, picked up the mic, smiled at his guests, and began.

"Well, I'm a little *boy*, maybe seven or eight years old, and there are only two things that are important to me— sports and insects. But today I add a third item to the 'most important' list." He gazed at Pearl for a moment, and then continued.

"The first two—sports and insects—are still on the list, but they've obviously moved down in order of priority.

"I don't know about you, but when I was a kid playing Little League baseball, I chewed a lot of bubble gum. And my gum of choice was Bazooka." There were nods of agreement from many in the room.

"Now if you remember Bazooka bubble gum, you open the package and there's the gum and also a little piece of waxy paper that has a cartoon on it featuring Bazooka Joe and his pals. The joke was usually really dumb, but you read it anyway. And there were also some words of wisdom on that paper, sort of like a fortune.

"I distinctly remember this one Bazooka fortune I got. I happen to have it right here." As the guests laughed, he took out his wallet and withdrew a small square of paper.

"'*You will meet a tall, dark rabbi.*' Jack paused. '*And you will marry her.*' More laughter. He again looked at his wife.

"Best damned piece of gum I ever had."

He sat down and kissed Pearl as the noise and applause continued.

The Comedian

At nine o'clock on a bright, sunny, Catskills summer morning in 1962, Sandy Wintergreen knocked on the screen door of the cabin, and Mrs. Solomon greeted him with a smile.

"Good," she said as she led him into the room. Over her shoulder, she asked, "When you're telling a joke, what's the most …"

"Timing!" shouted Sandy.

Mrs. Solomon joined her husband at a small table on which sat two cups of coffee and a glass of water.

"Boychik, come over and stand right there," Solomon ordered, pointing to a corner of the little two-room cabin. Sandy moved to the indicated spot.

"Go," was all Solomon said.

Sandy turned his back toward them for a moment, took a deep breath, then turned around. He had a smile—not only on his lips but in his eyes.

"So there's these four rabbis who like to play golf. They get together once a week every Tuesday.

"One Tuesday morning, they're playing ..."

Solomon interrupted. "How can they play? It's snowing."

"Oh yeah, I forgot."

"Start again."

Sandy closed his eyes, then began.

"So there's these four rabbis who like to play golf. They *love* to play golf! In fact, they get together as a foursome at least once a week, usually on Tuesdays, whenever the weather's good.

"One Tuesday morning—it was just a beautiful spring day, not a cloud in the sky, birds are singing, and they're out on the golf course. Each one is playing pretty well, but when they get to the third hole, they see people up ahead who are still putting."

"Okay, not bad," interrupted Solomon. "But I can't see the people up ahead. How do I know there are people? You're *telling* me there are people, but I can't see 'em."

"I can't see them either," said Mrs. Solomon.

"You can't see the people?" Sandy was confused. "There *are* no people. I'm just *telling* you there are people."

Solomon looked at the young man. "Of course there are people. You're telling me there are people, so there must *be* people. You just gotta make sure we can see them."

Sandy's face showed his puzzlement.

"Look, Boychik. You're an actor. You've got hands. Eyes. Imagination. Can you see the people?"

"I'm not sure."

"If *you* can't see the people, how are *we* supposed to see them? Where are they standing? What are they doing? How far away are they? How many? Two? Twenty? Sixty?"

Sandy closed his eyes. He imagined the people at the next tee; or were they on the putting green? He focused.

"There are six men and a woman. They're just milling

around and talking. They're arguing, wandering around, confused."

"I told you he was smart," said Mrs. Solomon.

"Good," said Solomon. "Start again."

Sandy started again.

"So there's these four rabbis who like to play golf. Boy, do they *love* to play golf! When they're giving sermons or teaching some bar mitzvah kid, what they're really thinking about is the next time they can knock some little white balls around the course.

"The foursome gets together whenever they can, usually on Tuesdays, if the weather's good. Sometimes they'll even play in the rain. Unless there's lightning. You don't want to play golf in lightning—even a rabbi knows that!

"So one Tuesday morning—it's a beautiful spring day, not a cloud in the sky, birds are singing, a perfect day, they're playing. And each one of them is doing really well, a very competitive situation. But when they get to the third hole, they see these people milling around up ahead on the next putting green—six men and a woman. They're stalled, and they're holding up the rabbis' game. The rabbis are not happy. And there's nothing worse than an angry rabbi.

"So they decide that one of them should go talk to these people and tell them they're holding up the game. The rabbis need to get back to the *mikvah*, or the cemetery—somebody's dying to get buried.

"They choose the rabbi with the longest beard—he should walk over and find out what the heck's going on."

Solomon stopped him. "Good, Sandy. *Very* good. What do you think, Mrs. Solomon?"

"A big improvement. But I'd like to see some more movement, to keep my attention from wandering. A little more body language."

"Listen to Mrs. Solomon. She knows from body language. But you're doing good, much better. I like the shtick about the mikvah and the cemetery. Nice touch. I'm gonna steal that from you."

"You're gonna steal it from me?"

"Sure. Why not? You think all the great jokes and stories were made up by one guy? No. Everybody steals from everybody."

"Oh."

"Don't worry about that. And also, you're already learning that you don't have to tell the story the same way every time. If you think you can improve it, if you have a new bit to add that'll freshen it up, go ahead. Make it your own."

"Well, yeah, I can see ..."

"And not only that. Pretty soon you'll be interrupting your own story to start another story. Or you'll be interrupted by some jerk in the audience—some heckler—and you're gonna have to put him down so you can continue your story."

"Those hecklers, oh my God, they're just terrible!"

"Nonsense. Hecklers are your best friends."

"My best friends?"

"Sure. Watch." Solomon stood up and said to Sandy, "I'm going to start telling your joke. When I get to about the second sentence, I want you to throw some insult at me. Anything. Tell me I suck and I should go back to Jersey or something. Okay?"

"Okay," Sandy said, a little bit unsure about the process.

Solomon began, "So there's these four rabbis who like to play golf. They love golf! No matter what they're doing at the temple, makes no difference. It's golf they're *really* thinking about ...'

Sandy yelled at him, "Hey, stupid! You're so fat you

probably couldn't even *see* a golf ball when you're standing up!"

Solomon stopped and pointed a finger at Sandy. "Wait a minute. I remember you! Aren't you the guy who was arrested last week at the zoo for humping a camel?" He looked at Mrs. Solomon. "Turns out the camel dropped the charges. It was the best sex she'd had in years."

Sandy started laughing. Then he looked at Mrs. Solomon, who was looking at him. He stopped laughing.

She said, "Do you see what Mr. Solomon just did? He turned the tables on you, the heckler. And he managed to toss off the joke about the guy and the camel in the middle of the first joke, which we haven't even heard yet.

"By the way, Solomon," she said, "I never heard the camel shtick before. That was good."

"Thanks. I just made it up. Now, Sandy, you gotta have a big bag of insults to throw at hecklers. You have the microphone. They're usually drunk, or they're jerks, or they're drunk jerks. You're not drunk, and you're smart. Sexually-related insults usually do the trick. Watch. Let's try it again. I'm gonna take it to the next level."

Solomon started the story. "So there's these four rabbis who like to play golf. Every Tuesday when the weather's good, they head off for the golf …"

Sandy shouted, "You imbecile! It's supposed to be 'A rabbi, a priest, a minister, and a nun are playing golf!'"

Solomon turned to him. "Hey! Aren't you the guy that was standing in front of me in the men's room and you got your shlong caught in the urinal?" He turned to Mrs. Solomon. "Lady, you wouldn't *believe* the size of this guy's member. When he flushed, it clogged up everything. There was water shooting all over the place. Geeze. I had to get the hell out of there quick and go over and use the ladies' room. That's okay, because I needed to buy some Kotex anyway."

Sandy started to laugh again.

"Sandy," said Mrs. Solomon. Sandy stopped laughing and looked at her. "Do you see what Mr. Solomon just did? Most of the time, if you want to belittle a man, you talk about how *small* his business is. But he switched it around and made it too *big*. Then he diverted the story and brought in a shtick about what happens when a man goes into the ladies' room. Boys are fascinated with the Kotex machine, right?"

"Well, yeah." Sandy showed a little embarrassment.

"By now, everyone's forgotten the heckler."

"I see what you mean."

"Sandy," said Solomon, "we're going to take a little break now. I want you to get out your notebook and write down a few words that will jog your memory about everything we talked about. It's a process. You don't need to write down everything. Just a few words. 'Urinal;' 'Kotex;' 'Sex with camel.' You get the picture."

"Sandy." It was Mrs. Solomon now, and he looked at her. "There's a wide range of comedy, from mild to disgusting, and your tool box has to be wide and deep. You need to know your audience, and you have to be able to do it all. Do you understand?"

"I do, Mrs. Solomon. Thank you." And he started to write in his notebook.

After the break, they began again. Sandy told the story about the four rabbis playing golf and continued to embellish it. Now the rabbis were short, tall, fat, bald. One guy's fly was open and his golf shirt had a little Jewish star on it.

The Solomons kept interrupting him. They both heckled him. Lightly at first, then more aggressively. Sandy responded

with a variety of defenses, making up his own material—
some of it mild, some of it stronger. He even insulted Mrs.
Solomon when she was the heckler. He watched the Solomons' reactions as they nodded, smiled, and even laughed a
couple of times.

They never let up, continuing to interrupt him and sometimes teaming up to throw insults at him. Sandy only got
stronger as the morning went on. He dug down into his
young life, bringing up potty humor, mild off-color jokes,
and a few zingers. He began to use his hands, torso, and once
even his feet. Periodically, Mr. Solomon stopped him, and
told him to write things in his notebook.

And through it all, he never finished the story about the
four rabbis playing golf.

They broke for lunch at noon, and walked over to the
dining room. Mrs. Solomon's arm was linked through Mr.
Solomon's arm, as always. Solomon's other arm was around
Sandy Wintergreen's shoulder.

During lunch, Mr. Solomon talked and Sandy listened.

"Boychik, you think being a comedian is fun? No, it's not
fun. It's hard work. You work for ten or fifteen years, then
maybe—if you're lucky—you get a spot on TV, and suddenly
you're 'an overnight success.'

"But it wasn't overnight at all. It was never overnight.
Everyone starts off in a place like The Lounge. Most give up,
but the great ones don't. And that's the way it goes."

"How about you, Mr. Solomon?"

Before he could answer, Mrs. Solomon leaned over and
kissed her husband on the cheek. "Sandy, Mr. Solomon *is* one
of the great ones. He's just not one of the *famous* great ones.
But if you listen to him, and have fire in your belly, maybe
you can be great *and* famous.

"Trust me, though," she went on. "There's a price you

pay for everything. You need to ask yourself three questions: *What do you want? How much does it cost?* and *Are you willing to pay the price?* If you really want it and you're willing to pay the price, then I say, *Go for it!*"

They finished their sandwiches, Solomon signed the check, and they left the dining room.

"Two things, Sandy," Solomon said as they walked back to the cabin. "First, this afternoon we are going to put together a dozen jokes for tonight's shows. And second, someday you are going to buy *us* lunch. And it won't be a sandwich!"

Sandy laughed. "I promise. Whatever you want for lunch, it's on me!"

Jack Moves In

After a romantic (and passionate) week-long honeymoon in Maui, Pearl and Jack came back to reality. It was time for them to finally move in together and for Jack to bring the rest of his stuff from his room in the Grizzly Peak house and find some empty space at Pearl's home.

She'd assured him that she'd made room for him in the closets, while at the same time reminding him that it was a "small" house. He didn't know what she was talking about.

"Three bedrooms and two bathrooms is a small house?"

"Men," was all she could say.

To her credit, she did clear a closet for him in what had once been her sister Ruth's room. Until there were children, that same room would serve as his study. Her own former bedroom was now home to her own desk and computer, more clothing, and books that spanned her life from the time she was in middle school to the present.

Whenever Jack opened a closet, what he saw was mostly black clothing and lots of shoe boxes. He wondered where all this stuff would go when they *did* have children. But, wisely, he said nothing.

Other than books about Judaism and religion (hers), and entomology and sports (his), which they kept in their respective studies, they merged their libraries on the living room bookshelves.

Of all the many books they owned, they were amazed to find only four duplicates: *The Amazing Adventures of Kavalier and Clay*, *The Bogleheads' Guide to Investing*, *The Joys of Yiddish*, and *The Adventures of Huckleberry Finn*. They shared a laugh about that.

He offered her his extra copy of *The Biology of Scorpions*, but she said she didn't need it. "I'm only into tarantulas."

He was able to fit all of his clothing and shoes into Ruth's former closet. It was the sports gear that was the challenge.

They donated, recycled, gifted, and discarded a lot of junk that had been left in the garage by former tenants, and that's where he started to move his stuff.

Pearl watched him as he removed his possessions from nine large, heavy-duty cartons that had been shipped by freight at no small expense from his parent's home in Florida.

She watched him as he arranged everything on the garage shelves. A volleyball, a basketball, several baseballs and softballs, tennis balls, golf balls, a football, some foam balls he said were Nerf balls, a rugby ball, and Ping-Pong balls. He even had a bowling ball that had belonged to his father. Then there were golf clubs; two tennis racquets; a lacrosse stick; table tennis paddles; two badminton racquets, a container of three birdies, and a net; and three baseball bats.

"Why three?" Pearl asked.

"Two are for baseball and softball. The metal bat's for college games," he said, as if this explained everything.

She saw a variety of gloves and mitts. He showed her a first baseman's mitt, a catcher's mitt, and his regular baseball and softball mitts. There was a football helmet he said he hadn't used since high school. He looked fondly at a professional bow that had been packed in a long cylinder with a quiver of arrows.

He also had a discus, a javelin, and a shot put.

"Why?" she asked.

"Decathlon," he replied. "I had a dream; life got in the way. But you never know. We might have a boy—or a girl—someday who'd like these. Too bad I couldn't keep my pole vault pole."

She decided to find out more about what had happened to his decathlon dream. First she needed to do some decathlon-related research.

Jack had cleats for baseball and some other sport. Snorkeling gear. An épée and face mask. A pull-up bar that he'd immediately installed in the doorway of his study. A dozen dumbbells. Pushup stands.

Finally, he put a fishing pole and a tackle box in the corner of the garage.

"I didn't know you like to fish," Pearl said.

"Actually, I haven't done much fishing myself. But one time I did teach a man to fish."

He said it so seriously that it took a second for Pearl to react.

"Cute. Real cute."

... To a Nunnery

Both Mary Fresa and Pearl had recently celebrated their sixteenth birthdays and were now juniors at Berkeley High School.

Mary's days as a pirate (or Israeli general) with an eye patch were long past. She'd been fitted two years earlier with an expertly designed and state-of-the-art prosthetic eye, with an iris as blue as her own. Only an eye professional or an extremely observant person could tell the difference.

Tonight, they were lounging in Pearl's bedroom for their weekly sleepover. There was a long pause in their conversation, and Pearl sensed there was something on her friend's mind.

"Fresa, what's bothering you?"

"I'm thinking about what I want to be when I grow up."

"And?"

There was another long pause. Pearl waited it out.

"I'm considering becoming a nun."

It wasn't what Pearl was expecting. She thought for a moment, choosing her words carefully.

"Is Mother Teresa hiring?"

"No. Seriously."

"I'm not sure what to say. Nuns are sort of outside my area of expertise."

"Yeah."

"Don't you want to get married?"

"What's the point? I can't have children."

"Well, I promised you that extra one you could keep. What do you want—boy or girl?"

"Stop. I'm serious."

"All right. Let me change into my serious pajamas."

Mary sighed. "Which ones are those?"

"The flannel ones, with St. Augustine."

"Pearl!"

"Okay. What's prompting this serious line of career choice?"

"I want to *serve*. I want to help people. I feel ... I feel a need to ... to do *something*. I don't know what."

Pearl realized her friend needed her help and support. Wasn't that what best friends were for?

"Fresa, I understand what you're saying. And if you want to be a nun, I'll support you all the way. I've never known anyone whose faith is greater than yours." She waited and watched as Mary closed her eyes, as if she were in prayer. Then Pearl continued.

"Look ... you've been around nuns your whole life. I haven't. But I have a feeling that it's not all Loretta Young and Ingrid Bergman." *Watching those old nun movies is finally paying off,* she thought. "Even Julie Andrews and Whoopi Goldberg—those women weren't nuns. They're all actresses."

Mary said nothing, and Pearl sat up in bed so she could see Mary more directly.

"Is being a nun your only option?"

A long silence. Then Mary spoke, softly. "I was actually thinking about nursing, too."

Although it wasn't easy to do, Pearl waited. Mary finally spoke again.

"I met a great bunch of nurses when I was in the hospital. They really took care of me. I loved them. They knew my mom had died. They dressed my wounds and cleaned me up and smiled and everything. They told me jokes and made me laugh. It helped a lot.

"There was one nurse who didn't have any children of her own. She talked to me for a long time about how she gave and received a lot of love being with other people's kids. She laughed when she told me that then she got to go home while the kids' parents still had to deal with all their problems."

Pearl remained silent. She'd observed her mother doing this sometimes—just saying nothing and waiting for the other person to speak. She could almost hear her friend thinking.

Mary quietly said, "Maybe I can talk to some of the nurses at the hospital about what I need to do to go into nursing. Would you come with me?"

"Of *course* I'll come with you. And I know my mom has friends who work at two or three hospitals. We can call and set up appointments."

"Thanks." Mary Fresa looked at her. "I'll remember this when I'm in the operating room covered with blood and guts."

"No problem. And one more thing you didn't consider."

"What?"

"Black and white are *definitely* not your colors."

"I know," Mary said. "They're yours."

Craig's Plea

"Shana Tova!" said Rabbi Craig Cohen from the bima of Lakeshore Temple. The building, with its large sanctuary and multiple balconies, was filled with congregants and their family members, friends, and guests, as well as many people who were not members of the congregation but needed a place to celebrate the holiest days of the Jewish year.

Tonight, September 26, 2003, was Erev Rosh Hashanah.

"Shana Tova!" many, but not all, responded.

Rabbi Pearl Ross-Levy sat on the bima, wearing her High Holiday white clergy gown and a new tallit and kippah she'd purchased especially for this night. She watched as the congregants settled in and Rabbi Cohen spoke again.

"Shana Tova!"

This time they were ready, and they echoed, "Shana Tova!" with exuberance.

Craig raised his cell phone in the air and said, "I want to remind everyone to turn their phones off and mute all pagers."

As always, this request prompted a flurry of activity.

"On behalf of Rabbi Ross-Levy and Cantor Sanders, let me welcome you!"

Everyone loves Rabbi Cohen, Pearl thought. He had a great smile, a handsome face, a confident presence, and a warm, empathetic personality. He himself would never consider himself charismatic; that was left to others.

Cantor Shelley Sanders took his place at the podium, smiled at the large congregation and nodded to Julian, who was sitting at the organ. The professional eight-member choir, seated on risers stage right, stood, and the music began. Twenty-five hundred people either sat back or leaned forward as they listened. Some quietly sang along.

Pearl sat next to Rabbi Cohen. She was enjoying the service even more tonight than she had the previous year, which had been her first High Holiday service in her new role of associate rabbi. Although Pearl had attended Rosh Hashanah services her whole life, and had led services as a visiting or guest rabbi during her years at the seminary, that first year attending the service as an ordained rabbi had been exciting and wonderful, scary and thrilling. It had been everything she'd worked for.

Now, a year later, life was going well. She was married to

a wonderful man she loved deeply, she lived in a vibrant and diverse city, and she was a rabbi in a great congregation.

Enjoy it, she said to herself. *If God is giving it to you, then thank God.* Which she proceeded to do, again, as she did every day of her life.

Pearl recalled the conversation she'd had the previous year with Rabbi Cohen.

They'd been preparing the High Holiday calendar when he told her, "Pearl, I'd like you to deliver the Erev Rosh Hashanah sermon this year. It may feel a little daunting to you, but it will be a great opportunity to get your feet wet in front of the entire congregation. Those congregants who haven't yet met you will see you in action. You're terrific, and I know you'll hit it out of the park!"

He added that he would deliver the sermon on Erev Yom Kippur—that was the evening that her sister Ruth had filled in at the eleventh hour to play Kol Nidre. It also started the two sisters on the road to a reconciliation that Pearl had long prayed for.

Yes. It had felt a little daunting as she worked on that Erev Rosh Hashanah sermon, making sure it contained the proper balance of humility, humor, and Jewish wisdom, as well as a brief account of her own rabbinical journey.

In describing that journey, Pearl had recounted Mary Fresa's fight for her life after the tragic car accident that had killed her mother. The new rabbi told how she had learned much about her own relationship to God from observing her best friend.

Without intending to, she'd brought many congregants to tears, and the outpouring of positive response had continued for weeks. Craig assured her that she had, indeed, hit it out of the park.

That was last year.

So Pearl was not surprised when Craig informed her that *this* year they'd be switching sermons—*he'd* speak on Erev Rosh Hashanah, and she would deliver the sermon on Erev Yom Kippur. Fair enough, she thought.

"But I need to give you a heads-up," Craig had told her.

She sensed a change in his demeanor—perhaps stress—that she hadn't observed before. She listened as actively as she could.

"There's something personal I need to tell the congregation this year. And I need to do it the first night. Otherwise it just won't work—not as many people come to the daytime services." He frowned as he spoke.

"And what I want to talk about isn't really appropriate for Yom Kippur. So this year, I'll take Erev Rosh Hashanah. Okay?"

Now Pearl was curious. What could he possibly have to say that "wouldn't be appropriate" for Yom Kippur?

She had no idea. All she really knew about his personal life was that he'd been a widower for about five years. Maybe he was just lonely and wanted to talk about that.

The thought crossed her mind that her mother might know someone who'd be appropriate for Craig. He'd certainly be a catch. She'd call her tonight.

But what she'd said to him at the time was, "Craig, please forgive me for saying this, and maybe I'm out of line, but my Spidey sense suggests you seem to be troubled about something. I only hope that whatever it is will be resolved."

Craig closed his eyes for a moment and then said, with a tired warmth, "Thank you for your concern, Pearl. My situation is very unusual, and you'll hear about it soon enough.

But I need to put your mind at rest. I'm in good health, and there's nothing you need to worry about. I'm not leaving my position or anything like that. Does that make you feel better?"

She relaxed. "Actually, yes. Thank you."

He looked at her. "Pearl, as you know, life is full of blessings and curses. I'm just dealing with my share."

And that was that. All she really knew was that there was going to be some kind of "reveal," and she'd just have to wait to see what it was. In the meantime, she'd talk to her mother about a possible fix-up for Craig.

And now, here she was on the bima in her white clergy gown and new tallit, gazing out at so many faces, many of which she now recognized. She smiled and listened to the wonderful music.

What she liked about Rosh Hashanah was that it brought together Jewish people in a celebration of their own New Year. Many of the readings were different or modified from those of the regular daily and weekly prayers, and the chanted melodies of the Torah reading were different as well. Many congregants wore white, and certainly most were dressed a bit more formally than they normally were. Many of the men were wearing ties. Only a few women wore hats. She reflected on how things were different when she was a girl. *I'm getting old,* she thought.

The choir ended its piece, and Pearl strode to the bima.

She read in English and in Hebrew and then welcomed guest readers who came on stage for a particular portion. Throughout the service there was a lot of kissing, hugging, and hand-shaking. The cantor led the assembly in song, chanted the age-old prayers, and the choir sang beautifully. It was a bit of heaven to listen to the lush harmonies in major and minor keys, the soaring sopranos and tenors, the mellow altos and basses, and Shelley's rich baritone.

Pretty much everything went as planned. No big surprises or screwups.

Seated on the bima, in addition to the three clergy and the musicians, were eight congregants. To be asked to sit on the High Holiday bima was an honor as well as a way of recognizing people for their service to the temple. Included tonight were a few past presidents as well as the current president of the congregation, several members of the board of directors, and at least one major contributor who had come to their rescue more than once. *You can never have too many angels,* she thought.

And then it was time for the sermon. Somehow people seemed to sense it and managed to be back from the rest rooms and sitting in their seats.

Everyone waited patiently as Craig walked to the bima, slowly and confidently. *What a pro,* she thought. He carried no papers or note cards.

"Once again, Shana Tova."

The congregation responded in kind.

"As we'll be reminded tomorrow morning—and I know all of you will be at services ..." He paused for the inevitable laughter because he knew many of them would *not* be present. "... the Torah portion will relate the miraculous story of Abraham and Sarah, the birth of Isaac, and the sad story of Hagar and Ishmael, who were 'sent away.'

"Then there's the vital story of the binding of Isaac. We all know how that turns out.

"In my professional life, my life as a rabbi ..." He paused, then said, *"your* rabbi ... I've always been struck by the observation that our Torah is filled with so many blessings and a multitude of curses.

"Blessings, curses; ups, downs; ins and outs. Life goes on until, well, until it doesn't."

He let that sink in, then went on.

"Instead of delivering a traditional sermon or drash to you this year, I need to ... I need to just talk to you. I need to talk to you about something that's been weighing heavily on my mind. And I apologize, but I just won't be able to rest until I share it with you."

This was not what the congregation was expecting. They quietly waited as he took a sip of water and returned the cup to a shelf under the podium. After taking a visibly deep breath, he continued.

Pearl realized that she was holding *her* breath. This was the "reveal" she'd been anticipating.

"Not all of you have known me since I first came to the temple twenty-five years ago, but many of you have. Those of you who have known me for twenty-five years, could you please raise your hands?"

Pearl wasn't surprised at the large number of congregants whose hands went up.

"Okay. Keep your hands up! Now, everyone who has known me as your rabbi fifteen years or more, please raise your hands as well. Great! Keep 'em up!"

People looked around them. There were certainly a lot of hands in the air.

"Finally, if you've been a member of the congregation or have been coming to services at the temple for five or more years, please raise your hands, too." Many more hands went up.

"Excellent! Now, look around you, front, back and sideways, and see how many hands are raised. Yes. A lot!"

Craig waited another few seconds, and said, "Okay, take a rest; hands down. But don't worry—you'll have another chance to raise your hands again soon. In fact, you might consider raising your *other* hand this time."

There were a few laughs, and people were smiling and commenting to one another about how many long-time congregants were present. Craig continued.

"Those of you who had your hands up have something in common, and perhaps you can guess what it is.

"Until five years ago, I was very happily married to my wife, Lorraine. She was a beautiful and lovely woman, with great charm, sweetness, talent, and abilities. She could leap tall buildings at a single bound; she could heal the sick, and raise the dead. She was my greatest blessing."

He paused while the congregation buzzed in acknowledgement. Although Pearl did not know Lorraine, she'd certainly been in the same room with her more than once when, as a teenager, she'd attended the bar or bat mitzvah service of one of her friends whose family belonged to Lakeshore Temple. Pearl's family had belonged to a Berkeley congregation.

"Five years ago, Lorraine succumbed to an unforgiving illness and passed. She died quickly and quietly, and I thank God she did not suffer too much.

"I suffered, however. I suffered greatly. In fact, everyone who knew and loved her suffered. It was the greatest of the curses that I personally have had to deal with. Blessings and curses."

Pearl watched him as he leaned down to get his cup of water and take another sip. *How was he doing this?* she thought. *Where does one get the strength?*

"All of you—my friends, congregants, and supporters, helped me through my year of mourning. You mourned with me. You comforted me. You made me laugh with your little comments and jokes, and cheered me up. You were there for me and I will be forever grateful.

"And God only knows how you fed me! *Oy!* I probably gained 25 pounds that year!" He laughed and everyone laughed with him, some with tears in their eyes. "But I made it through that year." He paused as he scanned the large congregation.

"When my year of mourning was over, I knew I had to move on. It's the Jewish way.

"And that's when it began. That's when I started to realize that my life was very different from the life I'd lived before. The life I expected that I'd live forever. Suddenly I was a man who had once been married but no longer was. I was a man who'd once had a partner, but no longer did. I was a man who'd once lived with someone and shared all the things one shares with a partner, but no longer could because that person was gone.

"Yes, that's when it began."

He paused and smiled.

"Okay, here we go again. Please raise your hands if you have ever—and I mean *ever*—introduced me to a woman you thought I might like. Go ahead!"

There were some nervous laughs. Several people on the bima raised their hands, smiling, and some in the congregation raised their own hands.

"Come on, people. I know you're out there, I can see you. If you've introduced me to a woman you know, raise 'em high! Don't be embarrassed. As you can see, you're in good company. And you were trying to do a mitzvah!"

More hands went up. People were smiling and pointing, and Craig turned around to see that Shelley had his hand up. He turned back to the congregation.

"If the Cantor's hand *wasn't* up, he'd be in big trouble.

"Keep your hands up. Now for the second group.

"If you have *not* introduced me to someone yourself,

that's fine. But if you have someone specific in mind that you *want* me to meet, a specific woman—or a man—raise your hand."

There was a lot of laughter and more hands went up.

"Now please keep your hands up as we add those who have been *thinking* of asking someone—perhaps a parent my age, if they know someone who's just *perfect* for me."

There was suddenly a lot of laughter and more pointing as Pearl's hand went up and a guilty smile crossed her face. Craig turned around, looked at her, smiled, and shook his head slightly as he raised his eyes toward heaven. He turned again to the congregation.

"Good. Now, before you put your hands down, take a look around. Okay, hands down." He waited until everyone settled down.

"So, you've all been trying to do a mitzvah, and I've been the recipient of those thousands of mitzvot. *Thousands of mitzvot.* Sounds like the title of a book. Just think what it's been like …"

At that moment, a cell phone began to ring. Everyone looked at everyone else. The sound was annoying, loud, amplified, and disruptive. People were looking accusingly at their neighbors. Craig looked around several times, then looked down, and pulled up his long white robe. He then took his own cell phone from his pocket, and looked at it, saying, "Oh my God, I am so terribly sorry! Please excuse me …"

Then he pushed a button on the phone, put it up to his ear, and spoke.

"Hi, Mom."

The congregation was stunned. There was some laughter, but it was quiet. No one knew what to say. Craig continued.

"Yes, Shana Tova to you too, Mom. You know, this isn't a very good time …"

He listened. Then he held the phone to his chest and spoke into the microphone to the congregation.

"My mother has a little dementia and doesn't remember that it's three hours earlier here on the West Coast. Just give me a second." He put the phone back to his ear.

"Mom, this isn't a very good time, I'm ... Yes, I'm glad your service was good. The sermon, too? Yes, he is a *very* funny rabbi!" Craig looked helplessly at the congregation.

"Yes...Yes...That's really sweet of you to think of me, but..."

He paused for ten seconds, looking off into the distance, then said, "No way! She was Miss Coney Island of 1968! You remember her from posters on the subway? That's remarkable. And she's still as beautiful as ever, even to this day!"

Craig once again put the phone to his chest and said into the mic, "She's a former beauty queen. And Jewish, too!" Laughter rippled through the room.

He put the phone back to his ear and said, "Listen, Mom, please don't give her my phone number ... You already did? Okay, I really need to go ... I'm in the middle of an important ... meeting. I love you too. Yes, I'm eating just fine." He looked up at the congregation.

"Gotta go." He hit a button on the phone, and placed it on the podium in front of him. As he did so, he looked offstage to his left where Duke Sniderman nodded, and put his own cell phone back in his pocket. Craig turned to face the congregation.

"Miss Coney Island. And Jewish! Try to top that!"

Pearl, who had witnessed the exchange between Craig and Duke, thought to herself, *How could anyone ever give a more dramatic Rosh Hashanah presentation than this?* She didn't realize at the time that it wouldn't be long before she *would* make her own dramatic presentation.

"Blessings and curses," Craig continued. "As your rabbi, I hear so many blessings and curses every day, every week."

He took a sip of water.

"I want you to know something. I don't think I've ever said it before, but I love you all. I have the best job in the world, the most wonderful congregants, the finest colleagues, and the greatest temple leadership any rabbi could ever desire.

"But *this must stop!* It's not easy to say this, but just do the math. Think of all those hands that went up.

"*Hear my plea!* Do. Not. Try. To. Fix. Me. Up. Don't even *think* about it! Do not ask anyone if they know someone who knows someone. *Please!*"

The congregation was silent.

"I am in good health, but this has been stressful. And stress is not good. Right?"

Affirmative nods and sounds from the room.

"I will always cherish the memory of my wonderful wife, and that's the way I want it to be. And I will not say this again. Do not try to fix me up. Even if she's a beauty queen from Coney Island.

"And let me repeat: I love all of you."

A lone voice called out, "And we love *you*, Rabbi!"

The applause began, slowly at first. Then it increased in strength and volume, and continued as people began to stand. Within a short time, everyone who could was standing.

Rabbi Craig Cohen stood there, overwhelmed. Finally, he wiped his face with his hands, composed himself and spoke into the microphone.

"Thank you. And let us say ..."

The entire congregation responded as one, "Amen!"

As Craig walked back to his seat, both Shelley and Pearl embraced him. Then the cantor moved to the bima, cued Julian and the choir, and the music resumed.

Pearl's hand reached towards Craig's as they sat side by side, and she held it tight. His eyes were closed and he did not open them for a long time.

A Talmudic Question

Pearl took a deep breath and readied herself for whatever might come up when Zinnia Chin came to her office for their regularly scheduled bat mitzvah study session. Her favorite student had already taught the teacher to expect the unexpected.

In an amazing demonstration of scholarship—genius, perhaps—Zinnia had virtually mastered her Torah and haftarah portions as well as all the readings and prayers necessary for the Shabbat service months in advance. Pearl had approved the drash she'd started writing on her portion, the Five Daughters of Zelophehad. It was quite entertaining as well as educational.

Zinnia knocked and entered, carrying a tome the size of a volume of Talmud. Pearl realized it *was* a volume of Talmud. *Now what?* she wondered.

"Hi, Rabbi." Zinnia was wearing what seemed to be new glasses, and today her long black hair was pulled back with a glittery scrunchie. Was she taller and thinner than the last time Pearl had seen her?

"Welcome, Zinnia. Make my day!"

Zinnia looked puzzled. "What does that mean?"

"It's just a line from an old Clint Eastwood movie."

To Pearl's surprise, Zinnia started whistling the theme from *The Good, the Bad, and the Ugly.* Pearl smiled as she was reminded that besides being incredibly smart,

Zinnia—at least according to the cantor—was a phenomenal musician.

"It's from a different movie, but go ahead. What's up?"

"Well, at the Kiddush lunch after services on Saturday, Dan and Bob were talking about how if you're Jewish and you get a divorce, you can also get a Jewish divorce, called a *get*. Like you 'get a *get*.' That's funny, don't you think?"

"Actually, I have always thought it was funny."

"Anyways, they told me there's a couple of books in the Talmud all about Jewish divorce. So, I was looking around the temple library and found them. The books are called *Gittin*—that's the plural of *get* in Hebrew."

"Yes, I'm aware of that," Pearl said, keeping a straight face.

"Oh, yeah, I forgot. You know Hebrew."

"No problem."

"Anyways, it's really cool all of the arguments these sage guys and rebbes are making. I don't have time to read the whole book now, maybe someday. But I sort of skimmed a little of it, jumping around, and came to this section I don't get. Ha! There it is again!"

Pearl laughed with her. *Will I ever have a daughter like Zinnia? Probably not. She's one of a kind.*

Zinnia placed the heavy volume on Pearl's desk and opened to a place she'd marked with a torn piece of paper.

"Here it is." She paused, and then began to paraphrase.

"So, this guy gives a *get* to his wife and says to the witnesses, 'If I do not mollify her within thirty days, then this *get* shall be a valid *get*.'

"Then it goes on and says, 'He went and attempted to mollify her but she was not mollified.' So this other guy, Rav Yosef, asks, 'How hard did he try to mollify her?'"

Zinnia looked up at Pearl. "I don't get it."

Keeping a straight face was getting difficult. She managed to say, "What don't you get?"

"See! There it is again. Ha! Anyways, what's with this 'mollify' business? I'm not sure I understand how they're using the word."

"Well, 'to mollify' means 'to satisfy,' right?"

Zinnia nodded, and Pearl continued.

"So the man was telling the witnesses that if he couldn't satisfy his wife within thirty days, then the *get* would be valid and they'd be divorced."

"Well, sure. But when Rav Yosef asks, 'How *hard* did he try to mollify her?' is that some kind of sex talk that he's slipping in there? Oops, well, you know what I mean—in the Talmud?"

Pearl grabbed a few tissues from the box and coughed, trying to mask her laugh.

"Rabbi? Are you okay?" Zinnia asked with true concern.

When Pearl stopped her fake coughing, she wiped a couple of tears away with her tissues. Zinnia, almost but not yet thirteen years old, just sat in her chair across the desk. Pearl stood up.

"Come here," she said as she opened her arms. The girl instinctively came in for a hug.

Pearl held her tight and said, "Zinnia, you are a very special young woman. I hope you don't mind me telling you that."

She let her go and held the girl at arm's length.

"As you get older and your maturity catches up with your intelligence, well, I just want to be around to see it."

Zinnia smiled up at Pearl and said, "That's funny, Rabbi."

"What's funny?"

"My mom says that sort of thing to me, like, all the time."

"I'm not surprised. Please tell your mother I said the same

thing to you that she always says. Now sit down, and let's look at the Talmud passage." Pearl moved the book closer and continued.

"And by the way, you're correct in questioning the business about 'mollification.' Although I believe they're talking about the husband giving the wife money, there could very well be a sexual component to it. The Talmud can often be difficult to interpret.

"But the line about 'how *hard* did he try,' well, that's an excellent observation of a subtlety on your part, but I think it would only apply in the English translation, not in the original text."

"Okay."

"People often say that something is 'lost in translation.' But in this case, we could say that you 'found' something in the translation."

Then Pearl added, "More or less."

She'd really wanted to say, 'As hard as that may seem,' but stifled herself. This was not Mary Fresa she was talking to. But she would certainly call Fresa later and tell her about the Talmudic discussion.

Pearl continued. "Zinnia, much of the Talmud contains discussions and arguments. The scholars and teachers often disagreed with one another. In fact, here's an example in this very book." She paged through a few chapters in *Gittin* until she found what she was looking for.

"I once wrote a paper about this. Do you know what a dowry is?"

Zinnia's eyes brightened. "Yeah, it's what the wife brought with her to the marriage in the olden days."

"Very good." Pearl was not surprised.

Zinnia went on. "My father once made my mom really

mad. He said that instead of her dowry being a cow or a goat, all she brought was fifty pairs of shoes. He thought it was funny, but she sure didn't!"

Pearl laughed. "No one seems to tell husbands about women and shoes, do they?"

"Yeah. And then she started talking about all his golf clubs and tennis racquets. I just went to my room and played the flute until dinner time."

"Good for you. Anyway, my point was that the rebbes argued back and forth about whether a certain dowry was property of the husband or the wife. And in the end, you see what it says here?"

Pearl pointed her finger at a sentence, and Zinnia read it aloud.

"*The Gemara concludes: The query stands unresolved....* Unresolved?"

"Yes. They couldn't come to an agreement, so they just left the argument and went on to something else. You find this a lot in the Talmud."

The rabbi and her student spent the rest of the session talking about the vagaries of Jewish law, in both Talmudic and modern times. Soon, their session ended. Pearl hugged Zinnia again, and the girl left, closing the office door with one hand while holding the heavy volume of Talmud with the other.

I love my job, Pearl said to herself.

The Rabbi Goes to Prison

Following the High Holidays, Rabbi Craig Cohen took a

much-needed two-week vacation. That was why Pearl was called in, like the Ninja Turtles—or Mighty Mouse—to save the day.

It seemed Warden Vernon Johnston at Folsom Prison was having a problem with his new "celebrity" prisoner. *Why couldn't they have sent this guy to one of the other state prisons?* he wondered.

The prisoner, Bruce "The Businessman" Steinblatt, had sent a message through his lawyer to the warden informing him that Steinblatt's mother's yahrzeit was coming up in a week. The prisoner demanded to see a rabbi so he could recite the special Kaddish prayer on the anniversary of his mother's death.

Warden Johnston looked up "yahrzeit" and "Kaddish" on his computer. As he typed on the keys, he adjusted his bulk in the "executive" office chair that supported his increasing mass. Once a powerfully-built law enforcement officer, he had little time to exercise anymore, and the only thing about him that could be considered "trim" was his graying mustache.

On the computer screen, the warden saw that these were, indeed, legitimate Jewish occasions and prayers of some type. He decided not to risk the bad publicity that might erupt from denying a prisoner a religion-related right.

He usually didn't have problems with his Jewish inmates, but this new guy, Steinblatt, had been a troublemaker from day one. So the warden did what he always did when he had a Jewish question—he put in a call to his favorite Jewish chaplain, Rabbi Craig Cohen, who worked at a big synagogue in the East Bay.

Unfortunately, the rabbi couldn't solve the warden's problem because, according to the woman he spoke to, Rabbi

Cohen was out of town and would not be back for ten days. Then she had added, for some unknown reason, that no one even *knew* how to contact him.

Warden Johnston and Rabbi Cohen got along well. After five years of working together they'd established a good relationship. The warden knew the rabbi had begun working at the prison following the death of his wife, and that for him it was an escape. Talk about irony.

There weren't too many Jewish inmates at Folsom, but there were enough to keep the rabbi busy; and of course he saw non-Jewish prisoners as well. The rabbi had once told the warden that he actually looked forward to the two-hour drive, his chaplaincy work, an overnight stay at the nearby Hilton, and the return drive the next day.

But now Rabbi Cohen was out of town, only God knew where, and the warden needed help. Jewish help. Pronto.

Esther, the woman at the temple, told him that she was directing his call to the associate rabbi, Rabbi Ross-Levy.

After he'd explained his predicament to the person he now thought of as "The Lady Rabbi," he was happy to hear her say that she'd be honored to substitute for Rabbi Cohen the following Monday.

Warden Johnston was gracious and sincere in his appreciation, and told Pearl that his assistant would make a reservation for her to stay at the same hotel that "Chaplain Craig" always stayed at when he came up to Folsom, and the prison would foot the bill.

After the call ended, Pearl and Esther went to work clearing the rabbi's calendar for Tuesday morning. Monday was Pearl's day off, but she hadn't mentioned that to the warden.

The following Monday morning, as the region was experiencing a mid-October heat wave, Pearl stopped by the temple to grab a couple of items before heading up to Folsom Prison.

Pearl hadn't thought much about the heat until she'd driven 45 minutes and heard a loud whirring sound come from behind the dashboard followed by a *clunk*. And then nothing. The car was still moving, but the air blowing through the vents was now hot instead of cool.

She sighed and cursed under her breath as she pushed the button to open the window. It wouldn't go down. None of the windows would go down. The sun roof wouldn't open, either.

So she just drove. *I'll make it,* she thought.

After another 30 minutes, she stopped at a gas station convenience center and went inside to cool off and take a bathroom break. A short, stocky woman stood behind the counter of the small store. However, it was not a service station, and there was no mechanic. Pearl bought a bottle of water.

I'll make it.

An hour later, her clothes damp with perspiration, she arrived at the prison. She tried to open the window so she could show her ID to the guard at the gate, but was quickly reminded that the windows didn't work. She opened the car door and handed the guard her driver's license. Pearl was relieved to hear that they were expecting her. She was directed to park in one of the chaplains' spots. She then headed into an air-conditioned hallway (*Thank you, God. I made it.*), where she went through numerous security checks and was given a temporary badge. She took another ladies' room break.

Pearl thought things were going smoothly until, twenty minutes later, she was led by a guard into a private visitors' room where Steinblatt was waiting for her. He wore a light blue prison-issue shirt, dark blue pants, a scraggly beard, and a mean scowl. Before the guard even closed the door behind them, Steinblatt spoke up in a loud, unpleasant voice.

"Who the hell are you?" was his greeting. It was not the greeting she'd been expecting.

"I'm the rabbi, Mr. Steinblatt. The warden told me you requested to see a rabbi."

"Where's Rabbi Ross Levy, the rabbi they told me was coming?"

"I'm Rabbi Ross-Levy. Pearl Ross-Levy. That's my name. Is that a problem, Mr. Steinblatt?"

The guard had not closed the door. He stood in the doorway.

"Sorry, lady. You're not what I'm looking for. I want a real rabbi. You can leave."

The guard said, softly, "Rabbi, tell me what you'd like to do."

Pearl sat down in a chair. She was tired, her clothes were wet, and she was getting hungry. Her car wasn't working right, and she felt anger building up inside her.

Time to be calm, Pearl, she said to herself.

She looked at the observation window on the wall of the room near the door.

"Officer, would you please close the door and watch us through that window?"

"Absolutely. If you need me, just look at me and I'll be in here in a second." He left the room and appeared at the window.

"You can leave too, lady. I'll be talking to my lawyer about this, and the warden …"

"Listen to me, you *shmuck!*" She said it with a tight smile and without blinking.

He looked at her in surprise. "Who are you calling ..."

"Shut your big mouth and listen to me, you stupid jerk!" She still maintained the smile on her face. "I just drove two hours in the heat as a favor to the warden so I can help you say the Kaddish for your dear, departed mother, whom I'm sure would be proud of everything you've done to get here."

"Hey, leave my mother ..."

"I told you to shut up! Now listen to me. You and I both know that you don't need a rabbi to say the Kaddish prayer. If you don't know it, I'm telling you now." She paused, and took a sip of water from the bottle in her bag. Then she continued.

"I am now going to tell *you* what to do, and you're going to do it. You are *not* going to call your lawyer, you are *not* going to threaten the warden, and most of all, you are *not* going to abuse me, you stupid *putz*. Because if you do, I'm going to call a press conference. *Listen* to me!

"I'm going to call a press conference. I am an ordained rabbi at one of the largest congregations in California. And I am going to be *happy* to reveal you for the fraud you are. A Jewish fraud. Don't expect for a second that anyone is going to care or give a damn what you have to say. Because *you* are a convicted felon. And *I* am a Woman of God. You don't stand a chance against me. Period."

She took another sip of water.

"Now we are going to play nicely for the benefit of that guard out there who would just as soon throw you off the roof as spit on you. Do you have a tallit?"

"No," he muttered.

"Here." She reached into her bag and handed him one, along with a kippah. "Stand up and put these on." He did what she told him as she stood, recited a prayer, and put on her own tallit.

Pearl took a small book from her bag. A card was holding a place in the book, and she handed the card to Steinblatt.

"We're going to read the prayer together. I don't care if you look at the Hebrew or the transliteration. Here we go."

She read it calmly and slowly. He recited many of the words along with her. In a minute, they'd completed the prayer. She reached for the card in his hand, but changed her mind.

"You can keep the card with the Kaddish prayer. Whenever you think about your mother, go ahead and recite it. And you can keep the kippah, too; but give me back the tallit."

He took it off and handed it to her. She folded her own tallit, then his, and put both in her bag.

"Now, smile at me for the guard, and say thank you." Steinblatt barely managed a smile, but he did say, "Thank you." Softly.

"We're done, Mr. Steinblatt. I hope your time here at Folsom is productive." She turned to the guard who had never taken his eyes off them. She nodded and he opened the door.

"Wait here, Steinblatt, while I escort the rabbi to the exit," the guard said. "Then I'll come back and get you."

A minute later, as the guard opened the door to let Pearl out of the secure area, he spoke to her in a soft voice.

"Rabbi, I want to disclose to you that there is an intercom system, and I was able to hear everything that was said in there. I should have told you that before I left the room. I apologize."

Pearl smiled at the guard, who somehow reminded her of Barney Fife, but with a modest pot belly. "Did you hear anything I shouldn't have said?"

Now the guard smiled back. "Actually, you said everything we all *wish* we could say to guys like him, but can't. So, I just want to thank you."

"You're welcome." She extended her hand, and he shook it. "Perhaps we'll meet again."

"I hope so. I know Rabbi Craig, and he's a really great guy. Please tell him 'hi' from Herman."

"I will, Herman." She turned and was about to walk through the door when she remembered her car.

"Herman," she said. "One more thing. My car's screwed up—the air conditioning's not working, and the windows won't open. I almost melted on the way up here." *It probably helped me deal with that idiot Steinblatt,* she thought.

He looked alarmed. "Rabbi, you can't drive back to Oakland with your AC not working, especially in this heat."

She laughed. "You're right, I shouldn't. But I'm staying overnight at the Hilton. So I figured, maybe you know of a mechanic where I can …"

He interrupted her. "Rabbi, you've come to the right place."

"Folsom Prison?"

He laughed. "That's a good one! No, I mean you've come to the right place—me! My brother and father run a garage not far from the Hilton."

He took out a pen and was looking for something to write on. She reached into her bag and handed him a grocery receipt. Herman wrote a name and address on the paper.

"Here's the address. It's right down the main road about two miles from here. Do you think you and your car can make it?"

"I'm sure we can."

"Good. I'll call my brother, and by the time you get there he'll be expecting you. You just leave the car with him and he'll drive you over to the hotel. Don't you worry about a thing. We'll take care of you."

Pearl, who now felt like she'd switched roles from the

tough-talking rabbi to the damsel-in-distress, thanked Herman, put the paper with the address into her bag and walked back to the security area where she reclaimed the items she hadn't been permitted to bring into the visitors' room.

Then she dragged herself out into the heat, folded herself into a *very* hot car, and headed down the road in the direction of the garage owned by Herman's brother—his name was Sherman. *(What was their mother thinking?)* She located it easily.

As promised, Sherman—a lumberjack-sized man who looked nothing like Barney Fife—was very accommodating. He took a quick look under the hood, and told her that her car would be ready by nine or ten the next morning. He gave her his business card.

"Just call me after you have breakfast. I'll come and pick you up." Then he drove her and her suitcase, in his air-conditioned pickup, to the Hilton.

Thanks to Herman the prison guard, the story of Pearl's visit with Bruce "The Businessman" Steinblatt had already begun to spread throughout Folsom Prison.

The Birth of a Star

Every morning, rain or shine, Sandy Wintergreen knocked on the Solomons' cabin door at nine, and they went to work. And every day at noon the Solomons took him to lunch in the dining room. After lunch, they resumed their sessions.

At five, they parted ways—Sandy to walk back to the restaurant for a light supper and to get ready for the seven o'clock show, and the Solomons to rest.

"This wasn't how we planned to spend our two weeks in the Catskills, is it?" Solomon asked his wife at the end of the second week.

"Are you having a good time?" she asked.

"The best."

"So, where's the problem?"

"I guess I don't have a problem."

"Solomon, we're helping the boy. You're finally getting a chance to share your vast comedic wisdom. And I'm doing what I always do, which is whatever I want to do."

"So, we're happy, we're doing a mitzvah, and all's well in the Catskills."

"Yes," she said. "And I have a good feeling about this. A very good feeling."

"Me too."

"What are you going to do about Manny?" she asked.

"Frankly, I'm not too worried. The Lounge has been getting busier every night. And you heard those people talking in the dining room this morning about 'that up-and-coming comic' in town. Manny's doing a good job getting the word out. You *saw* who was there last night."

"I did."

"A couple of them were taking notes. The pros are already stealing his material."

They sat quietly for a moment.

"Manny won't want to lose Sandy," Solomon said. "You'll see. Also, the kid needs more seasoning, at least a few months, before he's ready to go to a bigger resort. Then, maybe he can warm up the audience for the main act. We'll talk with the boy tonight."

"*After* we talk to Manny," Mrs. Solomon confirmed.

"You bet."

"Let's hear it for Sandy Wintergreen! Direct from Miami Beach! Put your hands together for Sandy! Wasn't he great, folks? And he's appearing *exclusively* at The Lounge. Please join us in our dining room for a late-night supper and drinks. But now, let's give Sandy one more round of applause. Sandy Wintergreen! We love you, Sandy!"

The ten o'clock show had been even better than the show at seven. Sandy Wintergreen was on a roll. The stories, jokes, heckler put-downs, and his physical presence just got better and better. The applause got louder because the room was packed. Manny had managed to stuff more cocktail tables into The Lounge. And the second week, he actually had the *chutzpah* to put a small sign on each table:

Five dollar per person cover charge.
Two drink minimum.

Mr. and Mrs. Solomon counted the house and calculated the take from the cover charge. It was a respectable amount.

At the end of the show, as always, Manny jumped onto stage as Sandy finished his routine.

Sandy took another bow and, waving, disappeared through the side door. As the audience exited, at least half headed for the dining room.

As they had done each night, the Solomons waited for Manny to join them. It took a while, since he was busy meeting, greeting, and *schmoozing* people in the dining room.

The Solomons waited patiently.

They'd told Sandy not to hang around after the show, and had given him the key to their cabin, and that's where he'd be now, waiting for them, knowing that it might be a while before they returned. They needed to talk with Manny.

And here was Manny now, all smiles, happy as a clam whose horse had just come in.

"There she is, the lovely Mrs. Solomon and her partner in crime." He sat down at the table and said, "Solomon, I've been looking for Sandy. Any idea where he is?"

"Manny, where he is, it's not really important. What's important is that he's not here."

Manny groaned. "I knew this was gonna happen."

"That's good, Manny," Mrs. Solomon said with a straight face. "You're starting to learn."

Manny sat back in his chair, his shoulders slightly slumped. "Okay. Talk to me. I'm ready."

"Probably not, my old friend. Probably not," said Solomon.

Silence. Solomon went on.

"So, as we all know, and at this point Sandy may even suspect, I've been paying him for the last two weeks. I've also been deducting my own agent commission from that pay."

"I know, I know. But how could I have ever guessed ..."

"Not important. Had Mrs. Solomon and I not intervened, he'd probably be back at your cousin Gertie's house in Queens, sulking and thinking about what a failure he is. Instead, he's a happy boy with a future.

"I think we can all agree, Manny. Sandy is a natural."

Mrs. Solomon was nodding.

Manny asked, "So, now what. Are you gonna steal ... are you gonna whisk him outta here and find him a deal at a resort?"

"Is that what you think we should do?" asked the agent, Solomon P. Solomon.

"It's probably what *I* would do."

"Yes. But I'm not you, Manny. And neither is Mrs.

Solomon. You're smart. We're smarter. Sandy is in our hands. God is watching out for him."

"Okay. I get the picture. Tell me what I gotta do to keep him here." Manny folded his hands in front of him.

Solomon reached into his jacket pocket and withdrew two folded pieces of paper. As he unfolded them, he placed one in front of himself, and the other in front of Manny so he could read it. The words "Contract Agreement" were in large, bold print at the top.

"Manny, I did not draw up this contract. My lawyer's office in Manhattan did. Not *my* lawyer. The lawyer in the office who deals with talent, artists, and show business stuff. It arrived this afternoon by Greyhound express. Read it."

Manny put on his glasses and read. His eyes opened wide a couple of times. He cursed under his breath more than once—but not loudly; he did not want to offend Mrs. Solomon. Finally, he spoke.

"A salary *and* twenty-five percent of the cover charge? Isn't that a bit much?"

"The lawyer suggested fifty percent. I told him you were my old friend, so he said, 'Okay, but no less than twenty-five,' which I agreed to."

Manny pointed to a sentence that contained numbers. "This weekly salary, Solomon. This is what guys get for warming up the major acts at the big resorts."

"Yes, isn't that amazing? Because I've already had two inquiries from the resorts offering just that. These were people who saw Sandy *last* night. Tonight he was even better."

Mrs. Solomon just loved to hear her husband lie. He was so good at it. She spoke her line, as they'd previously rehearsed.

"Solomon, Manny is getting ready to *hondel* with you.

I'm not in the mood for negotiating. It's been a long day."
She moved her chair back two inches.

"Wait!" Manny was so predictable. "Wait." He looked at
her. "Mrs. Solomon, you do me an injustice. I'm not gonna
hondel, not about the money, anyway."

He looked at the paper. "This deal, this contract," he held
it up, "is only good for two months."

"The lawyer told me to make it four weeks. I insisted on
two months because you're my old friend. And Mrs. Solomon mostly tolerates you."

"But what happens after that? What about next year?"

"Manny, by the end of August one of three things will
have happened. Listen to me carefully.

"One: Sandy will fail. He'll turn out to be a flash in the
pan, and he'll go back to your cousin Gertie's house. Eventually he'll become a CPA like she wanted him to do in the
first place.

"Or, Two: Sandy and his agent will get an offer—or
offers—that we won't be able to refuse, because, well, we
won't be able to refuse them. The money and the deals will be
too good. You know, the Copa, maybe a cruise ship, TV, Las
Vegas, whatever.

"Or, Three: You will make us a very generous offer. Let's
say a piece of the action—and The Lounge will be his 'home
base' for many years to come. You'll have a big sign outside
with his name and picture saying something like, 'Sandy
Wintergreen! This is where he started! And you can see him
appearing here on such-and-such a date.' And every season,
Sandy will do a couple of weeks in The Lounge. Meanwhile,
you will both be making a lot of money, because other new
comics will want to appear in 'The House That Sandy Wintergreen Built.'

"That's the way I see it. Anything to add, Mrs. Solomon?"

She turned to Manny. "Manny, don't be a *shmo*. Sign the stupid contact and pay Sandy what he's worth. You won't regret it. And if you do regret it, well, tough you-know-what." Solomon reached into his shirt pocket, extracted his thin gold pen, and handed it across the table. Manny, to his credit, took the pen and twisted it open.

He was about to sign, when Mrs. Solomon said, "Stop." She walked to the front door, stuck her head out, and came back into the room followed by a middle-aged man in a seersucker suit carrying a brown briefcase.

"Hello, Mr. Sondenheimer. My name is Kaplan, and I'm hear to witness and notarize your signature on this contract. Can I please see some ID? Your driver's license will do."

Manny could only shake his head again. He withdrew his wallet from his back pocket, fished out his driver's license, and waited until the notary recorded everything in a book. Kaplan also copied the information from Solomon's driver's license.

"Please sign here, here, and here, gentlemen." They signed.

Kaplan did his thing with a rubber stamp, and then smiled as he put his stuff away. "Mr. Sondenheimer, my fee has been paid by Mr. Solomon. Here's my card if you ever need a notary. I'm also a licensed real estate broker. It's been a pleasure." He shook hands all around, and disappeared out the door.

"Mazel Tov, Manny. You did good. God is watching over you," said Solomon P. Solomon. "Sandy will be opening at The Lounge next Friday night."

"Next Friday night?" A look of horror crossed Manny's face. "Tonight's Sunday! What happens in between? The Lounge will be dark!"

Mrs. Solomon sighed. "Manny. Listen to me. You have a lot of work to do. Clean this place up. Redecorate. Get more tables. Better signage. A big publicity photo outside in a glass-framed window. And this room and the stage need better lights, which you'll be buying from Solomon—if you have a brain in your head—at a deep professional discount. At cost, really."

"At cost?" Manny looked skeptical.

"He's not doing it for you. He's doing it for Sandy. Lighting is what Solomon does best. You are just the accidental recipient of his largess.

"And one more thing," she added in a more serious tone that surprised Manny. She actually pointed her finger at his chest. "You do *not* negotiate with Sandy directly. If you have a problem, a question, a concern, or you want to change his hours, or add music or dancing girls to his act, or do *anything* that has an impact on his performance, you call Solomon. Period. You got it?"

"Yes, Mrs. S. I got it. I really do."

Solomon said, "And in the meantime, Sandy will be living with us in Brooklyn, working his little *tuchus* off, learning new material and studying and polishing his act so that when he opens for you next Friday, he'll have a month's worth of material. After four weeks, he'll be off again for another five days."

Mrs. Solomon added, "By signing on the dotted line, you are helping to launch the career of a young comedian who will someday be a star. Someday years from now when we are all *alter kockers*, you'll be sitting around bragging to your cronies at the retirement home about how you discovered Sandy Wintergreen and gave him his first break. And how he helped you make a small fortune."

She stood up and added, "Unless you blow this deal." The two men quickly stood as well.

Mrs. Solomon leaned over, kissed Manny on the cheek,

and whispered, "Maybe you should just trust us. Know what I mean?" Manny gave a little nod.

After he'd shaken Solomon's hand, and the couple exited the building, Manny Sondenheimer looked at the sheet of paper in his hand. He then folded it, put it in his jacket pocket, and walked—a little smile on his face—into the dining room.

Craig and Pearl

When Craig returned from his vacation, Pearl informed him that after receiving an emergency request from Warden Johnston she'd subbed for him at Folsom Prison.

She did not go into any details about the encounter with the prisoner, her car troubles, or the assistance that Herman, the guard, and Sherman, his brother the mechanic, had given her. She didn't even mention that she'd stayed at the Hilton. She just told Craig that although Steinblatt was an obstreperous person, she'd succeeded in helping him recite the Kaddish prayer for his mother's yahrzeit, and that she wanted Craig to know about Steinblatt in case he had to deal with him in the future. She also remembered to say "Hi" from Herman.

Craig expressed his sincere thanks, and that was that.

He thought at the time, anyway.

Two weeks later, Craig drove up to Folsom for his regular chaplaincy visit, which would include an overnight stay with Grace.

When they checked into the Hilton at five, Leonard, the front desk clerk, greeted them in his usual friendly manner.

"Welcome back, Rabbi. Hi, Mrs. Cohen. Great to see you, as always. How are you both doing today?"

"We're just fine, Leonard. Good to see you, too," Grace said, charming him as she always did.

Leonard said, "I want to thank you and the warden for referring the other rabbi to us. I hate to tell you this, but she looked just exhausted—I think she'd had a bad day over at the prison."

Craig was a little flustered. Pearl had not mentioned anything about this.

"So ... she stayed here when she came up?" He exchanged a quick glance with Grace.

"Oh, yes. The warden's office called and made the reservation for her. I guess I shouldn't be telling you this since you pay for your room yourself, but the prison comped her for the night. They said it was an emergency visit."

"Yes, Rabbi Ross-Levy told me she'd filled in for me at the last minute at the warden's request." Craig felt like he was tap dancing on thin ice.

"Well," said Leonard, "I'm sure it would have gone better for her if the air conditioning in her car hadn't broken. But one of the local mechanics in town dropped her off here, fixed her car overnight, and she was good to go after breakfast. The guys at the garage really took good care of her. It probably didn't hurt that she's a rabbi," he said. "And men are always there to help a lady in distress, aren't they?"

"That they are," said Grace, with a smile. "It's in their DNA."

Leonard gave them their room key cards. "Well, I just told her I hoped she'd have a nice dinner and a good night's sleep.

"Oh, and I upgraded her room, too, at no extra cost. I told

her I was putting her in the same room that Rabbi and Mrs. Cohen always stay in when they're here."

Craig looked up, forced a smile, and tried to control his voice. "You did? You upgraded her to ... our room? You told her that?"

"Oh, yes. And she seemed really surprised. Maybe she'd never been upgraded before. But I told her it was something I can do for special guests, and she was certainly a special guest. Just like you are!"

Grace regained her composure first. "Well thank you, Leonard, for being so sweet. We appreciate that you took good care of Rabbi Ross-Levy. And Rabbi Cohen will be sure to give her your regards." She took Craig by the arm and gently pulled him away from the desk. He still wore an expression that bordered on mild shock.

Two days later, Craig waited until he knew Pearl was alone in her office. He knocked on her door, came in, and closed the door behind him. As he sat down in one of the visitor chairs, she noticed his grave expression and anticipated what was coming.

"Pearl, I owe you an explanation."

"No, Craig. You don't need to explain anything to me. Your private life is private, and I am not going to be judgmental about something I don't know about. You really don't have to talk to me about this." She added, "Do I tell you everything that's going on in my personal life? No."

Craig waited a while before speaking.

"It's not so much that I need you to know any details. It's more that I am carrying a burden, and it might help me if I know someone else understands. So if you don't mind—and since you already know—I really would like to talk to you about this."

"Of course." She picked up the phone and punched in a number. "Esther, Rabbi Cohen and I are having an important conference. Can you please hold any calls or visitors until we're finished? Thanks."

Craig smiled. "You really are very good."

"I learned from the best," she replied with a genuine smile.

Craig composed himself. "You never knew my wife Lorraine, but many of the congregants did. She was a lovely woman. You heard me speak about her at Rosh Hashanah. Although we never had any children, we had a very happy marriage. I loved her. And she certainly put up with me. By now you've discovered that being a congregational rabbi is challenging, time consuming, and complicated.

"One of the reasons I started working as a chaplain at the prison was that I needed an escape from the responsibilities I have here. As I like to say, I escaped to the prison." He paused, looked out the window, and then continued.

"About a year ago, I was at the annual chaplains' meeting at Folsom and met one of the Christian chaplains. Her name is Grace and she's quite a beautiful woman. She was also wearing a wedding band. Other than a quick introduction, we didn't talk.

"Later, when I went to a café during the lunch break, I saw her sitting alone at a table and asked if I could join her. We chatted for a while and learned that we'd both lost our spouses. One thing, as they say, led to another. And here I am, having a secret affair with a beautiful woman." He paused. "Who's not Jewish. We meet twice a month in Folsom and stay at the Hilton, where no one would ever find out about us. Until now."

"It *was* a strange combination of coincidences," Pearl said. "I'm really sorry."

He continued, "It's funny. When we go on a little trip together, we arrive at the airport separately and don't sit in adjoining seats on the plane. Just in case.

"We vacation on the East Coast or Mexico or Canada. We try to be so careful." Craig looked out the window again. "I miss her all the time we're not together."

Pearl grabbed a tissue from the box and caught the tear rolling down her cheek.

He smiled, sadly. "If I had my choice, I'd rather make you laugh than cry."

Pearl laughed.

"Better. So that's my story, sad but true. We enjoy our time together. Also, it will explain to you why I increased my scheduled visits to the prison to twice a month. Because of the situation, we can't have any friends. It's just the two of us. We're lonely together."

Pearl looked at him and said, "Craig, since your Rosh Hashanah sermon I've prayed that you would find happiness in your life. So I'm glad you found someone who cares for you. I know it wasn't necessarily your plan that it happen this way."

"But it did," he said. "I'm sorry for burdening you with my secret."

Pearl shook her head and said, "It's not a burden."

Craig rose to leave. "Thanks for understanding."

Pearl stood and embraced him. "God works in strange ways."

With his hand on the doorknob, he replied, "That She does, Rabbi. That She does."

How Old Am I?

Although she had never met the deceased, Pearl officiated at his funeral.

Bernard Pressman was 95 years old when he passed. She learned this during the ninety-minute interview with Bernard's son and daughter (and their spouses) prior to the service at the funeral home.

For the last seven years he'd been a resident at a well-regarded memory care facility in Walnut Creek. Before that, he and his wife had lived in Rossmoor, the large and very popular gated senior community, also in Walnut Creek. Prior to Rossmoor, the Pressmans had lived in the Crocker Highlands section of Oakland.

Although Bernard and his wife, Eleanor, had been members of Pearl's congregation for over 35 years, they had rarely participated in any activities (other than High Holiday services) for a very long time. And, according to what she was told, Bernard himself had not been to the temple at all since Eleanor's death ten years before.

Pearl assumed that his two children maintained their father's Temple membership for one of several reasons—the temple was a symbol of his past life; it was an act of charitable giving (and therefore a tax deduction); or (most probably) because he'd purchased two burial plots through the temple many years before, and it would be an act of continuity, if not simple convenience, to have the temple clergy officiate at his funeral. Probably, she thought, no one (including Bernard himself), expected him to live this long.

When Pearl had asked Craig about Bernard Pressman, he'd admitted to only a passing acquaintance with the Pressman family. They'd been active before his time. And now

Bernard's son and daughter were affiliated with congregations elsewhere in Northern California.

So Pearl met with the four family members, all in their mid- to late sixties, and learned what she could about the life of a congregant whom she'd never met. Mostly, they discussed how they'd like the funeral service to proceed and what role each would play.

"Oh, you can just do the Jewish stuff, Rabbi," said Elliot Pressman, the son. Elliot, wearing a well-tailored dark suit that fit his stocky frame nicely, appeared to be suffering quite a bit from his father's death. His curly hair and mustache were both gray. On his right hand he wore a pinky ring that featured a cabochon ruby. Every once in a while a gold Rolex poked out from under his left cuff. His wife, Judy, a petite blonde with blue-green eyes, sat close to him, holding his hand and rarely letting go.

"You know, say the Hebrew prayers, stuff like that." He gave Pearl a small smile. "Just make sure he gets put in the right section of the cemetery …"

"And goes into the right section of heaven!" added Beverly Pressman Manheim, Elliot's younger sister. Everyone laughed. "I'm sure he wants to be with his old friends so he can play pinochle again." Like Elliot, Beverly's hair was curly, but there was no gray to be seen. She wore a fashionable black pantsuit, a strand of pearls, and a diamond ring that Pearl coveted for just a moment. Looking at the taut skin of her face, Pearl suspected there might have been a face lift—at least one—at some point in the past.

Elliot added, with that sad smile, "I hope when he gets to heaven he remembers how to *play* pinochle … and who his friends are." At that point he had to grab some tissues; he wiped his face and blew his nose. Judy hung on to him.

Good wife, Pearl thought.

Elliot looked up at Pearl and said, "Like I told you earlier, Rabbi, my father was in the memory care facility for over seven years. The last five years he no longer knew any of us. He didn't even remember our mother, and, my God, he was married to her for what, sixty-five years?" He looked at his sister, Beverly, who just nodded. "He'd forgotten his entire career, the names of his parents and his five sisters. He couldn't even remember serving in World War II."

"Yes," said Beverly. "And that was something he'd always been proud of."

Elliot went on, not without some anger. "Rabbi, my father flew 44 missions in the South Pacific in a B-24 bomber during that damned war. And unlike a lot of others, he came back. There was a time he could rattle off all the names of his crew and tell us details about his plane and his years in the Army Air Force."

He gave a small laugh. "When my dad was about eighty, I was able to contact a couple of the guys in his bomber crew—I found them on the Internet. Six of them actually got together with their wives for a reunion in Chicago." He sighed. Then he continued with a sad face.

"But in the last four or five years, all he wanted to know was one thing. Tell her, Bev. I can't stand thinking about it anymore." Pearl thought he looked like he was going to cry again.

Beverly made a face, took a deep breath, and launched into it.

"All day long, Rabbi, it was the same question: 'How old am I?' *All day long!* He'd ask anyone who was in the room, 'How old am I?' I hate to say it, but it could drive you crazy."

Pearl said, "Dementia is a very cruel disease. It can take a tremendous toll on the family and the caregivers. I've seen it many, many times. My heart goes out to you."

She hadn't really seen it many, *many* times, but she had seen it enough, and knew that it was, indeed, cruel. Not so cruel for the victim, perhaps; but cruel and devastating for the family.

"So, Rabbi, please don't worry too much about the service," Elliot Pressman told her. "Just do the usual, you know, say whatever you feel is appropriate. There won't be too many people there. Just us, some of our friends, a few cousins, and our kids—the ones who could make it."

"Yeah. The ones who could make it," Beverly added, with a scowl.

Beverly's husband, Bill, put his hand on her arm and gently said, "Bev, let it go."

She took a breath. "Rabbi, our father didn't die the other day. He's been gone for years. We want to celebrate his life, not his death. Elliot and I will talk about him at the service. I just don't want to turn this into a tragic event. He lived a good, long life. Maybe *too* long."

The others nodded their heads in agreement, and Elliot said, "He saw the world. He helped win the war. He had a good marriage. His children were successful. His grandkids and great-grandkids are doing well…"

Beverly interjected, "Most of them."

Beverly's husband put his arm around her. "Bev, let's not get into it."

Pearl remained quiet during the brief moments of family dysfunction. She looked at her watch and then spoke.

"Okay. We'll be starting in about fifteen minutes. After a short preliminary service, I'll make a few remarks, and then invite each of you to come up and speak. Take as much time as you need. Then the pallbearers you've chosen will carry your father out to the hearse, and we'll all follow it to the gravesite, where we can put your father to rest while we chant the concluding prayer. You'll be given cards with the Kaddish prayer in Hebrew and in transliteration." They nodded, and she went on.

"As I understand it, you're going to a local restaurant afterwards. Thank you for your kind invitation, and I'd be honored to join you for a little while."

Beverly reached over and took Pearl's hand in hers. "I wish *we* had a rabbi like you in our congregation instead of that…"

"Bev," her husband interrupted, *"please* don't get started."

Beverly turned to her husband and gave him a look. "Maybe I'll quit and join *this* temple." He wisely said nothing.

Smart husband, thought Pearl.

Pearl stood and said, "Let's take a restroom break and then we'll go in." After the break, she led them into the chapel.

Funerals always brought out some kind of family tension, she thought. You just never knew what it would be. She was curious, of course, about the comments Beverly had made, but perhaps some things weren't worth knowing.

The funeral itself went smoothly. There were about forty friends and family members present. Elliot and Beverly spoke with warmth, humor, and more than a few tears about their father and mother. They told anecdotes from their own lives, and gave a creditable account of their father's long and rather interesting life.

There were more tears from many present when Beverly spoke about what it was like when your own father could not recognize you or remember your name. She also brought a few poignant smiles when she spoke about how, before his dementia advanced, her father would sometimes mistake her for his deceased wife.

When the eulogies were over, the pallbearers carried the casket out to the hearse, and everyone followed it, either on foot or by car, to the plot where Bernard would be laid to rest beside his wife.

Beverly had caused everyone to laugh when she explained that her mother and father would now occupy side-by-side plots in the same position they did in bed for over 65 years. Pearl filed that piece of information away for the future.

The Kaddish prayer was recited in Hebrew, with many joining in. Then family and guests lined up to toss shovels-full of dirt onto the casket, which had been lowered into the ground. From past experience, Pearl knew that this dramatic event often caused even the most stalwart to cry, and that was the case today. Elliot Pressman had to be consoled by several family members. *Yes, he was certainly taking it the hardest*, Pearl thought.

After the burial was complete, the family and guests returned to their cars and drove to a popular restaurant in Jack London Square for a buffet lunch in a private room. By the time they started eating and drinking, everyone was in a much better mood. In a short time, most were laughing and seemed to be having a good time.

Pearl watched and listened to Beverly, who was quite the raconteur. Elliot still seemed to be sad and subdued. Perhaps, Pearl felt, he was just a sensitive or emotional guy. Pearl was hungry, and she ate. She tried not to overdo it since she was, again, on a diet. After she'd schmoozed a little, she left.

One afternoon a few days after the Pressman funeral, Pearl sat at her desk working on an upcoming drash. Things were more hectic for her when Craig was out of town, as he was this week. These days, when he went out of town, he rarely

left a number where he could be contacted, preferring to
leave things in Pearl's hands.

"That's why you're here," he'd said to her. "You know
what to do. I trust you and promise to never second-guess
your judgment and decisions."

If asked about it, she'd tell the staff that Rabbi Cohen
needed some downtime. If Pearl didn't know where he was,
she at least knew who he was with.

Her drash was coming along, slowly, when Esther buzzed
her on the phone and asked if she had a few minutes to talk
to Elliot Pressman, who'd dropped by the temple in hopes of
chatting with her. Pearl went out to the small waiting area,
greeted him, and invited him into her office, closing the door
behind her.

She could feel the tension he brought into the room as
she sat at her desk and he collapsed in one of the two visitor
chairs.

"How can I help you, Mr. Pressman?"

His response was to bury his face in his hands and weep.

Pearl quickly came around the desk and sat next to him,
putting her hand lightly on his shoulder. She offered him the
tissue box and he helped himself, blowing his nose, and wiping his eyes.

"Rabbi, I have a confession to make. I need to tell you
about something I've done—I need to tell someone. I can't
hold it in anymore!"

"Mr. Pressman," she began, but he interrupted her.

"Call me Elliot, please."

"Elliot."

"I have to confess. I just can't take it anymore!"

"Elliot, please calm yourself," she said as calmly as she
could.

He took a deep breath. Pearl did too.

She spoke softly. "Elliot, I need you to understand something. While there is a tradition of confession in Judaism, it's a different type of confession than you may think; it involves God." She knew he was not in the right frame of mind for a theological explanation, so she tried another tack.

"We are not Catholics. I can listen to whatever you tell me, but I cannot absolve you of sin. And, I have to warn you, while whatever you tell me will be held in confidence, I may be obligated to report any possible threat to yourself. Or others."

She paused as he put his head in his hands and sobbed again. She asked, "Do you think you need a doctor? Or an attorney?"

He quietly said, "Maybe I do."

He then looked at her with an expression that she could only describe as horror, as he blurted out a sentence that froze her.

"Rabbi, I killed my father." He looked straight into her eyes and repeated it. "I killed him."

She sat stunned, and thought, *What am I supposed to do now?*

He went on. "I haven't told anyone yet, not even my wife. I need help. I'm desperate. And you're a rabbi. I thought maybe…" He sighed deeply, slumped in his chair, and closed his eyes. "I don't know what the hell I thought."

Pearl still had a hand on his shoulder. This was new territory for her. She took another deep breath.

"Elliot. Look at me." He did so, and she spoke softly.

"Elliot, we are going to get you help. Is there anything you want me to know before we move ahead?" She had to trust her own professional and personal feelings; and her intuition. Everything was telling her to stay the course.

Elliot Pressman stood up. "I'm going to tell you what happened, and then you tell me what I should do." He moved away from her, then turned to face her.

"Do you remember when we all met before the funeral?"

"Yes, of course."

"And do you remember my sister telling you that during the last few years of his life, my father only said one thing— he only asked one question, over and over and over again? Do you remember that?"

The tone of his voice was actually getting more forceful—angrier.

She responded, "Yes, of course, I do."

"What did he ask!"

It almost felt like he was taunting her. "He would ask how old he was."

"Yes! 'How old am I?' Over and over again. Rabbi, he asked everyone who came into that damned room, 'How old am I?' Endlessly."

"I remember."

"Rabbi, it drove me crazy. And I was only there once a week!

"All I wanted to do was have a conversation with my father. I wanted to communicate with him. I told him I loved him and I wanted him to tell me he loved me. Or that he was proud of me. Or remembered me. I wanted…anything! Anything but that damned question!

"'How old am I.' You'd tell him his age, but he'd ask again a minute later.

"'How old am I?' It sent me over the edge. My sister, too, but especially me. I don't know why.

"And Rabbi, the answer to the question only changed on his birthday, once a year.

"'You're ninety-two years old, Dad.' 'You're ninety-two years old.' I'd say that over and over for a year.

"And then it was, 'You're ninety-three years old, Dad.' 'You're ninety-three years old.' I'd say that for another year. I almost begged for the year to change so I could give him a different answer."

Pearl could hear the frustration in his voice. She felt a certain amount of empathy for him. Then she reminded herself that a few minutes earlier he'd told her that he'd murdered his own father. *Wait,* she thought. *Did he say* murdered *or* killed? There was probably a legal difference, but she didn't know what it was. *First degree? Second? Manslaughter? Voluntary? Involuntary?*

Her rambling legal thoughts were interrupted by Elliot.

"One day, after four years of him asking, over and over, 'How old am I?' I recalled a conversation I'd had with him maybe fifteen years before—years before he started to lose his mind, his memory—everything he knew.

"He was telling me about one of his good friends who'd just died in his early eighties. My father said that his friend had died too young. *Much* too young. I remember saying to him, 'Dad, eighty-two is not really too young to die. It's a pretty decent number of years.'

"And you know what he said? 'Not me, Elliot! I'm gonna live to a hundred! Yep, a hundred years old. None of this eighty-two or ninety-two business. A hundred. That's how long I'm gonna live!'"

Elliot then sunk back into the chair next to Pearl and shut his eyes. She waited until he continued.

"Last week, I was visiting him in his apartment. I was there for a couple of hours. And the whole time he kept asking me, over and over, 'How old am I?' How old am I?' And I recalled that conversation we'd had many years before.

"So you know what I did, Rabbi? The next time he asked me, *the very next time* he asked me, I said to him, 'Dad, you're a hundred years old.'"

Pearl sat still. She said nothing. But she felt a chill run through her.

Elliot said, "My father looked at me—he looked at me with a look I'd never seen before. And he asked me again. *How old am I?*' But the question sounded a little different than it usually did. It was just the two of us in the room. His caregiver was taking a bathroom break, or having a cigarette outside. I don't know. She'd gone for a break because I was with my father.

"I said it again. 'A hundred, Dad. You're a hundred years old.'"

"He looked at me kind of funny. Then he said, very quietly, 'I'm a hundred years old.' It was more of a statement than a question."

Elliot looked at Pearl. "Frankly, Rabbi, I was a little proud of myself. I'd gotten him to say something different. It was actually a relief."

Elliot smiled for the first time since he'd walked into her office.

"I watched my dad lean back and slowly close his eyes. Then he fell asleep. He had a little smile on his face—something I hadn't seen since my mother was alive. I left him there sleeping in his bedroom, and waited in the living room until Bianca, the caregiver, came back."

Pearl watched as Elliot Pressman stood once again and paced in front of his chair. He continued to speak, his voice shaking slightly.

"I told her that my father was asleep, that I was leaving, and that I'd be back for a visit the following week. We said goodbye and I walked down the hall, chatted with the woman at the reception desk, and was out the front door on the way to my car when Bianca came running over to me, yelling, 'Mr. Pressman! Mr. Pressman!' She was clearly upset.

"She caught up with me and whimpered, 'Oh, Mr. Pressman. Your father's not breathing! I think he's dead!'"

"I rushed back into the facility and heard the receptionist paging the medical director to go immediately to my father's room. He arrived seconds after we did.

"It was obvious, even to me, that my father had stopped breathing. The medical director confirmed this. He reminded me in a calm voice that there was a 'Do Not Resuscitate' form attached to the refrigerator, and there was no point calling 911. Instead, he called his office, which was on the other side of the building, and asked a doctor who'd been visiting another patient if she would come in and confirm what we both knew. The doctor came, did her evaluation, and confirmed that my father was, indeed, dead.

"And that was that. I told my father he was a hundred, and he died. Within minutes.

"I killed him, Rabbi, just as if I'd smothered him. I lied to him, and he just … died." Elliot once again sat down.

Pearl put her hand on his arm and said, "With a smile on his face."

"Yes, with a smile on his face." Elliot looked at her. "But what do I do now, Rabbi? I am wracked with guilt. I haven't slept in a week. I am a wreck. I killed my own father."

Pearl stood, and walked around her desk and sat down in the chair. She was deep in thought, and he waited. Finally, she spoke.

"Elliot, with your permission I would like to talk to a few people who might be able to help us with this … this dilemma. Because that's what it is. It is a dilemma."

He sighed and said, "I'll do whatever I have to do. Whatever is right. Yes, you have my permission."

Pearl made a quick decision. "Do not talk to anyone about this until I get back to you. Including your wife. You're staying here in town?"

"Yes, at the Marriott." He wrote down his cell phone number. "We're staying at the hotel while we wrap up my father's affairs and dispose of his furniture and so on."

Pearl stood and led him to the door. "I'll call by nine tonight." She gave him a hug, closed the door behind him, and sat back down at her desk.

And thought about what she should do next.

An Ethical Dilemma

After Elliot Pressman left her office, Pearl made some quick but deliberate decisions.

With Craig out of town, she was unable to confer with the person she would have turned to first. She was on her own. And she needed help, counsel, advice, and opinions. And she needed it all fast.

Pearl had promised to get back to Elliot that evening. He was distraught, suffering, and under intense stress. None of that was good. If she was going to help, it needed to be soon. Part of her was afraid of what he might do to himself— physically, emotionally, perhaps even legally—if allowed to continue without help.

Pearl took her pen and wrote three names on a pad of paper. Then she went into her contact list and wrote phone numbers next to each name—all except the last, which she knew by heart. She then buzzed Esther and told her that she'd be on the phone with some important calls for a while, and would then be leaving the office.

"No more temple business for today," she said.

"Got it," replied Esther.

Then Pearl made her first phone call. It was a long shot, but why not at least try?

"Hello?"

"Hello, is this Rebecca?" Pearl asked.

"Yes it is."

"Rebecca, this is Pearl Ross. You may remember me, although I haven't seen you in a few ... maybe a dozen years."

"Of course I remember you, Pearl. The sweet girl who came to my house and told me she wanted to be a rabbi. How could I forget you!"

"Thanks for remembering. It's good to hear your voice."

"And it's good to hear from you, Pearl. Don't think I'm unaware that you *did* become a Reform rabbi. Mazel Tov!"

"Thank you."

"Listen, Pearl, we don't live in a vacuum here," said the wife of the Chabad rabbi in Berkeley. "People say I know everything that's going on, and you know why they say that?"

"I think I do," said Pearl.

"You're right. Because it's true!"

Pearl laughed, remembering one Shabbos dinner, sitting at the "women's table" at the rabbi's large home in Berkeley. Even then she had marveled at how Rebecca Feldenstein walked the walk and talked the talk of a *rebbetzin*—the wife of a well-known, well-respected, and, Pearl thought, the most modern ultra-Orthodox rabbi she could imagine.

Rebecca herself was a marvel. She was a college graduate—Pearl thought she might even have a master's degree—yet, she wore a *sheitel*—a wig, but very fashionable, the best possible. She was a petite, beautiful woman, who'd had seven children by the time she was 40. She ran a tight ship both at home and in the congregation, which served the Jewish community not only on the UC Berkeley campus, but the surrounding area as well. And not just the Orthodox Jewish community. Conservative, Reform, and unaffiliated Jews often found themselves at Chabad House for services, classes, meetings, or just to see and hear Rabbi

Feldenstein, who was learned, funny, charismatic, and, most of all, wise.

"What can I do for you, Pearl? I'm at your service."

"Rebecca, I just spoke with the adult son of a recently deceased congregant. He's come to me with an incredible problem. Rabbi Cohen, our senior rabbi, is out of town, and I need help."

"The rabbi needs help," Rebecca replied. "It wouldn't be the first time, trust me."

"Is there any chance I can drop by and talk to your husband? And you, too? This is a tough one, believe me, and I need all the help I can get. I'm in a corner, and it's an emergency."

"Pearl, you can come over right now. I'll tell Mordechai to expect you and your problem. You remember where we live?"

"Yes, of course. Thank you so much! I'll be there in about an hour. Maybe sooner."

Pearl hung up, then made two more calls and set up two more meetings. Her luck was holding.

She grabbed her bag and jacket and made her way out the temple's front door, greeting a few people on the way.

Pearl made a five-minute stop at her house for a couple of items: she reached into the deep recesses of her bedroom closet and grabbed a long, loose, black skirt that had an elastic waistband. She'd worn it many times during her year in Israel when she needed to walk through certain neighborhoods in Jerusalem that required women to dress "modestly." She just pulled it on over her black pants. Then she opened her bottom dresser drawer and dug out a large multi-colored, paisley print scarf. She spent a minute in front of the mirror tying the head covering, making sure that her hair was not visible. Then swoosh, she was out the door, wiping off with a tissue what little lipstick she was wearing.

In less than half an hour she was in North Berkeley, parking in front of Rabbi Mordechai Feldenstein's large home. With their seven children, a large kosher kitchen, multiple refrigerators and pantries, and space for dozens of guests at their *Shabbos* dinner tables, the Feldenstein family needed a big home.

Pearl rang the doorbell and Rebecca greeted her with a smile, a hug, and kiss on the cheek. Pearl was a bit nervous but shoved that emotion to the part of her brain where the emotions lived. Rabbi Feldenstein may have been considered by some a modern Chasidic man, but in his world there were no female rabbis. She'd play it by ear. What choice did she have?

Rebecca looked Pearl up and down, and gave her a nod. Pearl wasn't fooling the rabbi's wife, but she needed to play her role, nevertheless. Her hair was completely covered, and there were no bare arms or legs—no skin showing at all other than her face and hands; and the rebbetzin would be with her during the meeting. So all was good in the land of the ultra-Orthodox. More or less.

Rebecca led Pearl into the rabbi's study. He was reading at his desk, but turned and then stood to greet her. He did not, of course, offer his hand, nor did she. Rabbi Feldenstein looked like a man who, if he was an actor, could play an orthodox rabbi in a movie. *Life imitates art,* Pearl thought. His longish beard was grayer than the last time she'd seen him, but his hair and eyebrows were still black. His eyes had a piercing quality behind wire-rimmed bifocals.

He smiled, and said, "Wait a minute, I was expecting a sixteen year-old girl!"

Pearl laughed. *What a kidder!*

She said, "Rabbi, it's so good to see you again. Believe it or not, I'm thirty and I'm a married woman. In fact, I'm married to a Levy! I go by Pearl Ross-Levy."

"Excellent! Please sit." She and his wife sat on a sofa while he returned to his desk chair. Although Pearl was at least a foot taller than Rebecca, when seated they were eye-to-eye.

Mordechai Feldenstein swiveled his chair around to face them.

"May I call you Pearl?"

"Of course."

"Pearl, I *am* aware that you are a Reform rabbi and work with Craig Cohen at Lakeshore Temple. Mazel Tov to you!"

"Thank you, Rabbi."

"It's the way of the future, I'm sure, although I doubt many of my colleagues would either agree or approve. But my philosophy is that Hashem often works in strange ways."

"Actually, that's my philosophy too," Pearl said and smiled. "You can't imagine how many times a week I say that."

"Good. I'm glad to hear it. Now, Rebecca tells me you have a problem that you think only I can solve."

Pearl took a deep breath, and said, "I'm not sure if anyone can really *solve* this problem. But I'm hoping that you can give me some guidance, maybe some direction, and hopefully some words of wisdom."

He nodded and waited.

Pearl told him and his wife the story of how, a few days after the death and funeral of one of her congregants, the son of the deceased had come to her with a confession—he believed that by lying to his 95-year-old father, who suffered from deep dementia, he had, basically, killed him. She spoke of Elliot's recollection that his father wanted to live to a hundred and how Bernard had been asking the same question, all day long, 'How old am I?' for years.

She told of Elliot's horror when he put two and two together in his own mind, feeling that his father wanted to make it to a hundred, and within minutes of believing he'd done that, Bernard had died—with a smile on his face.

The rabbi and his wife listened attentively as Pearl explained that she felt this situation had moral, ethical, religious, and, sadly, legal ramifications, and that she was not sure how, exactly, to proceed. Finally, she added, she had set up an appointment with a legal expert, whom she'd be visiting later.

Pearl looked at Mordechai Feldenstein and said, "But frankly, Rabbi, between you and me, I'm more concerned about how I should address this problem from a Jewish perspective. I keep looking at it from different angles and come up with so many different answers. And more questions."

Pearl sat back. She'd explained the situation as best she could. She was surprised to feel Rebecca's hand cover hers, and when she turned to look at her, she saw a smile on the rebbetzin's face that she could only describe as beatific. She was a very beautiful woman and conveyed much emotion with her eyes. The message Pearl was getting was that Rebecca approved of her.

The rabbi stirred in his chair. *His* face was not wearing a smile. In fact, he appeared quite grim.

"Rabbi," he said to her, which was quite a shock, "you present a wonderful Talmudic question. If I smoked a pipe, now would be the perfect time to puff on it while appearing wise, professorial, and prophetic. But I don't smoke a pipe. Maybe I should start."

He stood, and walked a few feet away. Then he turned to look at her again.

"Here's the story the way I see it. You've already thought this through and have done a good job summing up both sides of the question. Yes, you are right. There are ethical components to this dilemma; there are moral questions, legal ramifications, and personal, psychological, and religious issues.

"If you've spent any time with the Talmud, which I'm sure you have, you know that the rebbes and the sages would take a problem such as this and argue it forever. They'd compare it with my ox gored your ox, and an eye for an eye, and the son's intent, and the fact that he lied and thus did not honor his father, which is a commandment. Perhaps they'd discuss the mental competence of the father, and so many other things. Beis Hillel would argue with Beis Shammai; and Reish Lakish would argue with Yochanan; and Abaye would battle it out with Rava. And you know what would probably happen after a lot of back and forth, and accusations, and nitpicking?"

Pearl responded without thinking too much about it, "They'd probably leave it unresolved."

The rabbi looked at his wife and smiled. "Rebecca, we have a very smart girl … excuse me, a very smart woman here. A real daughter of Rashi. Do we have room in the house for her? Maybe she can move in and we can study together."

"I *told* you," said his wife. "I knew when she was a teen-ager." The rebbetzin patted Pearl's hand again.

Feldenstein sat down in his chair. "I would say you hit the nail on the head, and I'm not going to waste your time. There is, in my humble opinion, no clear way out of this problem."

Pearl just sat there on the sofa. There was nothing she could think of to say.

Feldenstein spoke again. "Certainly, in my opinion anyway, I don't believe a court or a jury would convict this man of killing his father after they heard the facts. He loved his father. He'd visited him regularly for years. He cared about him. He took care of his needs. He did not smother him, or strike him, or give him an overdose of drugs.

"Yes, he did lie to him, perhaps dishonoring him. But that was an exception to his usual behavior. Like you alluded to in your excellent narrative, if someone were to tell a person with a weak heart that her only child had just died in an accident, yes, she might suffer a coronary and die from the shock of the bad news. And if that news about the dead child turned out to be either a lie or a mistake, the bearer of the news *might* be culpable in some way. Might be. This kind of thing has, I'm sure, happened during wartime, perhaps even in our own modern times.

"But what jury is going to send your congregant's son to prison? What court of sages is going to subject him to lashes or have him stoned?

"Should I call some of my colleagues and convene a *beit din* and proceed to judge him? We don't have that power in today's society. And who is going to want him to suffer more than he already is suffering?" He paused, and then added, "Well, maybe there *are* some people who would point a finger and accuse him. There are always such people.

"But this man's intent was not to harm his father. It seems his intent was probably to calm his father, and maybe give him some rest from his constant questioning about his age. How could he know that this answer, 'You're a hundred years old,' was what his father was waiting for so he could allow himself to die? All of that is only apparent after the fact.

"We all know of people who live to a hundred and two, or a hundred and five. I do. And dementia, as you know, is a cruel disease.

"There's no easy solution to this problem—unless you have a magic wand you can pass over this man's head to cure him of his guilt. Perhaps, hopefully, with time, with the help of the Eternal, and maybe with some professional counseling, he'll come to forgive himself. That's all, I'm afraid, I can hope for, and all I can say to you.

"Rabbi Ross-Levy, I wish I could help you more. But I can't. I'm sorry."

Pearl nodded. He'd given her the honor of addressing her as "Rabbi" twice. It was a great honor, and she appreciated it. Rebecca squeezed her hand again. The meeting, Pearl knew, was over.

She thanked them both again, and after the rebbetzin had led her to the door, the two women hugged.

"I am so proud of you, Pearl. I've never heard my husband speak to a woman in the way he just spoke to you. As a peer. As a colleague. Thank you for coming here and blessing our home with your presence."

"Thank you for having me. I appreciate it so much."

"And please say hello to your mother for me. I remember her well. I've actually sent a few clients her way. Maybe you know that."

"I didn't. I'll give her your regards."

And with that, Pearl was out the door and into her car. She slipped off the long skirt and removed her head scarf, shook out her hair, and in a minute was on her way to Oakland's Piedmont Pines neighborhood for her next appointment.

Pearl felt sad, and in some ways the heaviness that she had in her heart for Elliot Pressman was even greater now than it had been before. Where was that magic wand when she needed it?

"Rabbi, come in, please. What a pleasure to have you here!"

She walked through the front door of Jimmy Rohrbach's home and shook his hand as he kissed her on the cheek. He had, Pearl thought, a lawyer's handshake—firm, confident, and two-handed. He wore a perfect smile and a perfect hair-cut, and even without a suit and tie—he was wearing a sub-dued Hawaiian shirt and tan slacks—he exuded friendly power. His wife, Lily, who was blonde, pretty, and looked younger than her sixtyish husband by at least a decade, greeted her as well. Jimmy and Lily were longtime congregants. He was a former member of the temple board, and she was a current member.

The smells of dinner were in the air.

"I hope I'm not interrupting your dinner."

"Rabbi," Lily said, "we'll eat when you're finished talking to Jimmy. Unless you'd like to join us?"

"Thanks, Lily, but frankly, I don't have time. Perhaps on another occasion when I'm not, well, on business."

"Come this way, Rabbi." Jimmy led her into his study and closed the door behind her. She sat in an overstuffed chair, and he sat in a similar chair a few feet away.

"Okay, let me have it. When you called, you implied an urgency."

Jimmy Rohrbach was an attorney. But more than that, he was a criminal defense attorney, with quite a reputation. Pearl didn't even want to think how much this meeting would cost her if she were a paying client. She laughed to herself—being a member of the clergy had its privileges.

"It's complicated, Jimmy. I'm not sure where to start."

"Start at the beginning."

So she did. Having explained the situation to Rabbi Feldenstein, it was easier the second time. Rohrbach sat patiently, nodding occasionally, smiling once or twice, and nodding again.

After she was finished, he looked at her and said, "Rabbi, I'd love to defend your client. This is a great case."

"Terrific! But can we win?"

"Who the hell knows? But boy, would we get publicity on this one. TV, newspaper headlines, the politicians would be all over it. Christians and Jews would be lining up on both sides. This case would go viral. International! I could write another book. You know why?"

"Tell me."

"Because it goes to the deepest core—the heart—of the legal systems the world has been struggling with since Biblical times."

"*Oy.*" Pearl couldn't come up with a better response.

"*Oy vey!* Even better."

"Yes," Pearl agreed.

"If I were a Hollywood agent, I'd want this story. It's a classic. I'd be casting it before the ink was dry on the contract."

"I can't believe I'm hearing this from my legal counsel."

"Believe it. And you know the craziest thing? I have no idea—absolutely no idea—how the movie ends.

"I can guess, maybe. I can assume. I can posture. I can hope and pray. But I don't *know. That's* the problem, Rabbi."

"You don't know." She felt stunned. Again.

"Not really.

"Oh sure," he went on, "I doubt a jury would convict the son of murder, or manslaughter, or involuntary manslaughter, or whatever some prosecutor would try to throw at him. But that's not the real issue here. And I'm having to step out of my legal role for a second. Because the real issue is the guilt that this poor *schnook* is now carrying and probably will for the rest of his life. That's the sad truth.

"If *I* were a prosecutor and I really wanted to nail this guy—and believe me, there are plenty of jerks who would try, maybe because they're new or they have to prove themselves or they're holier-than-thou—then sure, I could come up with evidence and so-called experts who would testify that the son was directly or indirectly the cause of his poor father's death. There are, as you know, cases where something said to a person *can* kill them. It's happened."

"Yes. I've thought about that."

"But Rabbi, we're talking about a victim who's ninety-five years old. Do you realize that some expert would be called on to testify how much money, exactly, the life of a ninety-five-year-old is worth?"

"Really?"

"Sure. It's an actuarial thing. If a young man dies, his life is worth X. If a woman has two young children, her life is worth Y. If it's some famous actor who earns ten million dollars a year, his life is worth Z. And so on. That's the world I live in. You want in?"

Pearl laughed. "They actually mention this in Leviticus."

"Why am I not surprised."

"So where do I go from here?" Pearl was getting frustrated. "What do you think I should do?"

Rohrbach sat back in his chair and thought for a minute.

"I'll tell you what I think, and I'll tell you where I believe you should go from here. You should put on your *SuperRabbi* costume with the red cape and handle this from a strictly spiritual and pastoral position. This is my unsolicited—well, it *is* solicited, but it's free—advice. Get the legal aspect out of the picture. It's stupid. No one wants the son to suffer more than he already has by throwing him into the legal arena, the lion's den, as it were. Don't do it. Get that out of his head as soon as you can.

"Use your best persuasive skills. Hey, you're a woman— you know what to do. Lie to him if you have to—hell, I do it all the time."

Pearl kept a straight face, but it wasn't easy.

Jimmy went on without missing a beat. "Tell him that

you've spoken to a world-famous legal expert who said that he absolutely, positively, did *not* kill his father, no matter what he thinks. Pound it into his head. Then, work on him to get counseling, some therapy, maybe some drugs, whatever it takes to get him back to normal. Have him focus on what a long and wonderful life his father led."

"You think he'll buy that?" Pearl asked.

"Rabbi, I tell you what. You go ahead and turn this into a heart-warming family story. Twist it around. Make it sound like the son did his father the greatest mitzvah anyone could ever imagine. He helped his father reach his goal; he shortened the poor man's suffering. Hell, the old man's quality of life was *bubkis*. Am I wrong? No. And now he's in heaven with all his old buddies playing golf."

"Pinochle."

"Whatever. He's with his wife. He's getting laid again. Sorry, Rabbi. Anyway, what a deal. What a mitzvah he did. The best thing the son could have ever done for the father he loved. Blah, blah. You get the picture."

Pearl was taking it all in as fast as Jimmy was throwing it out, and he hardly took a breath.

"Listen, you're a rabbi. That's almost like being a magician. Same union. Let me tell you—it's all magic—smoke and mirrors. Just make it happen. You can do it. Trust me."

Pearl couldn't help herself. She was laughing. It was the first time she'd laughed all day. Now she knew why Jimmy Rohrbach could charm the juries he faced. That was his reputation.

They both stood up. He opened the door for her and she was about to walk out of the room, but she stopped and turned to him.

"One more thing. I want you to promise me something."

The flamboyant attorney looked at her and said, "Sure. Anything, Rabbi."

"Promise me that if I'm ever accused of murder, you'll defend me."

"Rabbi, it would be my greatest pleasure to take your case. To the Supreme Court if necessary."

They were laughing as they walked into the living room, where Lily seemed surprised to see the change in mood that had occurred since the rabbi's arrival.

Pearl hugged them both, said goodbye, and went out to her car. When she got behind the wheel, she just shook her head in amazement before she headed to her last appointment of the evening.

Pearl had done a lot of driving in a short time, and was now headed back to Berkeley. She was hoping that she'd make her self-imposed deadline of talking to Elliot before nine o'clock. It was 7:30 as she walked through the front door of her parents' house. She'd called Jack earlier to tell him not to expect her for dinner; not a problem, he'd said—he had plenty to keep him busy.

The first thing Shayna did was sit her daughter down at the kitchen table and put a plate of food in front her—stir-fried chicken and vegetables on brown rice.

Shayna watched her daughter eat, just like she had when the girl was twelve. Pearl looked up to see her mother sitting there with a smile on her face.

"Trust me," her mother said, "someday you'll know how enjoyable it is to watch your child eat."

"I trust you, Mom. That's why I'm here." Pearl finished

up, wiped her lips, and stood. "Let's go into the living room and relax. Where's Dad?"

"Monthly faculty dinner meeting. Now that he's the assistant dean, he has to go to these things all the time."

"Meetings," Pearl groaned. "I'm always in meetings."

They made themselves comfortable, and sipped the hot tea Shayna had prepared.

"Talk to me Pearl. You sounded stressed on the phone."

And Pearl talked, occasionally looking at her watch.

She told her mother Elliot Pressman's story, which was getting easier each time she told it. Then she gave her a capsule report summarizing the visit with Rabbi Feldenstein and his wife, Rebecca. Shayna was pleased to hear that the rabbi had treated her daughter with such respect and that the rebbetzin sent her regards.

Pearl followed this with a short version of her meeting with Jimmy Rohrbach. Shayna smiled as she listened to her daughter do an impression of the well-known defense attorney.

"Tell the son he did his father the greatest mitzvah anyone could ever imagine! Listen, the old man's quality of life was bubkis. And now he's up in heaven playing golf with his buddies and having sex with his wife again—best sex he ever had. Better than when they were alive. Heavenly!"

Shayna laughed.

"So what do *you* think, Mom. I've heard from a rabbinical sage, a renowned defense attorney, and now, ta-da, here's the famous shrink herself."

Pearl smiled at her mother, and Shayna responded.

"No good will come from making the son's burden greater. He's already carrying a lot of guilt, and that will not go away quickly or easily. He *feels* responsible for his father's death, and that feeling is very strong right now. It may last for a long time.

"He needs therapy—says the therapist—and I'll be happy to give you a few names of people near where he lives. He may also need to be medicated.

"The other thing is, he's going to need the support of his wife. Do you think she'll be supportive?"

"From what I observed, yes."

"That's good. He seems to trust you, and you are, after all, 'The Rabbi.' You need to help him escape this downward spiral; it's dangerous. I'm with the lawyer. You really do need to move this away from the legal arena to a more—let's call it 'spiritual'—playing field. And I'd say you should strongly urge him to begin therapy—I recommend you call it grief therapy—as soon as possible."

Pearl was nodding her head in agreement. It all made sense. She was formulating her plan as they spoke.

Her mother gave her a few more pieces of counseling wisdom. Rabbis and cantors did what was often referred to as pastoral work, but Pearl's training was basic, and a lot of what she did in her role as a counselor was intuitive and natural. She was fortunate to have grown up the daughter of a professional therapist.

Pearl decided to call Elliot from her mother's house. He answered on the first ring.

"Hello?"

"Elliot, this is Rabbi Ross-Levy."

"Oh, thank you for calling, Rabbi. Judy and I are sitting here in the room just watching TV. I told her I'd spoken to you about my dad and that you'd be calling."

"Elliot, would it be okay if I came over now and spoke to you and Judy? I have some important information to give you, and it'll be easier if I shared it with her at the same time.

She's your partner, and she loves you. We can't keep this a secret from her."

There was a short pause, and then he said, "I'm so glad you said that. Yes, absolutely. You don't mind coming over? We have a little sitting area with a couch."

He gave her the room number at the Marriott, and she told him she'd be there in a half hour or so.

Pearl kissed her mother goodbye, and headed off to downtown Oakland.

She let the valet parking guy take her car. She'd give the receipt to Duke. She was, after all, on the job.

Elliot was waiting for her with the door open and led her into a small sitting room separate from the bedroom. The nighttime view from the window on the twenty-third floor was beautiful. Pearl sat in a comfortable chair while Elliot and Judy sat on the small sofa facing her. They were holding hands.

"Judy, I'm going to give you some background first, and you'll understand why I'm here. I want you to know that Elliot has been under more stress about his father's death than is apparent. Much more."

Judy looked at Elliot, and he nodded. She held his hand tighter and turned to Pearl.

"Okay. Tell me."

And Pearl did. She slowly and carefully summed up the situation, starting with Elliot's visit to her at the temple earlier in the day, and her subsequent appointments with a well-known rabbinical scholar, an esteemed legal expert, and a respected therapist. She did not name names. Judy sat and listened, nodding occasionally, sometimes looking at her husband, but never letting go of his hand. Elliot himself had tears running down his cheeks, which he occasionally wiped away with a handkerchief.

Now it was time for Pearl to be *SuperRabbi*. To wave her magic wand. To put it all together.

"Elliot, listen to me carefully. I agree with the three experts. You are *not* responsible for your father's death. He was waiting to die. In fact, he couldn't wait. You freed him from his prison. You rescued him from the captivity of his dementia. You said the magic words that released him from a terrible and evil spell. Somehow, you realized what those magic words were, and once you spoke them, your father's shackles were broken and fell to the ground.

"You did an incredible mitzvah, Elliot. No one could have done it but you. No one. If your father could speak to you now, he would thank you with all his heart and soul. You honored your father, as the Fifth Commandment tells us, in one of the most awesome and remarkable ways that could ever be imagined."

At this point, Elliot and Judy began to cry, almost uncontrollably. They held on to one another. She showered him with kisses. Pearl watched as the couple embraced and displayed their deep love for one another. After several minutes, they dried their eyes, breathed deeply, and sat again, facing the Rabbi, who had wiped tears from her own eyes.

"Elliot," Pearl said. "You must now continue with your grieving. Judy, you can participate in any way you wish." Judy nodded.

Pearl reached into her bag and handed Elliot a folded piece of paper. "This is a list of several highly recommended therapists who live near your home. Call one tomorrow and begin the grief therapy process as soon as possible." Both of them nodded.

"And, most important. Listen to me carefully. Other than with the therapist, you must not speak with anyone, including your sister or other family members, about what transpired with your father and what you said to him and how you initially felt you were responsible for his death. They will not understand and don't need to know. Each will go through the grieving process in his or her own way.

"You have confided in me, we have received expert opinions and advice, and that's where it ends. It ends with the wonderful mitzvah you performed for your very ill father. Do you understand?"

They both said, "Yes."

"Do you both agree with what I'm telling you?"

Elliot spoke first, "Oh, yes, Rabbi. You've lifted a weight from my heart that I never thought would disappear. I never could have done that without you. Thank you."

"Yes, thank you, Rabbi. My husband has been suffering so much in the past few days, and now I know why. But what you've said, oh, my God, it's *you* who have given him his life back. You are so wonderful."

Pearl reached out and hugged them both.

"I want to tell you something else," said Pearl. "It's personal, and I hope you don't mind."

They waited for her to speak.

"My husband and I have only been married a short time, but I hope and pray that when we reach your stage in life, that our relationship and our love is as strong as yours. You have a very special bond. I saw it when I first met the two of you, and I've seen it again just now. Thank you."

She stood, and they stood with her. They all embraced again, and she left them in the room, holding hands, standing very close to one another. They were looking at each other. Smiling through their tears.

Several weeks later, Pearl was sitting at her office desk when Esther knocked and entered. She was carrying a desktop arrangement of cacti and succulents in a clear glass planter.

"This just came for you, Rabbi. It's from Mr. and Mrs. Pressman. There's a card marked 'Personal.'"

They both admired the arrangement. The center cacti sported a large red flower on top, and the plants were surrounded by small, polished stones.

Pearl gazed at her gift, recalling those frantic hours as she'd driven back and forth between Oakland and Berkeley, the change of clothes, the intense conversations, the questions, the answers, the good rabbinic advice, the tears, and the magic. She'd written a thank-you letter to Rabbi and Mrs. Feldenstein as well as to Jimmy Rohrbach, the attorney she hoped she'd never need to defend her. She'd even written a note to her mother.

As Esther cleared a place on the credenza near the window for the bowl, Pearl opened the envelope and read the enclosed letter to herself.

Dear Rabbi Ross-Levy,

I will never be able to thank you enough for what you've done for my husband. You probably saved his life. And if not his life, then certainly his sanity.

Elliot has begun grief-therapy sessions with one of the people you recommended; she is a lovely, professional person. I've joined him for some of the meetings, and I can only say that as good as I felt our marriage was before, it's getting even stronger.

In my opinion, you are more than a rabbi, more than a spiritual leader, and more than a compassionate person. You are, in a word, a magician.

You have my—our—lifelong appreciation and sincere thanks. God bless you, Rabbi.

With warmth and heartfelt affection,
Judy Pressman

Pearl folded the letter and just sat for a moment, her eyes closed.

Esther asked softly, "Rabbi, besides the funeral, what did you do for these people?"

Pearl opened her eyes and looked up at her.

"I did my job, Esther. I just did my job."

Jack Catches the Torah

It was Thanksgiving Day, and Pearl and Jack were hosting the holiday dinner for the first time as a married couple. Pearl's parents were there, as were Ruth and Samantha. Jack's parents, Mort and Shayna Levy, were present as well—they had flown in the week before and spent a few days in Napa and Sonoma. Eight for Thanksgiving dinner seemed just right.

The five women crowded into Pearl's kitchen while the three men sat watching football on TV in the living room; it was, Shayna Ross observed, a typical sorting of the genders. Samantha, it turned out, had superior food skills as a result of six months spent at a culinary academy, something no one, including Ruth, knew about. Samantha wound up carving the bird—that year and every year ever after.

At one point, Jack's father called, "Shayna!" from the living room, and both mothers-in-law had simultaneously answered, "What?" The women were still laughing about it.

The dinner conversation was lively, especially as the meal continued and more fine California wine—the result of the Levy's trip to Napa—was drunk.

Over dessert, Shayna Levy, whom more and more Pearl thought of as "bubbly blonde," looked at her daughter-in-law and asked, "Did Jack ever tell you about the time he caught the Torah?"

Pearl looked at Jack as she responded. "No. For some reason he's never told me about the time he caught the Torah. Maybe he'd like to share that with us."

Jack closed his eyes for a long moment, then opened them and said, "Mom, why don't *you* tell the story? You do it so much better than I ever could."

Without missing a beat, his mother began her narrative.

"So, Jack is at Shabbos services one Saturday a few weeks after his own bar mitzvah—he did a simply marvelous job, by the way. Everybody said so. But this was the bar mitzvah of one of his good friends from Hebrew school. Jack was sitting with some boys on the other side of the temple from where Mort and I were.

"Anyway, the bar mitzvah boy—I remember he was quite small and, apparently, not very strong—was supposed to carry this big Torah around the sanctuary. Everyone could tell he was struggling with it.

"And … as he walked up the aisle, he tripped and started to fall!"

Shayna paused for dramatic effect. She looked around and seemed satisfied that everyone was paying attention.

"Oh, my God! The whole congregation held its breath! The worst thing in the world is to have the Torah fall on the ground!"

In spite of the fact that she didn't get the overwhelming agreement she'd hoped for, she went on.

"Anyway, there was Jack, standing at the end of the aisle right where this boy was falling, and somehow Jack *leaped* forward and caught the Torah just as the bar mitzvah boy was going down!

"You can imagine the pandemonium! The rabbi, who was

walking behind the boy, came over, and Jack, who was lying on his back, handed the Torah to the rabbi. At that point, everyone started to applaud! The music never stopped, and the rabbi carried the Torah the rest of the way around the sanctuary.

"Even while they were still marching around with the Torah, people wanted to congratulate Jack on performing this heroic mitzvah. But he'd obviously hurt himself—he actually limped out of the sanctuary. I was so worried. We didn't see him again until the kiddush lunch.

"Everyone came over during lunch to shake his hand. We were so proud of him."

She smiled, proudly, as she finished her story. And as always happened when she told it, everyone at the table clapped and raised their glasses in a toast.

Pearl leaned over to kiss Jack and whispered, "Did that really happen?"

He whispered back, "Sort of. I'll tell you later."

The rest of the evening went well, and at the end everyone was hugging and kissing and telling Pearl and Jack how much they had enjoyed it.

Later, when they were in bed holding hands, she looked over at him and said, "Okay, tell me."

He was shaking his head. "You know, with all the honors and trophies I ever won—by myself or as part of a team—scholarships, awards, degrees, whatever … *that's* what she's most proud of. *That's* the story she always tells."

She could sense a note of sadness, almost bitterness, in his voice. She waited for him to continue. Jack sighed.

"One of the kids in my Hebrew school class was, well, he was like the proverbial ninety-eight-pound weakling—a nice kid, but not a friend of mine, really."

"Do you remember his name?"

"Yes. Vladimir. Never Vlad. He always called himself Vladimir. His parents were Soviet Jews, and they somehow wound up in Florida. Their last name was something Russian and difficult to pronounce, like Raskolnikov."

She was surprised, and it showed in her voice. "How do you know about Raskolnikov?"

He turned toward her. "Hey! You think you're the only person in this family with culture?" He pronounced it "cultcha."

She realized too late that she'd inadvertently insulted him. "Sorry."

"You're not the only one in this bed who went to college!"

"Sorry."

"I'm gonna call a foul on you!"

"I *said* I'm sorry!"

He grabbed her ass under the covers.

"*Stop!* Don't distract me. I want to hear the story!"

"All right. Anyway, it's true, I was standing at the end of the aisle. Vladimir was carrying the Torah—the same Torah I'd carried a few weeks before. Of course, I had about thirty or forty pounds on him.

"We were all standing waiting for him to pass by so we could touch our tallit fringes to the Torah. I could see he was having a hard time holding it—it was the biggest one they had."

"He wasn't an athlete?"

Jack laughed. "No."

"Soccer? Tennis? He didn't play *anything?*"

"Pearl. He played chess."

"I see," she said.

"So, as he was getting closer to me, a person on one side of the aisle reached over to touch the Torah while at the same time a lady on the other side stepped forward, accidentally tripping Vladimir. I swear, everything seemed to go into slow motion. I can see it now." Jack paused for a second.

"As he was going down, our eyes met. He was letting go of the Torah to break his fall and I just dove for it. I managed to grab it just before it hit the floor. I wasn't really thinking about it; I just did it automatically.

"As I went down, I twisted, so the Torah was on top of me. I was on my back, holding it above me like you do when you dive for a fly ball and want to show the ump you caught it before it hit the ground."

She realized she was holding her breath. "Incredible!"

"Yeah. But my mother doesn't know the rest of the story. There I am on my back, holding the Torah up, and the damned rabbi rushes over to grab it and while he's leaning over me he manages to kick me in the nuts!"

She laughed.

"Sure, laughs the person who doesn't have nuts. It may sound funny now, but it wasn't then. You can't know what it's like to be the temple hero who caught the Torah, but you can't even stand up."

She tried to stop laughing. "I'm sorry. So what happened then?"

"Well, the show went on. They kept on marching around the temple, but now the rabbi was carrying the Torah and Vladimir was following behind."

"What about you?"

"Me, I struggled to get up and then limped out of the sanctuary. I went into the temple kitchen and got some ice, and then sat in the men's room for forty-five minutes icing my testicles.

"The only good thing about all this was that I didn't have to sit through the rest of the service."

"Typical."

"By the time the kiddush lunch started, I was okay. It was embarrassing, though. Everyone came over to congratulate me and shake my hand, including the rabbi. I felt bad for Vladimir."

Pearl sighed. "I can understand."

"It gets worse."

"Worse? How can it get worse?"

"There was a video. They filmed the whole thing."

"No way!"

"Yeah. If ESPN knew about it, they'd have shown it on *The Play of the Day.*"

Pearl groaned. "Once a jock, always a jock."

"You know, I often wonder what happened to that video."

She did not indulge him with a comment.

"Vladimir thanked me at the time, but I don't think he ever spoke to me again. I hate to say it, but that's what people will forever remember about his bar mitzvah. My mother isn't the only one who still talks about it."

Pearl was quiet for a while, then whispered, "As the Talmud says, no good deed goes unpunished."

"Does the Talmud really say that?" he asked.

"It may as well."

Mildred Babson

"Good morning, Esther," Pearl said into the phone in response to the intercom buzz.

"Hi, Rabbi. Your ten o'clock appointment is here. Her name is Mildred Babson and she just joined the congregation. I've given her a tour of the temple, and she'd like to meet you and chat for a few minutes."

"Sure, I'll be out in a minute."

Pearl walked out to the reception area, and was quite surprised to see that her visitor was none other than Millie, the woman she'd observed having sex with Bert Standish at Grand Lake Towers.

"Good morning, Ms. Babson." Pearl said, putting her best foot forward, holding out her hand, and holding her breath at the same time. Millie stood as they shook hands.

"Yes, Rabbi. We meet again. But this time I promise to keep my clothes on."

There's something about this woman that I like, Pearl thought as she led the tall, thin red-head to her office.

After they were seated, they just looked at each other for a moment.

"I know you're wondering what the hell I'm doing here."

"Well, I know you just joined the congregation. Welcome!"

"Thank you. And please call me Millie."

Pearl said, "And it isn't as if I haven't thought about you once in a while since our … encounter. These days when I visit Bert, I do my best to avoid bumping into his …"

"His girlfriends. Yes. I know I wasn't very nice to you, Rabbi. Bert's son, the lawyer, threatened to take away my conjugal visits. He can be such a *shmendrick*. You think it's easy for a woman my age to find someone in that facility who still knows how to have a little fun?

"Anyway, this is not about my sex life, as it were. I'm having a personal problem, and when I thought about it, I decided I needed a rabbi. I was wondering if there were any female rabbis around here, and I remembered you. Maybe it wasn't a coincidence you showed up when you did."

Pearl smiled. "As my husband likes to tease me, 'Hashem works in strange ways.'"

"Yeah. That Hashem, what a card.

"Look, Rabbi, I've just been diagnosed with lung cancer. I quit smoking forty years ago, but I'm seventy-five now, so I still puffed away for almost twenty years. You know, it was the thing to do when you considered yourself a modern woman. Smoking, drinking, never thinking. I was so sophisticated, and now it's come back to bite me in the butt. Well … the lung."

Pearl was smiling her saddest smile. "I'm so sorry to hear about your illness."

"I'm going in for surgery in a couple weeks to remove a tumor—well, part of my lung, really. My doctor says it looks like it's just Stage I. I'm supposed to feel good about that."

"I understand. What can I do for you?"

Millie opened the same train case that she'd been carrying when she visited Bert. Pearl wondered briefly if it was filled with lubricants and condoms. But what Millie pulled out of the little box was a white handkerchief, bordered with purple flowers. She dabbed at her eyes. Pearl wanted to move closer to her, but her instincts told her not to.

"I'd like you … I'd really like you to visit me in the hospital. Maybe put in a good word for me, you know?"

Pearl was taken by surprise. "Of course. Yes."

"I just joined your temple. I wrote a check to the woman in the office." She looked up at Pearl. "I guess I'm paying for you to visit me in the hospital."

Pearl sat back. How should she handle this? It was a tough one. But she was talking to a tough woman.

"Millie, let me tell you something. I've been paid to marry people. I've been paid to bury people. I've even been paid a couple of times to sing—and I'm not a great singer. But I would never, ever, take money to visit someone in the hospital. That's ridiculous, and you need to know that."

Millie composed herself. "I'm sorry. I keep insulting you."

"I've been insulted before. You should only know." Pearl thought of her visit to Folsom Prison. "I can handle it."

Now it was Millie's turn to smile. "I like you. You're good.

You're the kind of person I wish I had working for me when I had my company."

"Tell me about your company."

"Did you ever hear of Smart Girls Curls?"

Pearl lit up and touched her hair. "Of course! These curls are natural. My mother used to buy the shampoo for me."

"That was my company. I founded it, I ran it, and I made a ton of money from it, and then I sold it for another ton of money to some conglomerate that ignored it and parceled it off to some other multinational that also ignored it. And now it's gone. Rest in Peace."

"Now that you mention it, I haven't seen …"

"This is what happens when you give up control. Never give up control for money. Never."

They sat quietly for a minute.

Pearl said, "Besides visiting you in the hospital, is there anything else the temple can do for you?"

"I don't know. Do you have any good-looking men my age who can still do the deed? And I'm talking about someone who might remember me five minutes later."

"That's a hard one."

"Yeah, I know that joke, too."

"Well, I'll put your name on the Mi Shebeirach list for starters, and you'll begin getting the Temple Bulletin so you can see what's going on here. We're a fairly large congregation with lots of activities. What do you like to do, besides, well …"

Millie laughed. "You're okay, Rabbi. Your mother must be very proud of you."

"She's a shrink."

"Even so. What do I like to do? I read. I go to plays. I sing—I'm an alto—must have been all those cigarettes. I used to play Mah Jongg."

"Bingo."

"I don't like Bingo."

"No, Mah Jongg. We have a regular game, a couple of tables. I play sometimes."

"You're kidding."

"No, really. I learned when I was in rabbinical school. Also we have a couple of book clubs, a choir, a Purim Spiel, and many other activities. I think you'll like it here."

"If I live long enough."

"Let's assume you will." Pearl paused as she looked at Millie. "Please let Esther know when you're scheduled for surgery. You won't be alone. I'll make sure."

"Thank you. I do appreciate it."

"I didn't ask if you have any family."

"Don't ask."

"Fine. We're your family now, Millie. We have almost a thousand family units in this congregation, and that's a lot of people. And a lot of, let's say, personalities. You have no idea."

"I'll take your word for it. Regardless, I'm used to being by myself, even though I'm not always the easiest person for myself to get along with, if you know what I mean."

Pearl smiled as she stood. The meeting was over. Millie gathered up her train case, shook Pearl's hand, and did not look back as she went through the door.

That's one tough lady, Pearl thought.

The Blackhawk Doctors Jam

One day while doing his rounds at the hospital, Dr. Stuart Chin bumped into one of his colleagues, Rod Kleinman, in the physicians' break room. Besides working in the same medical center, Kleinman was also a member of Lakeshore Temple. Stuart and his wife, Dana, occasionally socialized with Rod and his wife, Leah. They'd attended the Kleinman's son's bar mitzvah—he was a few years older than Zinnia.

"Hey, Stuart, what are you doing this Sunday?"

"Honestly, nothing that I can think of. What's up?"

"Well, there's a jam session that's been going on for many years. You and Dana should come. I think you'd like it. It's mostly docs and some other professionals who are amateur jazz musicians—some of them are really good. I'm one of the drummers. Why don't you join us? Starts at two. It's at Fred Carter's house in Blackhawk. You can't miss it—he's got the place covered with Christmas lights and reindeer and stuff."

Stuart thought for a second. "You know, this sounds great. But I think Dana's on call Sunday. Would it be okay if I brought my daughter? She loves jazz."

"Absolutely! Wait. Zinnia plays the flute, doesn't she? Tell her to bring it along if she wants. What is she now, eleven?"

"Twelve. Her bat mitzvah's coming up next July. You guys are invited, of course."

"Sounds great! How's she doing with the bat mitzvah prep?"

"Well, frankly, that's Dana's department. I'm the Chinese goy in the family. But Zinnia's doing well, as far as I can tell. She's studying with Rabbi Ross-Levy, and seems to love her. So, I guess things are going okay."

"Yeah. You know Beth's on the temple board? And she likes Pearl a lot, too. She gets along really well with Craig and the cantor. The temple's lucky we got her.

"Anyway ... let's see ... oh yeah, the jam session is a pot luck, so bring something to share. Girl Scout cookies, whatever. Anything will be fine."

When Stuart told Zinnia about the jam, she sounded excited. Well, as excited as Zinnia got about anything.

"Dr. Kleinman said you should bring your flute."

"You think? These guys are probably really good players."

"Well, Z, the flute doesn't take up much room, so why not?"

"Okay."

Fred Carter's home in Blackhawk was gigantic and, as described by Rod Kleinman, surrounded by lights, Santas, reindeer, and elves.

Inside, white carpets covered the first floor, and a beautiful white grand piano stood front and center in the living room. Someone had set up a professional sound system, and there were seven or eight musicians playing when Zinnia Chin and her father arrived. Two dozen folding chairs had been set up alongside the sofas and lounge chairs. A fire was roaring in the gas fireplace, above which were five red and white stockings.

All we need is snow, Stuart said to himself.

People would come and go, eat some of the buffet offerings from the dining room table, and then return to listen, drink in hand. The Chins, father and daughter, filled their plates with appetizers, got something to drink, and settled into their chairs.

Zinnia was thoroughly enjoying the music. She watched closely, observing how the musicians interacted, traded fours, and decided on the fly who would take the next solo. Her flute sat in its case next to her chair.

About twenty minutes into the session, Zinnia leaned over and whispered to her father. "Dad, I know this song pretty well."

"You do?" Even he recognized *Autumn Leaves*, although he wondered how Zinnia might know it.

"I don't think they'd mind if you played."

"You sure?"

"Let me check." He walked over to Rod Kleinman, who was standing to one side while another drummer was playing.

"Rod, do you think it would be okay if Zinnia played? She says she knows this song."

Rod whispered something to the trumpet player who nodded his head, then smiled and gestured to Zinnia to join them.

It took just a few seconds to put her flute together and breathe into the head joint to warm it up. She stepped to the periphery of the group and waited as several of the musicians, all middle-aged men, took their solos.

Eventually, the trumpet player motioned to her that she was up next. He told her to play into the microphone, which he adjusted for her.

When the top of the song came around, Zinnia began to play. It was the same as she'd been doing at home for a year, jamming with the Jamie Aebersold play-along track on her CD player. It was the same, but different. It was better. Because today it was live. *She* felt alive.

Because Zinnia's eyes were closed, she did not see the other band members smiling and nodding to one another. When she came to the end of the chorus, she opened her eyes and saw the trumpet player waving his finger in a circle, the sign to "keep going."

So she kept going. She listened to the piano, bass, and drums playing behind her, comping her riffs, pushing the song forward. She'd started off playing some half notes and quarter notes tied to other phrases, fooling around with the melody, adding some little figures and trills here and there, echoing some notes from the altered chords being played by the pianist.

Zinnia let her ears and fingers take her to another level as her solo progressed. Occasionally she'd execute a scale that seemed to work, maybe something from one of the Coltrane CDs she listened to all the time. Or she'd throw in a scale fragment from the book the guy at Forrest's Music in Berkeley had recommended to her, Sigurd Rascher's *158 Saxophone Exercises.*

Zinnia played, and mostly it worked. She was aware that she was playing note combinations and phrases she'd never played before. Some of the things she played sounded, well, "wrong." But not *that* wrong. She knew that both Thelonius and Miles had said "there are no wrong notes."

So she just kept playing—more and more sixteenth-note phrases, with notes cascading up, down, in and out.

Her eyes were closed so she didn't see the musicians grinning and shaking their heads in disbelief. *Who the hell* is *this kid?*

Stuart Chin knew something special was happening, but he wasn't sure what. He was, however, a trained and careful observer, and he was trying to record memories of these moments to share with his wife.

Eventually, at the end of four choruses, Zinnia had said what she wanted to say, and lowered her flute. Behind her, the other musicians picked up the head of the song and she joined in.

Then *Autumn Leaves* was over. The applause was instantaneous as one by one each musician turned in Zinnia's direction and began to clap. Other guests joined in, including many who'd come into the room to listen when the word about the girl playing the flute spread through the house.

She was puzzled by the attention, and even felt a little embarrassed. But she smiled. This was *so* cool. And a lot different than playing in the middle school band. A minute later, the next song started.

When she began to go back to her seat, the trumpet player whispered, "Honey, don't you go anywhere. You stay right here with us."

Zinnia realized much later *that* was the moment she became an official member of the Blackhawk Doctors Jam.

Millie's Soliloquy

Mildred Babson sat in her darkened apartment. She was alone, eating dinner by candle light, listening to a recording of the Bach *Cello Suite No. 1*, and thinking about a cigarette. After forty years, she still had a craving.

"Addictions," she muttered aloud to no one. She thought about her own addiction to cigarettes—nicotine, actually—and the addictions that had affected the most important people in her life, killing a few of those most dear to her. *And now me. Maybe.*

She took a sip of her Pinot Grigio and gazed out the window of her twentieth-story apartment in Grand Lake Towers, the upscale, high-rise retirement facility in which she lived.

The night sky was gorgeous, she thought, as she viewed Lake Merritt below, its "necklace of lights" surrounding what many called the Jewel of the City. It was a mild December night, and people were still strolling around the lake—singles, couples, parents pushing baby strollers, more than a few joggers, and some homeless people. Or street people—she wasn't sure what they were called these days, but they'd been a fixture everywhere she'd ever lived. *Some things never change.*

The hills, the night sky, the lake—it was all beautiful. *Forget the addictions for now,* she told herself.

Instead, she thought about her visit that morning with Rabbi Pearl Ross-Levy. A beautiful tall girl, with dark curly hair, whose mother had bought Smart Girls Curls shampoo for her. The rabbi was probably around thirty. About the age her own granddaughter would be. If she had a granddaughter. Which she didn't. Because her son, Emile, had committed suicide at age twenty, and her daughter … Well, her daughter, Fay, was a question mark. Maybe there was a granddaughter someplace, or a grandson, but Millie didn't know.

And what difference did it make at this point. Her daughter wanted nothing to do with her and had generally succeeded in eluding the private detectives Millie had periodically sent out to find her. Oh, they'd eventually find her, and Millie would try to open a line of communication through any number of means—personal letters, attorneys, counselors. Nothing worked, and her daughter would soon disappear again. What was the point in trying?

Someday, another private detective would locate her daughter and inform her that Millie had died and Fay had inherited a large sum of money. *What would Fay do?* she thought. *Take the money?* She'd never wanted Millie's money. Who knew what she'd do? Because of these unknowns, Millie's will and trust contained contingencies that spelled out a variety of situations.

And once Millie was dead, perhaps her daughter would … Maybe she'd regret … Maybe she'd reconsider … *Maybe.*

Another sip of wine. Another bite of steak. The steak was good, but no longer warm; she was eating too slowly. *So what?* she asked herself.

Millie recalled all her planning and efforts to find the right place to live once she'd sold her home in Marin and her apartment in New York City. The Marin house was too big. And she just didn't need the New York apartment anymore. She was too old to keep traveling from coast to coast, and the glorious New York she'd enjoyed twenty, thirty, even fifty years ago, was gone.

She loved the Bay Area, and Oakland tended to be a little warmer than San Francisco most of the time. It was also a widely diverse community with a great selection of ethnic restaurants. So that's where she chose to live. She could get to San Francisco quickly and easily enough if she wanted to, although she didn't go now as much as she had in the past. These days it was just the opera, a few museums, not much more.

When she wanted to hear classical music, she attended the Oakland Symphony performances; that was easy since there was a little shuttle bus that went from her facility right to the Paramount Theater. She also liked going to the Woodminster Playhouse up in the Oakland Hills to see some of the old musical theater shows that were presented each summer. The series was called *Under the Stars*, but often it was under the fog. She bundled up for those shows just in case.

Walking around Lake Merritt on a beautiful day and looking at the many varieties of ducks, pelicans, geese, and other wildlife, as well as the wide variety of people—that was a three-mile walk she truly enjoyed. And the lake was just a block away from her building.

More and more, she went to restaurants and events alone. She'd call a limo service that ran a tab for her. Money had stopped being an issue years before.

For breakfast and lunch, she ate in the dining room downstairs, which was just fine. But for dinner she preferred to go out. Or she'd eat in her own large apartment. She generally ate dinner at home three times a week, and when she did it was prepared by a personal chef, Suzanne, who knew just what Millie liked and didn't like to eat.

The young chef had been recommended by BrendaLee Marcus, a friend in the restaurant business and someone whom Millie had helped years before when BrendaLee was just getting started in the food service industry, a notoriously dangerous business. After a few years, BrendaLee had become quite successful, and eventually joined the expanding network of high-powered businesswomen that Millie had established in the early 1980s.

Suzanne was a wonderful chef, and Millie put her on a monthly retainer. If Suzanne couldn't deliver a meal personally, she'd arrange for a colleague to do it. Millie never complained, although she did occasionally make minor requests or suggestions. She did not want to rock the boat and always tried to support a young woman making her way in the business world.

So, once again, here she was, eating alone—a tender beef fillet, fresh green beans with slivered almonds, and an incredibly delicious yam, as she sipped a very nice white wine. Thinking.

How could a person as smart as I am, as strong, as successful, and rich as I am, have screwed up as badly as I have?

Wait. Don't be so rough on yourself, Millie, she told herself— as she'd told herself a thousand times before. She sighed and wondered if maybe she'd just lived too long. *Maybe.*

The irony was, she knew, that she was no worse off— make that, she was much better off—than virtually any other old, single woman she could think of. And at least she'd had it all. Seen it all. Done it all.

She'd met presidents and first ladies, kings and queens,

actors, producers, financiers, movers and shakers, musicians and composers, the good, the bad, the ugly. Many were now dead or half dead. Including herself. Life was fleeting.

Millie ate what was now a room-temperature green bean. It was excellent.

She could buy, go, wear, eat, visit, or pretty much do anything she wanted.

She thought about her first husband, Gregory, with whom she'd had her two children. He was a nice-looking, well-built, sexy man she'd met when she was just out of college. A successful stockbroker who loved to talk, laugh, and drink. Over the years, the drinking began to exceed the talking and laughing, and after the kids graduated from high school, she told him she'd had enough.

He remarried a few months after the divorce was final, and had probably had the other woman on the side for a long time. She didn't really care. She'd realized she'd never truly loved him. Let some other dame take care of him. And the other dame did just that for ten years as Gregory continued to deteriorate. He eventually croaked from the effects of alcohol and who knows what else.

One thing she managed to gain from the marriage was a working knowledge of the stock market. She also got half of the stock portfolio and other assets, which helped her land on her feet after the divorce. She only wanted half, and that's what she got.

Then there'd been Martin, whom she'd met a few years later, around the time she'd started her own business. He was an architect and a partner in a San Francisco firm. They'd really hit it off, and anyone could tell they were in love. She'd never had so much sex in her life—before or since. Incredible. He was the love of her life. In addition to her business, which was beginning to take off.

Who could have known she'd strike gold in the cosmetics business with her Smart Girls brand? First came shampoo, then conditioner. These were followed by nail polish, foundations, moisturizers, eye liner, and mascara. Things were really coming together.

But Martin and she were not coming together as often, because she was not around. She was in New York, or Paris, or Geneva, or Milan, or Melbourne.

They had "the talk," and she chose her company. It was not the money, she tried to explain. He said he understood. They had one last incredible and tearful goodbye love-making session, and he married the next woman who came through his life. His new wife knew about Millie, and was cordial to her the couple of times they'd met. But the visits ended decades ago, and that was fine with all concerned.

Every year on his birthday, she would write Martin a letter, bringing him up to date on her life. Closing each letter, she would tell him that she loved him, and was happy that he was happy.

And each year, around her birthday, he would write to her. In each letter, he too expressed his love. It was that kind of love. An old, warm love.

Over the years, the letters became emails.

In Martin's most recent message, he'd said something she was still smiling about:

"Dear Millie, after all these years, I hope you still have a place for me in your heart. Or wherever it is you keep the memory of me."

How right he was. An old, warm love.

A sip of wine. A forkful of yam. Delicious.

And today she'd written a check to the temple so she'd be sure that the tall, pretty rabbi with the lovely black, curly hair would visit her in the hospital after she had surgery in a few weeks to remove part of her lung. The same girl who'd observed her having a quick orgasm with old Bert Standish. As long as she had a heartbeat, a partner, and could do the deed, she would.

Millie thought about the few times, after she'd turned seventy, when she'd paid men to have sex with her. She could do that again, she supposed, but preferred not to. The young men always overdid it, trying to make it look like they were really enjoying screwing an old woman. Probably much like a female hooker acted while having sex with an old man. Lots of theatrics, moans, and groans.

Of course the old men with their young female hookers probably believed it was all real.

Millie, however, knew it wasn't, and no longer hired male escorts (oh, just call them whores).

Bert—or some other old guy—would do. Or she'd just go without. Maybe after the lung surgery she'd be dead and wouldn't need to think about it anymore. Or maybe everyone in heaven had great sex all the time. She smiled. *Maybe.*

A sip of wine. A bite of pie. What was this pie? Some kind of berry. Elderberry? Boysenberry? Huckleberry?

Millie wasn't sure why she'd decided to join a temple now. She'd never denied her Jewishness; she just hadn't paid much attention to it. She knew a lot of people who felt the way she did. But now she was being drawn to her faith by some intuitive feeling. And she knew enough to trust her intuition; it rarely failed her.

Occasionally, a new product idea would pop into her head, just like in the old days. But these days it was enough to just think about it—not execute it. She was now seventy-five. She had many millions in banks and investment accounts and didn't need to pitch or execute any more product ideas.

Sad, isn't it? she thought.

Millie looked again at the necklace of lights around the lake, and the many traffic lights on dozens of street corners jumping from red to green, just like the Christmas tree lights she saw on distant houses.

Another bite of pie. Not bad.

She thought about how at one point she'd realized she had more money than she needed. Not as much as God, but perhaps as much as God's ex-wife.

Many years before, when she was still married, Gregory had mentioned a company that was buying other companies; he said it was run by a really smart financial innovator. He'd bought some shares of the company, Berkshire Hathaway, for his own account. The shares continued to increase in value, and Millie took half of the shares in the divorce settlement. After she'd located a competent female stockbroker, she acquired more shares. And more.

Each year, she carefully read the Berkshire Hathaway annual report and often attended the yearly stockholders meetings. Those meetings allowed her to meet other women who were successful in business, and her network expanded.

That network, which started with just a few women, grew through the years to include many hundreds. Whenever she encountered a woman who was starting out on her own, or who was in a profession where women were in a minority (the "oldest profession" was the exception), she'd exchange contact information and let them know of others whom they might like to meet.

Over the years, the Network expanded to women pretty much everywhere, and included members of Congress, doctors, lawyers, accountants, and women in the entertainment industry. She was shocked when she realized that people referred to it as "Millie's Network."

Mentoring young women became a passion for her. Often she'd get a frantic *"Millie, I'm desperate! What should I do?"* call, and if she didn't know what the woman should do, she knew another woman who did.

She continued to acquire more shares of Berkshire Hathaway, and now she had those shares of stock, plus shares of other companies, mutual funds, bonds and bond funds, and cash. She'd made a fortune when she sold her thriving business to a large conglomerate. She wasn't sure she wanted to sell, so she asked for a stratospheric—no—an astronomical—price. And they'd given it to her. Those were the go-go years. She took the money and ran.

And then she'd sold her home and her apartment—each of which was worth millions. She was a very wealthy woman.

I wonder if my lung tumor knows that, she thought, as she finished her pie, sipped her wine, and watched the candles on her table flicker.

Millie thought again about the rabbi and the temple.

Esther, the young woman who'd helped her with the membership application, had taken her on a little tour and shown her the sanctuary, which was just grand—over a hundred years old. Some elements had been upgraded, she saw, and others hadn't.

Later, the rabbi had told her that the congregation was now her family, and she seemed sincere when she said it.

Maybe, after her surgery, she thought, she could join a temple book group or go to a Friday night service or sing in the choir. Maybe she'd play Mah Jongg. *Maybe.*

Or she could help in some other way. Millie had more and more been dabbling in philanthropy, and these nonprofit organizations often struggled financially. Maybe she could be an angel. Did Jews believe in angels? She'd have to find out.

Millie closed her eyes for a moment. *I've had a good run,* she thought. She smiled. *I really shouldn't complain.*

She took another look at her glorious view. As long as she could smile, how bad could things really be?

The Bitter Dream

The Monday morning after her meeting with Millie, Pearl woke from a strange dream with a terribly bitter taste in her mouth. She couldn't remember the dream, but there was no denying the taste. She'd never experienced anything so bitter before in her entire life. *Angostura bitters times ten,* she thought.

She mentioned it to Jack, but he was preoccupied with a lecture he had to give that morning, and didn't have any brilliant suggestions regardless.

Monday was her day off, and she was joining her mother for their regular lunch date.

At noon, she and Shayna were sitting in a café on College Avenue, sharing a salad and a sandwich. Each had ordered a glass of white wine. Shayna's short auburn hair looked like she'd just had it done, and she was wearing a violet suit jacket over a black silk top. Even when Pearl was a teenager, she'd always considered her mother a smart dresser. No black pants suit and white blouse for her.

In response to her mother's question about what was new, she mentioned that she'd had a strange dream.

"Tell me about it. I never get a chance to analyze dreams these days. People are only concerned with feelings." She took a sip of her Chardonnay.

"There's not much to analyze, Mom. I can't remember any of the details of the dream, but I woke up with this terribly bitter taste in my mouth. It was very bitter."

Shayna looked at her daughter with a knowing smile.

Pearl, lifting her wine glass to take a sip, said, "What?"

Before the glass had touched her lips, her mother reached over, took the glass out of her hand and moved it to her own side of the table. As she did this, she said, "Mazel Tov!"

"Mazel Tov *what?* And how come you took my wine?"

"No more wine for you for a while, Pearl. You're pregnant."

Pearl just stared at her mother and waited.

Shayna said, "What would you say if I told you I had that same bitter dream when I was pregnant with you and Ruth?"

Pearl was surprised. She'd never heard about this before. "I wouldn't know *what* to say."

"And what if I told you that both my mother and my grandmother had that same bitter dream during each of *their* pregnancies?"

Pearl reached down for her wine glass, but it wasn't there. She took a sip of water instead.

Shayna said, "Think of it as a family tradition."

Pearl paused, then asked, "What can you tell me about the dream?"

"I can only tell you that the dream gets more complicated the more pregnant you get. It's filled with shadows and ancient men. I never could figure it out. But the bitter taste is a constant. I can't explain it, but I'll put money on your condition. In fact, lunch is on me. I'm going to be a grandmother!"

On her way home, Pearl stopped at the drugstore. Since she hadn't even missed a period yet, she decided to buy two home pregnancy kits. That night the test was negative, but she made an appointment to see her OB/Gyn, Liat Morgenstern, the following week.

A week later, she repeated the home pregnancy test, and it was positive. Her mother had been right. Dr. Morgenstern confirmed the test the next morning. She then put Pearl on prenatal vitamins, estimated her due date, gave her verbal and written information, and scheduled her next office visit. They also talked about how much weight she might gain. Pearl groaned.

At dinner, Pearl broke the news to Jack.

"Remember last week I told you about my bitter dream?"

"Yeah. Very weird. What was that all about?"

"Turns out it's my mother's home pregnancy test. She predicted I was pregnant, and guess what?"

"No way!" Jack said. He sat stunned for a moment at the news, but quickly recovered and came around the table, kneeled down next to her chair, and held her close.

Pearl's mother might not have known what the dream meant, but *she*, the rabbi, did. Or, at least, she had an idea.

"Drinking the bitter waters," she knew, was a test described in detail in both the Torah and Talmud. It was a test given to a *sotah*—a woman suspected of adultery. How it related to her own dream, she had no idea; but she wanted to know more.

Her first step when she got to the temple the next day was to look at the Torah portion *Naso*, which addresses priestly duties and blessings, the Nazirite, and the consecration of the tabernacle. It also speaks about the wife accused of unfaithfulness (the *sotah*).

Next, she went to the Talmudic tractate *Sotah*, which she

found in the temple library. She doubted the volume had ever been opened, even by Zinnia. She began to read the English translation, but realized it would take too long. She put a note with her name and the date on the shelf where the volume had been, and lugged it back to her office.

She'd get to it when she could. As she knew from personal experience, you can't rush when it comes to the Talmud.

'Twas the Night Before Surgery

Millie lay in her hospital bed, gazing out the dark window.

"Are you comfortable, Ms. Babson?" asked the nurse as she straightened the sheets and blanket.

This reminded Millie of an old joke, and she responded with the punch line. "I make a living."

The nurse, who was of some ethnicity Millie could not identify, just said, "Good, very good," grabbed some papers, and left the room.

Millie's surgery was set for early the following morning, and so far the doctors and staff at Alta Bates Hospital had been efficient, respectful, and pleasant. Her surgeon, Arjun Dhari, was a no-nonsense, self-assured man. He was not without a sense of humor, which gave Millie cause for hope. Research she'd done had revealed him to be a graduate of one of the top medical schools in the U.S., and he had plenty of experience.

Dr. Dhari had been strongly recommended by her new primary care physician, Jessica Rofrano, who was a member of the Network and thrilled that *the* Millie Babson was now her own patient. Dr. Rofrano, almost 50 years old, had training in both internal medicine and gerontology. She spent her vacations working for Doctors Without Borders. Her numerous awards were stored in a couple of boxes in her coat closet. Although only five-foot-two, she was strong, both physically and verbally. She smiled with her eyes.

Millie's first visit to Dr. Rofrano three months before had resulted in a barrage of tests that revealed the lung tumor. And here she was. In the hospital.

The food left something to be desired, but Millie, a "foodie," knew that her pre- and post-surgical diet would be limited for only a week. So what difference did it make? She'd survive the food. The surgery? That was another question.

Her main goal at this point was to avoid feeling depressed or sorry for herself. So she turned to her main defense against all that. She just became fatalistic. That felt better.

As Millie processed her emotions, the door opened and in walked Rabbi Ross-Levy, wearing a cream colored blouse, black pants and jacket, a black leather shoulder bag, a colorfully crocheted kippah, and a smile.

"Hi, Millie."

"Rabbi. Here you are, as promised. Thank you. I appreciate it."

"I just wanted to make sure you're ready for your big day."

"My big day? Who the hell writes these lines for you?"

"I make 'em up in my own head, believe it or not." Pearl pulled a chair up to the bed so she could be closer to this woman who could be her grandmother.

As she sat down, she looked at Millie, and said, "You know, if you want, you can just call me Pearl."

Millie laughed. "Let me explain something to you, sweetheart. I have lots of pearls. Lots and lots. Many kinds and colors, a wide variety of sizes and lengths. If I put them on all at once I'd fall down." Millie took a sip of the apple juice that was sitting on the hospital table near her bed.

"But I only have one rabbi, and you are she. So, you call me Millie, and I'll call you Rabbi. Okay?"

"Fine with me."

"Pearl is a somewhat old-fashioned name."

"I know. I was named for my grandmother who died too young."

"Unlike myself."

Pearl laughed in spite of herself. She looked around. "Anything you need? Anything I can get you?"

"Yeah. Get me a cigarette."

Pearl swung her head around to see that Millie was smiling. Pearl leaned back and relaxed. If it weren't for the fact that she was visiting a cancer patient who would be having major surgery the next day, she could relax even more.

"Rabbi, tell me a little about yourself. If you have some time."

"Sure. I have plenty of time." Pearl's last lie of the day. "What do you want to know?"

"Tell me about yourself. Where did you go to school, what are your parents like, who's your best friend, what's your favorite book, how you came to be a rabbi. How you met your husband. I saw him at the service last week. He's a hunk."

"That he is," Pearl replied. "Truth be told, he's one of a new breed: 'The rabbi's husband.' There aren't too many of them yet, but there will be. I believe half of the Reform rabbinical seminary is now female."

"I'll bet it takes a certain kind of man."

"It does. And he's it. Of course, he has his own field, which is pretty fascinating. He's a professor of entomology at Cal."

"Bugs."

"Yeah. That's what I said when he told me. We both started our jobs at about the same time."

And then Pearl told Millie about her life, the highlights. She spoke of her parents—her father the chemistry professor and her mother the therapist; and her sister, the cellist; and her best friend, Mary Fresa, a nurse in Chicago; and about growing up in Berkeley.

Pearl spoke briefly of her years at Stanford and then at rabbinical school in Cincinnati, her year living in Israel, and learning to speak Hebrew. And finally, she talked about how she'd just gotten her position at the temple when she met her husband, Jack, who was being recruited by the university, and how they'd both known "right away."

Pearl realized she'd been talking for almost half an hour, often gazing out the window as she spoke. When she looked down at Millie, she saw that the thin redheaded woman who'd insisted on calling her "Rabbi," and teased her about wanting a cigarette, was asleep.

Pearl sat back in her chair, then reached into her bag, pulled out a small book, and opened to a specific page. Quietly, she chanted the Mi Shebeirach prayer for healing, closed her eyes, and added a little silent prayer of her own for this successful businesswoman who liked sex and had broken through the glass ceiling on her way to the top. She'd probably broken a few hearts along the way as well.

Pearl closed the book, put it back in her bag, and rose. She was about to walk out the door, when Millie spoke.

"I heard every word about your life, Rabbi. And thanks for the prayer. Can't hurt, I suppose."

Pearl smiled. "It might even help."

"You're a lucky girl. And smart. Must have been the shampoo."

Pearl laughed as she touched her dark curls.

Millie continued. "Thanks for coming and telling me about yourself. I'll see you after they've cut me up and sewn me back together. Hopefully."

"It's a deal." She was half-way to the door when Millie spoke again.

"You know, Rabbi, I told you this once before: I wish I could put you on my payroll."

Pearl walked back to the hospital bed, picked up Millie's cool hand, and held it in hers.

"Millie, you're a member of my congregation. I *am* on your payroll."

Millie looked at her, but didn't say anything.

Surgery Day

They wheeled Millie into the operating room early the next morning following the lengthy prep and protocol procedures. She looked up at her gowned and masked surgeon. Through an increasingly sedated consciousness, she said, "Good luck, Doc. Knock 'em dead."

Although she'd regained partial consciousness following the surgery as they moved her from one place to another, Millie recalled little of those moments. She drifted in and out of sleep during the afternoon.

Now, she opened her eyes, taking a few moments to focus. It was dark outside. She looked up. Above her bed she saw three bags hanging from a metal stand, each full of stuff bubbling its way down tubes into her arm, which was immobilized at her side. She was sure she had a catheter stuck up inside her. Her bed had those irritating side rails up, as if by some miracle she could even move enough to fall off. The back of her bed was raised slightly.

In the subdued light, she became aware of someone else

in the room. She did not recognize the woman sitting nearby, reading a book. Millie decided to test her voice.

"And you are?" she asked.

The woman, who appeared to be in her mid-to-late fifties, set her book on a small table, stood, and moved to a chair closer to the bed.

"I am the woman who bought my daughter Smart Girls Curls shampoo. And look what happened."

Millie managed a faint smile. "Tell me your name—what should I call you?"

"Please call me Shayna."

"I'm Millie, as you know. It's a pleasure to meet you. I guess I should ask why you're even here. I'm surprised, although it's an honor."

"Millie, I'm here because my daughter asked me to be here. Actually, that's not entirely true. I'm here because I'm accustomed to dealing with a variety of crises, and your surgery has set off the type of crisis that the temple is not used to. So Pearl suggested to Duke that he call me to help deal with the situation."

"A crisis? And who's Duke?"

"Duke Sniderman. He's the executive director and administrator of Lakeshore Temple. You couldn't find a more efficient person anywhere, including Washington, Beijing, or the Kremlin."

"Maybe I should hire him for my own use."

"If you did, my daughter would cut off your oxygen supply."

Millie started to laugh, but the pain from the exertion was excruciating.

"Oh, my God, that hurts! Holy crap!" She actually groaned.

Shayna Ross strode to the door, said something to

someone outside, and in fifteen seconds a nurse swept in, fiddled with the bags and tubes, and seconds later Millie's face was calm again.

The nurse showed Millie how to operate a button that would release a dose of pain medication. Then she checked the urine level in the bag attached to the bed, typed some sentences in a nearby computer, and left the room.

"Wait. She didn't ask, 'Are you comfortable?'"

"She knows you're not. The type of surgery you had is typically very painful. I'd probably be screaming my head off."

"I doubt it," replied Millie. After a moment, she added, "The rabbi said you're a shrink."

"My daughters like to refer to me as that. I'm not sure why, but they always have."

"There are worse things. When my children were young, they referred to me as 'the Bitch.'"

"I see what you mean. I've been advised not to talk to you about your children."

"Yet somehow I opened the subject, didn't I."

"That's why I'm the shrink and you're not."

"Shayna, here's the short version. My son committed suicide when he was twenty, and I don't know where my daughter is. She ran away, and every time I've managed to locate her, she runs away again." Millie closed her eyes for a few seconds. Shayna waited until she opened them before replying.

"Millie, I doubt that you've been without counseling during your life. But right now you're recovering from major surgery and I'm here to help. Okay?"

"Yes. Could you please get me a sip of water?"

"Of course." And she did.

"Millie, I know you've been a successful executive, and you're a very capable person. So if you're up to it, I'd like to give you an update and assessment of what's going on. If you're too tired, we can wait until tomorrow."

"No, go ahead. Whatever the nurse pumped into me did the trick. I'd appreciate an update on 'the crisis.'"

"I'll make it quick.

"First, in your great wisdom, you wrote the name 'Rabbi Pearl Ross-Levy' as your temporary custodian on a paper the hospital gave you to sign. Do you remember doing that?"

Millie smiled weakly. "Here's my answer to that: In *her* great wisdom, your daughter said to me, quote, 'We're your family now, Millie.' So I entered her name in the blank space. It was either her or my lawyer, who's a very sharp cookie, but right now she's probably either in Acapulco or in jail. Or in a jail in Acapulco. So that's how that happened. I certainly didn't mean any harm. Also, frankly, I'm pretty much alone. And between you and me, this whole thing has been scary."

"All right. I understand. But what you could not have predicted is that somehow word of your surgery leaked out, and Alta Bates has been inundated … is there a stronger term than inundated? Yes … absolutely overwhelmed by calls, wires, cables, telegrams—I didn't even know people could send cables and telegrams anymore—from hundreds and hundreds of people, all women, it seems. From around the world. Millie, you are also being swamped with flowers. We've decided to not have any in your room. The scent would be suffocating."

Millie's face showed consternation. She was deep in thought. "There's only a few people who knew who could have done this, and we know it wasn't the rabbi or my doctor. So my bet is it was my chef, Suzanne. She probably told the woman who referred me to her—even though I asked her not to say anything—who then told some people in the Network, and it spread from there."

"The Network?" Shayna asked.

"It's a long story. Women in many fields who support each other. I am so, so sorry."

Millie looked like she was ready to cry, so Shayna softened her voice.

"What's done is done. Relax."

"Thank you." Millie took a breath.

"Since you gave Pearl an element of control, we've taken steps to sort things out. We've begun to compile a list of who's called, sent cards or flowers, left messages, and so on. When you've recovered sufficiently, we'll give you a printout of the spread sheet."

"Good idea."

"'Good idea,' she says."

Millie asked, "So, who's on first?"

"Who's *not* on first? You've received get-well messages from women in politics, finance, Hollywood, the press, sports, the Sorbonne, medicine, and science."

Millie couldn't help smiling as Shayna took a breath.

"Millie, is there a woman in a high place whom you do not know?"

Millie took Shayna's question seriously. "I'd always wanted to meet Mother Teresa."

"Well, if it helps any, there is a get-well message from the Vatican."

"Not the same."

Shayna was about to speak when the door opened and two people walked in. One was Millie's surgeon, and the other was Pearl.

"So, how are we doing?" asked the ebullient Dr. Dhari.

"Shayna, can you please explain to me why doctors always say, 'How are *we* doing?'"

Millie looked at the doctor. "*We* are doing just fine from

where you're standing. *We* are doing just miserably from where I am, lying on my back with a damned tube shoved up my …"

"Great! Glad to hear it, Millie. Especially from a young woman like yourself who just lost one of the lobes of her left lung. I forgot where I put it."

"Would someone please get this comedian out of here?" Millie said to no one. The doctor just looked at her chart and then at the computer in the room. He took Millie's pulse and put his stethoscope on various parts of her body. Then he spoke.

"I know you weren't sure you wanted to, but you're going to live. The further good news is that the tumor was *not* the size of a grapefruit as you insisted. As *I* predicted, it turned out to be the size of an M&M."

Millie grunted, and said, "Plain or peanut?"

The surgeon ignored her, and went on. "You and I have spoken before about how this type of surgery is painful. We'll be tapering you off pain meds as soon as we can, so get used to the pain. The faster you're out of bed and moving, the faster you'll heal. What's helped a lot is that you're not overweight, you eat a healthy diet, you exercise regularly, and I'm one of the best surgeons in the world."

Even Millie smiled at this. "Yes, doctor. Your skills are only exceeded by your modesty."

The doctor continued. "And Millie, I've informed the rabbi here that although I did take a phone call from one woman in the Surgeon General's office and another at NIH, I will *not* be answering any more questions about your surgery. This is not the White House!"

He said goodbye to those present, and left the room.

Shayna squeezed Millie's foot. "There are strict orders from 'the rabbi here' that you are to have only one visitor at a time at this point. So, it's been great talking to you, and we'll meet again."

Shayna picked up her book, gave Pearl a kiss on the cheek, and left.

Millie took a deep breath, which seemed to hurt. She pressed the button, which gave her a squirt of pain medication.

"Rabbi, your mother is the real thing."

"That she is." Pearl sat down in a chair she'd pulled close to the bed. "She's always given me courage to confront any obstacle in my path."

"Tell me what's happening out there. And by the way, I had no idea I was going to burden you with my care. I'm sorry the word got out. I do apologize."

"Yes. I asked Duke Sniderman to take over, and he put Esther Robinson on the job. You met Esther when you joined the congregation. She's sitting outside your room now. The get-well wishes, flowers, and notices of charitable donations made in your name are pouring in. We've decided to save the cards but donate all the flowers to other patients in the hospital, except for one beautiful bouquet of roses, which we placed at the nurse's station. They're from a certain governor who …"

"I know who."

"They tell me the local florists are flooded with orders."

"Rabbi, could you do me a favor? Your lovely mother said someone is making a list of who's sending get-well greetings. Is that Esther?"

Pearl went to the door, spoke, and Esther came in, holding a laptop computer.

"Millie, you've met Esther. She's now 'on loan' from the temple office and is in charge of, well, what's going on."

"Yes. Esther, I apologize for what you're having to go through."

"Are you kidding? This is incredible! Do you know all these people? Actresses? Women in Congress?"

Millie just nodded vaguely, and asked, "Esther, do you know who Suzanne is?"

"Yes. Your chef. She's called a couple of times and wants to know if you'll be needing meals delivered."

"Please call and tell her to come see me tomorrow. No, make it the next day. Tell her if she's the one who told anyone about my surgery, I'm going to kick her ass from here to Menlo Park."

"Menlo Park. Got it." Esther left the room, and the door closed behind her.

"Rabbi. I know I can't steal Duke Sniderman from you. How about Esther?"

Pearl smiled. "Don't even try. I'll sic my husband on you."

"Is he coming to visit me?"

"I'll see if I can get him on the list. Maybe he can bring some of his gay buddies from the Grizzly Peak house. They're gorgeous."

"I don't know what you're talking about, but I'm sure it's an interesting story."

"It is. Millie, it's time for you to rest. If you're up to it, the visitors begin tomorrow. I know we have your friend, the judge, coming by in the first fifteen-minute slot, and …"

"Fifteen-minute slot?"

"Yes. Esther told her that's all she can have."

"Okay." Millie exhaled.

"You have a problem, you ask Esther or Duke."

"I want to meet Duke."

"Duke's the one who put the security guard outside your door. I won't tell you who we had to turn away today."

"*Oy.*"

"Don't worry. We put everyone on your visitor schedule."

"Rabbi ..."

"Our senior rabbi, Craig Cohen, is out of town, but he'll be visiting when he returns."

"Rabbi ..." Millie tried to interject again.

"Yes. One last thing. Do you like cello music?"

"Rabbi, I *love* cello music."

"Good, because your next visitor is going to play for you for fifteen minutes. Then, lights out."

And with that, Pearl held the door open and Ruth Ross, dressed in black and holding her cello and bow, came in. Ruth smiled, sat down, and began to play softly. Millie thought it sounded like a lullaby.

The sonorous notes lulled her into a pain-free sleep.

Visitors

Although she'd been an early riser her entire life—you had to keep up with the competition, or ahead of it—the nurse in her room managed to wake Millie the next morning.

Doors and drawers opening and closing, metal utensils and pans banging, and chairs scraping—it was enough to wake the dead, she thought.

Wait, she wasn't dead. She decided quickly that was a good thing until the first burst of pain hit her.

"Holy crap—that hurts!" she said to no one as she reached for the pain button and pressed it.

"Ms. Babson," the nurse said, "the doctor is lowering your IV pain med later this morning. Just keep that in mind." This was a new nurse, who spoke as she bustled around the small room.

"You've got a busy morning," the nurse continued. "I'll be removing your catheter in a few minutes, and then we're going to help you onto the toilet so you can have a bowel movement. Are you hungry?"

"Let me see … Bowel movement. Breakfast. Catheter. I think I got it."

The nurse offered a little smile. "You should save your humor for when we get you out of bed and that pain med wears off. Let's take the catheter out now."

Millie put herself in the nurse's hands and was happy to have the bed rails come down and the catheter removed. She hoped she wouldn't get a urinary tract infection.

Then the nurse helped her move her legs off the bed and stand up. Carefully pushing the metal stand that held the IV still stuck in her arm, Millie shuffled over to her bathroom with the nurse's help. She was barely aware of her butt sticking out of the hospital gown.

She sat. She waited. *Success!*

Then she shuffled back to her bed, which the nurse propped up for her. If it were not for the pain in her chest, breakfast in bed might have been fun.

Halfway through some shredded wheat, her primary care doctor strolled in.

"What's up, Doc? How are we this morning?"

Millie loved her doctor, who exuded confidence and had a wonderful professional bearing.

Dr. Rofrano smiled. "We're fine and we're watching you eat your … shredded wheat. That's making us very happy. You're a good patient, Millie," she said.

A moment later, Millie's surgeon walked in, and the two doctors greeted each other. Her surgeon glanced at the nurse, who opened the door and told someone outside they'd need privacy for a few minutes. She then returned to assist the surgeon as he took a look at Millie's chest and drainage tubes. The two doctors chatted, Millie bore the pain, and the exam was soon over.

Dr. Dhari said, "If every patient had a security guard outside the door, my job would be easier. I'm switching you from intravenous pain medication to pills over the next day or so. That way we can get you the hell out of here soon and end this craziness."

"Don't blame me. Somebody ratted me out."

"You could have warned us," Dr. Rofrano said gently.

Millie sighed. "Doctor, it's been ten or twenty years since I've had any contact with most of these people. I'm truly sorry."

"Okay. But you owe the rabbi and the temple staff. Big. They have formed a wall around you twelve feet thick. A Sherman tank couldn't get through."

The surgeon nodded in agreement, and said goodbye as he ducked out of the room.

Dr. Rofrano chatted with Millie as the nurse propped her up on pillows, made her as comfortable as possible, and then left the room.

"By the way, Millie, there's a very important member of our network waiting out there to see you," said the doctor. "Can I tell Esther you're ready for a visitor?"

"A very important … ?" Millie had forgotten who was coming.

The doctor opened the door and Justice Emily Blauberg swept in. The doctor gave her a quick hug, said goodbye, and left.

Emily leaned over and gave Millie a quick kiss, sat down

in the chair and asked about her well-being. Millie had mentored the judge when she was an up-and-coming lawyer and then public prosecutor. There'd never been a doubt that she'd rise to the top.

"Why the hell didn't you tell me you were sick?" asked the judge. "I know people. I know doctors. Thanks to you, I know everyone!" They spoke about the old days and other women that Millie knew. They were having a grand old time.

The judge was thus surprised when Esther entered the room and said with a professional smile but in a firm voice, "Thank you for coming, Your Honor, but I'm afraid it's time to say goodbye to Ms. Babson."

Blauberg was about to offer a protest, but thought better of it. She squeezed Millie's foot and blew her a kiss. "Let me know if you need anything. Anything!"

"Emily, send over a cigarette and a virile eighty-year-old man. Unmarried would be best."

The judge laughed as she waved goodbye.

Sitting in her chair outside Millie's room a few minutes later, Esther looked up to see Justice Blauberg's aide—a young man in a jacket and tie—standing in front of her.

"Judge Blauberg wants to know if you'd be interested in applying for a job on her staff."

Esther smiled at the young man. "Please thank the judge and tell her I'm flattered by the offer. But I'm the personal assistant for two rabbis and a cantor, I have a great boss, and I work in a House of God. So, sorry, but no thank you."

As the aide departed, Duke Sniderman came around the corner.

"Was that Emily Blauberg I just saw getting off the elevator?" he asked Esther.

"Yes, but don't worry. I'm not jumping ship."

He gave her a quizzical look, but just asked if there was time to talk to Millie.

"Yes. Cantor Sanders is scheduled in ten minutes. And by the way, thanks for Rodrigo. He's making my job easier." She nodded to the uniformed guard, who nodded back. Even without a gun, the man was an intimidating presence.

"Thank the rabbi." With that, Duke knocked and entered Millie's room.

"Wait. Don't tell me. Duke Sniderman," said Millie as she looked up.

Duke said, "That's what they call me."

"And they call me clairvoyant."

"I see. So tell me, oh, clairvoyant one. What do I have in my pocket?" he replied.

She looked him up and down. "Well, I don't see a banana in your pocket, but I still hope you're happy to see me."

Duke laughed, came over and gently squeezed her outstretched hand, and then settled into the armchair.

"Duke, please don't ask, 'How are we feeling?'"

"Promise. Have you been made aware of the logistical situation? If you're not feeling well, we can talk later."

"I'm aware, and I apologize. This was never my intent."

"Actually, it's nice to have some excitement once in a while."

They were alone in the room. "Can I speak to you in confidence?" she asked.

"Better me than some straight guy with a big mouth."

"Good. I plan to reimburse the temple for any expense it's incurring on my behalf. Whatever ..."

"That's fine, Ms. Babson. On behalf of Lakeshore Temple, I accept your offer."

"Call me Millie, please."

"Millie. You can even do it anonymously if you want. It's such an unusual situation."

"Good. We'll settle up later. Promise."

"Great."

"Next, tell me, does the temple have, say, accounts where people donate funds for special occasions, things like that?"

"Hang on a second." He opened the door and asked Esther if she had a Temple Bulletin, which she did, of course. He came back, closed the door, and opened the Bulletin to a specific page.

"Here it is. The rabbis and the cantor each have discretionary funds. We also have the literacy project, the religious school, social action—all kinds of needs. The temple's a non-profit, Millie."

She felt a sharp pang, grimaced, and pressed the button. Some of the pain remained. Obviously they were already cutting the dose.

"You okay?" He looked at her with concern.

"Yes. No. Whatever. Where's the most need now?"

"I'd say religious school and general fund."

"If I split a donation between the two, will that help?"

"Of course. I'll be sure it's anonymous."

"Plus Rabbi Ross-Levy."

"Frankly, between you and me, the rabbis need it the least right now. People love them, and they're always donating to their discretionary funds. Have you met Rabbi Cohen?"

"I saw him at the Friday night service I went to. He's very good-looking."

Duke laughed. "Yes, he is. Unfortunately you missed his famous Rosh Hashanah sermon this past fall. He made a plea to the congregation to stop trying to fix him up with women. It was a classic. People will talk about it forever."

"He's single?"

"A widower."

"Ah."

"Anyway, when you meet him, I'd steer clear of the subject. He's really tired of it; and whatever's going on in his life, the real message is, let him do his rabbi job and leave his personal life personal."

"Gotcha."

There was a knock on the door. Duke stood and opened it, letting the cantor in.

"Millie, this is Cantor Shelley Sanders. Cantor, this is Ms. Babson. Call her Millie. Esther says you have fifteen minutes. I'm leaving. See you, Millie. It's been a pleasure." With that, he was out the door.

"May I sit?"

"Of course."

He sat.

"Cantor, thanks for coming. But we don't have a lot of time now, so please tell me a little bit about yourself, your wife, and your family. The *Readers Digest* version—you know what I mean?"

Shelley laughed. "Yes, I do."

"If I close my eyes, that doesn't mean I'm bored or sleeping or not listening, okay?"

"Got it." And he told her the brief version of his life in the theater and his subsequent career as a cantor. He also included a glowing description of Susan, and a four-sentence version of his two children that only a father could give.

He was finishing up as Esther poked her head in the door, made a "T" with her hands, and said, "Bellezana just called. She's eight minutes away." The door closed, but Shelley's mouth was open.

"Bellezana? You know Bellezana?" he asked with astonishment. Millie ignored him as she pushed the pain button again. Not much happened, but she took a few deep breaths and rested.

"Okay." He rose to go.

"I'd like to meet your wife, Cantor. She sounds truly special."

"She is. I don't know what she sees in me."

"I do. Take care. I need to rest before Bellezana gets here." She closed her eyes as he left the room.

Bellezana

Esther did not recognize the woman standing in front of her—until she smiled. *Incognito,* thought Esther, smiling back.

"Hi. I'm here to see Millie. Sorry I'm late."

Bellezana was wearing a cloche hat, a dark blue silk blouse, skintight jeans, and red Converse sneakers. Her skin was the most unusual color Esther had ever seen, and reflected what she'd read about the entertainer's parents and grandparents—a mixture of Mexican, Chinese, Jamaican and British. Bellezana's hair under her hat might be any color, and was never one fixed shade. She carried a small, nondescript purse.

"Good morning. She's looking forward to seeing you." Rodrigo moved aside as Esther led Bellezana into the room.

"Millie! I'd say you look fantastic … if you did!" Bellezana kissed Millie on the cheek, pulled over a chair, and sat. Then she turned to Esther and asked, "How much time do I have?"

Esther looked at Millie. "Fifteen?"

"No. Let's make it twenty, Esther. I have a little business to discuss with Bellezana."

"Uh-oh!" said the pop star and singer-dancer-turned-actress. "Now I'm in trouble! Thanks so much, Esther."

Esther closed the door behind her and thought about how she'd just been in the presence of one of the best-known and most talented women in show business, and maybe one of the wealthiest as well. Very soon, Esther would learn that Millie was quite wealthy herself.

"Okay, Millie. Talk to me."

Millie brought Bellezana up-to-date on the surgery and gave her a quick overview of how she'd unwittingly put herself under the protection of Rabbi Ross-Levy and the temple.

"You could have called me. But it looks like you're in good hands."

"The best," Millie said.

"So, what's up with the 'business' business?"

"*Smart Girls*. I miss it."

"Your old company?" Bellezana was surprised. "I'm sorry, Millie, but I was just a little girl when you had your company. By the time I found you—you found me, whatever—you'd sold the company."

"I know. But I'm getting bored. It's not easy being an old lady, trust me. Also, this surgery and the way people have been taking care of me have been affecting me in strange ways."

"Millie, this is not about money, is it?"

Millie laughed. "Hell, no! But thanks for asking.

"I'm actually thinking of setting up some kind of non-profit or foundation attached to the sale of product, you know, like the Newmans did with spaghetti sauce and salad dressing?"

Bellezana smiled her famous smile. "I get it. Totally! Did

you know I have a charity foundation? Really! It was my agent's idea. She set the whole thing up through an L.A. attorney who does this sort of thing for a lot of Hollywood people.

"And Millie, listen to this—the lawyer's a member of your network. She's really great. She'd love to help, I just know it."

The Network. Again. Seeds she had sown thirty, forty years before were now mighty oaks. Oakettes.

"Good. Just what I need."

"I'll send her contact info over."

"Thanks."

Bellezana paused for a reflective moment. "If it weren't for you, I'd still be working on my GED."

"Don't exaggerate."

"Whatever. Anyway, I hope you get better soon. I want to see *Smart Girls* back on the shelf. Maybe I can do a TV commercial for you, or a magazine spread. You just let me know. I'm serious."

She leaned over and kissed Millie. Then they chatted for a few minutes until Esther opened the door.

"Esther, your timing is perfect. You should be in show business. Or come work for me."

Esther looked embarrassed. "Thank you. I just want to tell you what an honor it is to meet you. You're one of my role models."

"Baby," she replied, "if you're looking for a role model, you just look at that lady over there. She's *my* role model."

And with that, Bellezana made her exit.

When Esther looked over, Millie's eyes were closed. She appeared to be fast asleep, but wasn't. She was thinking about a yet-to-be-made TV commercial.

That afternoon, after lunch, a breathing therapy session, a

long walk up and down the hallway, and visits from her doctors, Millie was sitting in her bed thinking about a dozen things when the door popped open.

"How are we doing?" Pearl asked with a laugh. Millie laughed too.

"We're doing just swimmingly. Good to see you, Rabbi. How are things over at the temple?"

"The same old stuff. Challenges. B'nai mitzvah lessons. Committee meetings. Religious school meetings. Meetings to plan meetings." Pearl sat down. "Millie, I'm wondering if you're up for some visitors? Do you have any energy left after this morning?"

"Sure. Does someone want to see me?"

"Hang on." Pearl left the room and a moment later the door opened again as Rodrigo came in carrying a folding card table and four folding chairs. He and Pearl cleared a place at the foot of the bed and set up the table and chairs.

Pearl asked, "You ready to play?"

"I sure am!"

They helped Millie out of bed, draped her robe around her, and sat her in one of the chairs, her IV stand off to the side.

Pearl then opened the door. "We're ready!"

Three women entered, one carrying a Mah Jongg case. Each introduced herself as they set out the tiles, racks, and cards.

One woman, Bernice, said to Millie, "I don't know about you, but I use a large print card. I brought my extra one for you."

"Perfect. Thank you so much! And remember, I haven't played in years."

"Today, we're not playing for money, right girls?"

All agreed. Pearl stood by as the sorting and choosing of

tiles began. The others reminded Millie about some of the rules and procedures as they went along. No one rushed her.

The rabbi slipped out of the room as she listened to the women's voices and the sounds of the tiles.

"One bam."

"Three crak."

"Call ... flower."

She asked Esther, "How's it going? Having a good time away from the office?"

"It's just incredible. Justice Blauberg was here this morning. And then Bellezana!"

Esther paused, then said, "Rabbi, who is Millie, anyway?"

"We're finding out, aren't we?"

"She knows everyone. Famous people. Calling, sending cards and flowers."

"All I can tell you is that she was a very successful businesswoman who has been a mentor to other women trying to break through the glass ceiling. It's still hard, but not as hard as in the past. She sacrificed a lot and gave a lot, and frankly, I think she suffered a lot along the way." Pearl sat down in the chair Esther had vacated. She was tired and needed to pee, but could wait.

"When I was a young girl, I used the shampoo that her company produced. I didn't know who she was then, of course. If you look her up, though, you'll see that she was— and still is—on a lot of lists. Women's lists in particular."

"Like, is she really rich?"

"Esther, you'll find that 'rich' is a relative term. We know Bellezana is rich, but she's a celebrity. I'm not sure how to answer your question.

"This morning, a famous entertainer came to visit Millie in the hospital. Before that, it was a federal judge.

Congresswomen and presidents of big companies have sent flowers.

"But I believe that tonight, when Millie thinks back on this day, it'll be the Mah Jongg game with the temple ladies that will bring a smile to her face."

Esther was deep in thought, digesting what the rabbi was saying.

"Sure," Pearl continued. "She's happy that her protégées have remembered her and are coming to see her or calling or making donations and sending get-well greetings. But I don't believe she's thinking much about money. Perhaps she's happy to just be alive. She survived her surgery, and now she's playing Mah Jongg.

"Millie came to us because she needed *our* support. And we're supporting her. We're helping her heal."

"I understand," Esther whispered.

"In spite of having money, Millie's life hasn't been easy. Things aren't always what they seem."

Esther nodded her head. "That's for sure, Rabbi."

"I've gotta run. You're doing a great job. More than one job, really. Thank you."

She gave Esther a hug, and was gone.

Esther thought about how lucky she was to be working for this incredible woman.

Millie and Esther

The following morning, Millie woke up to pain, but it was bearable. It seemed less than the day before. A nurse, as usual, was moving things around the room. She helped Millie to the toilet. Then the surgeon showed up and checked out his handiwork, pronounced it wonderful (as usual), and departed.

Millie ate her breakfast. She read. She wrote in her journal. She rested. There didn't seem to be much happening, and that was fine with her.

At nine, Duke knocked and entered.

"Good morning, Millie."

"Duke. Good to see you."

"Change of plans today. A few people from the temple caring community are covering your phone. Esther couldn't make it, but she wrote up some notes for the volunteers. They'll know what to do. Some of these same people will be helping out in a few days when you go back to your apartment. Do you have someone to help with your personal medical care?"

"There's a nursing aide who's coming by."

"Good."

"But Duke, what's happening with Esther?"

Duke sat down in the visitor chair and sighed.

"Her aunt was admitted to Highland Hospital last night at two. Something to do with her heart. On the way home, Esther's car broke down again, and she had to call a taxi. This morning, Esther needed to take two buses to get to the temple. I loaned her my car and she dropped me off here. Then she went back to Highland."

"Why did she even come to work?"

"I *told* her to take the day off, but she insisted on coming in to the office after lunch. There's no point arguing with her."

"She's a serious young woman," Millie said.

"Esther's been burning the candle at three ends—doing her regular job, coordinating what's going on here, and now dealing with her aunt. This is the woman who raised her and is, for all intents, her mother. She and her cousin are trying to do it all without much help. It's a mess. Esther is super, but without a car, she's just screwed."

Millie shook her head and exhaled. *It's always something,* she thought.

"Duke, can you help me for about a half hour? Now?"

"Sure. What can I do?"

"What's the name of that big car dealer on Broadway in Oakland."

"There's a couple. Downtown Toyota ..."

"That's it. Can you get them on the phone for me, please? Put it on speaker, if you would."

In a minute, Duke had them on the line.

"Downtown Toyota. How may I direct your call?"

Millie said, "Good morning. Do you have a female salesperson on the floor who's available right now?"

"Yes, we do. Shall I connect you?"

"Yes, please."

A few buzzes later and a woman's voice came on the line.

"Hello. This is Chloe. May I help you?"

"Chloe, this is Ms. Babson. Do you have a few minutes? I need to buy a car."

"Sure. What do you have in mind?"

"Now look, Chloe, here's the situation. I'm buying this car for ... my niece. I'm currently at Alta Bates hospital, and I don't have a lot of time or energy. I want this to be a fast transaction. Can you do that for me?"

"Yes. Just tell me what you need, Ms. Babson."

"I want a Prius, used—under 5,000 miles. The best one you've got."

"Got it. Hang on, I'm looking at our current inventory on the computer right now."

Millie and Duke heard keyboard clicks.

"I have two vehicles, each less than six months old, that

fit your criteria. The white one has forty-nine hundred miles, and the light blue one has forty-two hundred miles. They're both very clean and come with a one-year warrantee. If you want an extended warrantee …"

"That's okay," Millie interrupted. "Give me the prices."

Chloe quoted two prices; the blue one was eight hundred dollars more.

Millie spoke softly to Duke. "Do you think she'd like the white one or the blue one?"

Duke mouthed, *blue.*

"Chloe, we want the blue one, but you need to give me a better price."

"I'll be right back. I need to talk to my sales manager. Can you hold?"

"Yes. Tell your manager we want to buy today."

A minute later, Chloe returned. "He said we can reduce the price on the blue Prius by one thousand dollars, but not a cent more."

"Good. Go back to him, and tell him that if he makes it fifteen hundred I'll take it. And Chloe, I don't want that coming off your commission, do you understand?"

"Yes, Ma'am. I'll be right back."

Another minute went by, and she was back. "He told me to say we can split the difference and make it twelve-fifty. Is that okay?"

"He also told you that if I refused, he'd give me the fifteen hundred dollars off, right?"

Chloe laughed. "Are you a mind reader?"

"I'm clairvoyant. We'll take the fifteen hundred reduction and the car. Tell Chuck or whatever the hell his name is, 'Thank you,' and please get the car cleaned and prepped and make sure it's in beautiful condition by one o'clock. Can you do that?"

"Absolutely."

Millie said to Duke, "Can you take her over after one?" He nodded yes.

"Chloe, Mr. Sniderman will be coming by between one and two with Esther, my niece, and my credit card. The bank will accept the charge; call them if you need to. Please title the car in Esther's name, and I don't want to see any extra charges for B.S. add-ons or stuff like that. *Claro?*"

"*Claro*, Ms. Babson." She paused for a moment. "I wish I could meet you. The receptionist said you specifically asked for a female sales agent. Is that true?"

"Of course it's true. You're in a tough business. We need to stick together. I hope you make a few bucks on this sale."

"It'll help me make the rent this month for sure."

Millie paused for a moment, then said, "Mr. Sniderman will have a piece of paper with the titles of a few books you should take out of the library and read. Do that for me, Chloe, will you?"

"I will, Ms. Babson. You've got a lucky niece."

"She's worth it. Thanks, and good talking to you. Bye."

"Goodbye."

Duke picked up the phone and clicked the off button. He looked at Millie. The transaction had obviously tired her out, and she'd closed her eyes. He waited for her to open them.

When she did she said, "Thank you, Duke." She fished a card case out of the hospital table drawer and handed him a credit card. "Could you please call the number on the back of this card? It's too damned small for *me* to read."

Ten minutes later, with the bank having received her approval for the transaction at the car dealer, she scribbled the names of a few books about business and personal finance for women on a sheet of paper, and handed it and the credit card to Duke.

"You know what to do. Thanks so much. If Esther objects, tell her that I'll be talking to her about how she can pay me back over time, and to just not worry about it."

"Got it." Duke took the card and the paper and left the room.

Millie fell asleep immediately.

That evening at nine, Esther slipped into the room. Millie was writing in her journal, which she closed as the young woman sat down in the visitor's chair. The room was lit only by the lamp above the bed, and seemed very calm and peaceful.

"You didn't have to do that," Esther said quietly.

Millie looked at her. "Esther, you need to be able to get to work, to the hospital to visit the woman who raised you, to the store, maybe to school, go on a date, get to the airport. You need good transportation. This is not New York City, where you can hop on the subway and you're in Brooklyn."

"But a car. It's too big a gift. I've never ..." The tears started to flow. She reached for the tissue box.

"How's your aunt?"

"They say she's stable. We're taking her home tomorrow. In the new car. When she sees it, she'll think I've been turning tricks or something."

"Here's the deal, Esther. The car's a gift. But I need your help, and that's how you can repay me."

"You need *my* help?"

"Yes. I would like you to be my part-time personal

assistant for the next couple of years. You can work for me two to four hours a week."

"But I work full-time for the temple." Esther had a worried look on her face.

"It won't be a problem. This would be at night—after work, or before work, or on the weekend. It would be a very flexible schedule. I don't want it to conflict with your job at the temple. The Rabbi would kill me."

Esther laughed. "Well, I'm sure I could do that. At night? Or in the morning, or on the weekend?"

"Yes. For example, you could come to my apartment near the lake at seven, we could have a 'working dinner' together, and you could leave at nine. That would be two hours."

"Well, that sounds good!"

"That would be two hundred dollars worth of work."

"Wait. A hundred dollars an hour, to have dinner and work?"

"You think it's not enough?" Millie was holding back a smile.

Esther turned her head to one side and gave Millie a suspicious look. "Hold on. You're playing with me."

"No. A good personal assistant is worth a hundred dollars an hour. And you're good."

Millie took a sip of her apple juice. "Esther, how many of my friends have offered you a job since I've been here?"

"A few, actually," she answered with embarrassment. "Plus your surgeon."

"That guy, I'm gonna …"

"I turned them all down. I like working for the temple, and the rabbis, and Duke. They're good people."

"Yes, they are."

"But I'd like to work for you. Or, do whatever, like, to

repay you for the car. It's really beautiful, by the way. I love the light blue color. Thank you."

"Okay. Let's be clear. This is not a real job. The car is my gift to you. I just need some help. Think of it as an internship."

"All right. I understand. That feels good. What will I be doing for you?"

"Okay. I've got a project in mind. It's complicated, and I can't keep track of everything myself. I don't have the computer skills. You do. I can't keep up with all the calls and messages. You could. I'm an old lady. You're not."

"From what I've seen the last few days, you can pretty much do anything. And you just had surgery."

"You ain't seen nothin' yet."

Esther laughed.

Millie said, "I did not make up that line."

Esther got up to leave, but turned back before she reached the door.

"One last question. Chloe, the lady at the Toyota place, kept calling you my aunt. What was that all about?"

Millie closed her eyes. "Goodnight, Esther."

Zinnia's Project

"Zinnia, you still have some time, but you should start thinking about your bat mitzvah project. Here's a list of suggestions and examples of projects others have done over the years. Whatever you choose, it should be something that allows you to contribute in some way—to the city, to the community, or to the world. The project should be completed before your actual bat mitzvah date."

"Okay."

"And if possible, try to make a connection between your project and your Torah portion, and mention it during your drash. If you can do that, it would be great."

Pearl had already learned that nothing fazed Zinnia Chin. As she gave her these instructions in April, three months before her upcoming July bat mitzvah, Pearl had no doubt that Zinnia would come up with something interesting.

That was the moment the baby decided to make its presence known to its mother. Pearl closed her eyes and wrapped her arms around her own waist.

"Are you okay, Rabbi?"

Pearl paused as she savored the moment. "I'm fine, Zinnia. Would you like to feel the baby kicking?"

"Wow! Of course!" She walked over and allowed Pearl to guide her hand to where the action was taking place. "Whoa, that's weird. And very cool!"

"This is the first time I'm feeling it."

"Is she—or he—just kicking, or what? It feels like it's rolling around or something."

"Maybe all of those things." Pearl smiled at her.

"This is great! I can't wait to tell my mom."

One Sunday in mid-May, Zinnia's mother said she was taking a donation box to Second Chance Dress for Success, a charity that collected clothes for battered or homeless women trying to return to the work force. Dana asked Zinnia to go through her own closet and dresser to see what she might want to include. After putting a half-dozen items in the cardboard box, she joined her mother as they drove to the donation center.

"Great! Dress shoes!" the woman checking their box said. "We *never* have enough high-quality dress shoes, especially like these!"

"That's interesting," said Dana.

"Suits, jackets, blouses, yes. But not enough nice shoes. If you know anyone else who has good women's dress shoes to donate, we sure could use them. Spread the word!"

During the drive home, Zinnia said, "Mom, I'm thinking about what that lady said about shoes. Do you think that if I got people to donate dress shoes for Second Chance, that would be a good bat mitzvah project?"

Dana said, "It sounds good to me. Why don't you ask the rabbi?"

After the Shabbat kiddush lunch the following Saturday morning, Zinnia told Pearl about her experience at Second Chance and asked whether she thought the shoe collection project was a good one.

Pearl said, "Not only is this an excellent idea, but I'm going to be one of the first to contribute to your bat mitzvah project! If you come by the temple Tuesday or Wednesday, I'll have a few boxes for you."

"Awesome!"

Pearl continued. "But before you start asking people for shoes, put together a one-page outline of the criteria people need to follow when making their donations."

The word spread quickly through the temple office and community.

A week later, Dr. Stuart Chin mentioned at dinner, "Is it my imagination, or are there a bunch of shoeboxes in the garage that weren't there before?"

"Yeah, Dad. They're for my bat mitzvah."

"Wait. How many pairs of shoes do you need? This is a bat mitzvah, not a Chinese wedding."

"Zinnia, your father can't help himself. He's thinking like a man."

"Yeah, Dad. You know what Mom always says."

"I know, I know. You can never have enough shoes."

"Anyways, these are not for me. They're for my bat mitzvah project. I'm collecting them for the Second Chance women's center."

The shoe collection continued to grow so rapidly that Zinnia's father needed to install several new shelving units to accommodate the growing number of boxes. They worked out a system whereby the shoeboxes were categorized by both size and style. If you needed a size 7 in a white dress shoe, Zinnia could show you exactly where to find it. It was soon apparent they'd be running out of space—not just for shoe boxes, but for the actual shelving units.

One night, Dana tentatively asked her, "Uh, Zinnia, I'm going to a reception at work tomorrow night. Do you happen to have anything in my size in a black patent leather?"

Zinnia consulted the chart she kept on a clipboard. "Actually, I do, Mom. But you'll have to donate a pair in exchange."

Thus was Zinnia's Women's Shoe Exchange born.

With just a few weeks to go before her bat mitzvah, Dana answered the phone one evening as they finished dinner.

"Yes. Yes, it is. Okay. Hold on a second. I'll put her on.

"Zinnia, it's a reporter from KTVU. She'd like to speak to you about shoes."

Zinnia took the phone. "Hello?"

"Good evening, Zinnia. This is Gloria Salas from KTVU. How are you tonight?"

"I'm okay."

"Here's why I'm calling. One of the women who works here at the station says that you have a very interesting bar mitzvah project going on."

"Actually, it's a *bat* mitzvah project."

"Uh, okay. I'll check the spelling on that. Anyway, I'm told you're collecting shoes for a homeless shelter, and ..."

"Well, it's a little more complicated ..."

"And how many pairs have you collected so far?"

"Well, let me take a look."

"Take a look?"

"Yeah, I'm just looking at the inventory list. Not counting the boxes that were dropped off today, I have 242."

Her father murmured, "And growing fast."

"Who was that?"

"Oh, that's my dad. He's in charge of, well, stocking the merchandise. He keeps saying that my bat mitzvah can't come soon enough because there's no more room in the garage for his car."

"I guess your father doesn't know about women and shoes."

"My mom tried to explain, but ..."

"Zinnia, the TV station would like to do a little story on your project. Would that be okay?"

"Mom, they want to do a story about the shoe project on TV. Is it okay?"

"I guess so. Why not?"

Stuart mumbled, "Yeah, maybe they need some shoes over at the station. Tell 'em to bring a pickup truck."

Gloria continued, "May we come over tomorrow afternoon, around five o'clock?"

"Mom, they want to come at five tomorrow?"

"Okay. I'll be here."

"My mom says that's fine."

"Great! I'll be there tomorrow at five with a camera crew." She confirmed the address and said goodbye.

The next day at 4:50 p.m. Gloria Salas showed up with her two-person crew and fourteen boxes of shoes. Stuart looked at what was going on, groaned, and left the room.

After telling the story—on camera—about how her project started, Zinnia then led everyone out to the garage to view her increasingly large, but very organized, collection. When the crew finally left, the Chin family sat down to dinner.

Stuart gazed toward heaven. "Shoes! When I was in med school we *never* talked about shoes."

Dana cheerfully replied to her husband, "Really? When *I* was in med school we talked about shoes all the time!"

Donations continued to come in. Every morning as Stuart Chin left for work, or when he returned in the evening, there were inevitably more boxes of shoes stacked on the front steps and porch.

At work, his male colleagues were talking about it as well. "Hey Stuart, we saw your kid on TV. She's really great! I've got a few boxes of shoes out in the car that my wife sent with me."

And then there were the female doctors and nurses. Every night, his back seat was filled with shoe boxes.

"I feel like Captain Kirk in 'The Trouble With Tribbles,'" he complained to anyone who would listen. They all laughed.

"Sure, laugh!" he said. "You can probably fit *your* car in the garage!

The following week, it went Code Blue.

Both Drs. Chin were preparing dinner and Zinnia was setting the table when the phone call came. Once again Dana answered the phone.

"Hello? No, this is Dr. Chin, Zinnia's mother." After listening for half a minute, she said, "Yes, Mr. Epstein, I understand. I'll put her on.

"Zinnia, Mr. Epstein is calling you from Boston. He's in the shoe business and heard about your bat mitzvah project from his own rabbi, who's a friend of Rabbi Ross-Levy." Dana handed the phone to her daughter.

"Hello?"

"Good evening, Zinnia. My name is Nathan Epstein. I'm calling from Boston. How are you tonight?"

"I'm okay."

"That's great, Zinnia. Glad to hear it. As your mother just told you, the rabbi at my congregation near Boston is a friend and classmate of your rabbi's, and she told me about your bat mitzvah project. She thought I might be interested because my family is in the shoe business. We import women's shoes and handle a number of major brands."

"Cool."

"I like the idea of your project, helping women trying to get back into the job market." He paused. "Back on their feet."

"I guess, yeah, sort of. Wait—is that a joke? Ha!"

"Anyway, we'd like to help out. Every month we get a certain number of returns from stores that we can't send back to the manufacturer. They're basically new but they might have minor flaws—very small things wrong with them. We call these 'seconds.'"

"Sure, I've heard of seconds. But they're in good shape and in the original boxes?"

"Absolutely!"

The phone call continued, but her parents could only hear Zinnia's side of the conversation.

"Yes," said Zinnia. "Okay. Chai. Sure, chai's great. Thank you. You'll send them here? Okay. You have my address?" She gave it to him. "Okay. Just as long as they're here really soon, because Second Chance will be picking them up July eighth, and my bat mitzvah is on the tenth."

A moment later she said, "Okay. Thank *you*. Sure, I'll tell Rabbi Ross-Levy about your rabbi."

There was another long pause, and then Zinnia added, "Oh, that's really nice of you. Thanks, Mr. Epstein.

"Sure, I know. One six-and-a-half and two sevens. Great. And please make sure to send me your address so I can mail you a thank-you. My mom says that's important. Yes. This is awesome.

"Goodnight."

Zinnia hung up and resumed setting the table. In a few minutes, they all sat down, said the *motzi* prayer, and Zinnia dug into her food. She didn't say a word.

Stuart finally broke the silence. "So what did Mr. Epstein have to say?"

"Well," she said between bites, "his rabbi is a friend of our rabbi, who told her about my project. And because he's in the shoe business, he's going to donate some shoes." She resumed eating.

Dana joined in. "I heard the word chai mentioned. Is he sending you eighteen pairs of shoes."

"Not exactly."

"Not exactly? Then how many?"

She looked up. "He said he wanted to send me 'a multiple of chai.' So he's sending a hundred and eighty boxes."

Stuart dropped his fork and choked. *"What!* Where are we supposed to put a hundred and eighty shoe boxes? Do you realize that we're already up to our …"

Dana interrupted. "Do you know anything about the shoes he's donating?"

"Yeah. He said they're all good brands—he actually said 'major' brands. But he said they might have a little thing wrong with them—like flaws and stuff—that make them seconds."

"That shouldn't be a problem."

"No, he said hardly anybody would even see the stuff—the flaws."

Stuart muttered, "A hundred and eighty shoe boxes. Dear God."

Zinnia added, "But he's also sending some extra shoes. He said it's a special gift for my bat mitzvah."

"Well, that was very sweet—and generous," said Dana.

"But it's kind of weird, Mom. He said my shoes are not seconds. They're firsts, I guess. And brand new. And they're designed by that actor who played the Hulk on TV."

"What?" Dana said, obviously confused.

Stuart, now recovered, said, "You mean Lou Ferrigno? The body builder? He designs shoes?"

"Yeah, *that's* who he said."

Dana gasped. "Ferragamo? He's sending you a pair of Ferragamo shoes?"

"Yeah, maybe *that's* who he said."

"Stuart, Ferragamo shoes sell for five hundred dollars or more. A pair."

Zinnia looked up and smiled. "Cool." She kept eating.

Her father just said, "Another 180 shoe boxes. I think I've lost my appetite." He left the table, shaking his head.

Dana sat silently. Thinking. Then she spoke.

"So let me get this straight. My thirteen-year-old daughter is going to be wearing a pair of Ferragamo shoes for her bat mitzvah. What am I supposed to wear? Chopped liver?"

"Oh, he says he's including an extra pair for you, too. And the rabbi. That's why I had to give him your size. You and Rabbi Ross-Levy wear the same.

Dana smiled. "Well, now that's *very* cool!"

"But Mom, you're gonna have to write your own thank-you note."

When the Epstein shipment came, Stuart was beside himself. He was, at this point, counting the minutes until Second Chance picked everything up. Shoeboxes were now stacked in the living room, the hallways, the garage, the kitchen, the bedrooms, and the bathrooms. Dr. Stuart Chin feared the fire marshal might find out. He was even thinking of calling the fire marshal himself. But the way things were going, the fire marshal's wife would probably send him over with twenty boxes of shoes.

When the day *did* come, it went more smoothly than anyone could have imagined. Dana and Zinnia had recruited some volunteers to help sort and carry shoe boxes into an empty moving van that showed up at six on Thursday evening. As the inventory was carried from the house and the garage to the truck, Zinnia checked off boxes on her clipboard and gave the okay.

In two hours, they'd loaded over 800 boxes of shoes onto the truck. Dr. Stuart Chin almost cried in relief. He'd ordered pizza and sodas delivered for the volunteers. After everyone had eaten and been thanked, he parked his car in his garage, went back to the house, and thanked God for delivering him from the shoe business. He then collapsed onto the bed and fell into a deep sleep.

He still had his shoes on.

Zinnia's Drash

Shabbat Shalom!

I want to welcome all my friends, family, and everyone from the temple. Thank you for celebrating my bat mitzvah with me.

Now that I'm considered an adult member of the congregation, my dad says I can start paying my share of the temple dues. I told him he should take it out of my allowance.

Rabbi Cohen always likes to remind me that he's known me since I was born. There's a family legend that he once changed my diaper.

When my parents and I first went to his office to talk about studying for my bat mitzvah, he asked me if I'd be willing to study with our new rabbi, Rabbi Ross. He said that I'd really like her and that she'd like me.

I said, "Sure." And he was right—she's awesome! If it weren't for Rabbi Ross-Levy—that's her married name—I wouldn't be wearing these great new shoes.

Working with Cantor Sanders was also a lot of fun. And I gotta tell you that he really knows about all kinds of music. We talked about everybody from Al Jolson to Norah Jones. You may not know this, but the cantor does a great impersonation of Al Jolson. It didn't mean much to me until I watched an old movie called The Jazz Singer. *I think the cantor did a better job than Al Jolson.*

I often think about what it would be like if I lived in the olden days, like a hundred years ago. Well, first of all, I wouldn't be here. I'd probably be living in a shtetl *in Eastern Europe. Or else on a farm in China. Or nowhere, really, because my parents never would have met and gotten married a hundred years ago.*

And I wouldn't be standing on the bima or reading from the Torah, because girls couldn't do that in those days; just boys.

And we wouldn't have a female rabbi sitting here. Or even a female board member, like we do. Or two female senators in California. Or two Jewish female senators in California. By the way, I sent bat mitzvah invitations to both senators, and even though they couldn't come, I received nice notes back from both of them. One said the reason she couldn't come was because she had to go to her own granddaughter's bat mitzvah today.

I bring this up because the reason we now have female rabbis and cantors and senators and might even someday have a female president of the United States can all be traced back to my Torah portion today.

When I talked to my mom about the Five Daughters of Zelophehad, she said, "I'm not sure I know about this story. Have they been keeping it a secret?" That was surprising, since my mom knows just about everything.

Here's the story—it's from the book of Numbers:

> The Five Daughters of Zelophehad … came forward. They stood before Moses, Eleazar the priest, the chieftains, and the whole assembly at the entrance of the Tent of Meeting, and they said, "Our father died in the wilderness. He was not one of Korah's faction, which banded together against Adonai, but died for his own sin; and he has left no sons. Let not our father's name be lost to his clan just because he had no son! Give us a holding among our father's kinsmen!"

People talked funny in those days.

Anyways, it was like the Five Daughters had just filed a lawsuit and they wanted justice. I agree that they were being deprived of their rights. Don't you? It's because the system favored men, and women didn't have *any rights. Also, the daughters didn't want their family name to disappear.*

*So Moses thought about it and decided to bring their law-
suit case before God, and God said,* "The plea of Zelophehad's
daughters is just; you should give them a hereditary holding
amongst their father's kinsmen; transfer their father's share
to them."

Even God talked funny in those days.

*I like to think of this story as one of the first steps in the fight
for women's rights and equality.*

*When I talked to the rabbi about this, I asked her why it
wasn't, like, a famous bible story taught to every kid—especially
to every girl. Because it sounds to me like this is where the struggle
for women's rights really got started. And my mom agrees with
me.*

*The rabbi got that look she gets when she's thinking really hard
about something. Then she agreed that, yes, it is a very important
story. But one reason it's not one of the big-time stories is that
there's no miracle in it. She said most of the really famous bible
stories have a miracle—like Noah and the flood, or Moses and the
burning bush, or the parting of the Red Sea.*

*My mom says that considering that men ran just about
everything in those days, letting women inherit property was a
miracle.*

*Rabbi Ross-Levy then suggested that I look at the story as
if it were a play. My dad helped me write this. He's a funny guy
sometimes.*

Dawn breaks over the wilderness and we see the
tents of the Israelites. A small group of people gath-
ers near the entrance of one of the tents. *(Cue Israeli
desert music.)* Inside, Moses is sleeping. His wife,
Zipporah *(that name still reminds me of a zipper)*,
shakes his shoulder and says:

"Moshe! Moshe! Wake up!" *(Moshe is, like, the
Yiddish name for Moses.)*

Moses is still pretty sleepy, and grumpy, too,
and he says, "Why are you waking me up so early?
You know I had a late night."
"I know it's early, but you have to wake up.
Here—I brought you a cup of hot tea—it's made
from manna." *(My dad made that up about the manna.
That's pretty funny.)*
"Moshe, wake up and get out of bed. You have
to talk to the girls!"
"Girls? What girls? You woke me up to talk to
some girls?"
"Yes, the Five Daughters of Zelophehad. Now
get up before I get angry!"
"Okay, I'm getting up! I'm getting up!" *(Moses
sounds just like my dad sometimes.)*

*When I first thought about the Five Daughters, I pictured
girls about my own age. But the Talmud tells us that they were
"righteous women in their forties." And it says that later they
all got married and had children. My mom said, "See—another
miracle!"*

*In preparing this drash, I looked at a few books about famous
women through the ages. I'd already heard of Eleanor Roosevelt
and Madame Curie. But most of them, I didn't know, even though
they did really brave things. I learned a lot about the struggle for
women's rights and equality, and about all the things women did
in World War II and Vietnam.*

*My mom is a doctor, and she told me about how hard it used to
be for women to get into medical school. I read in one book that the
percentage of women medical students went from nine percent in
1969 to about 50 percent now. That's a pretty big increase. In law
schools, more than 50 percent of entering classes are now women.
It used to be, like, less than five percent in the 1950s and '60s.*

The rabbi told me that Hebrew Union College ordained its

first female rabbi in 1972, and now about half the students there are women.

So things have come a long way for us women.

But sadly, the story of the Five Daughters doesn't end as well as we might like it to. Moses was pressured by the men to change God's decision, and the daughters were forced to marry into their father's clan. That way their inheritance wouldn't go outside the tribe. Can you imagine these guys changing God's decision?

My mom says, "Some things never change."

And my dad says, "You always have to follow the money." (He also says, "Cherchez la femme.")

Anyways, it doesn't seem fair, does it?

But I think the takeaway—that's like the moral of the story—is that the daughters fought for the right to inherit, and they got it. The right to keep it took another few thousand years.

Pause for effect ... Oh, wait, I wasn't supposed to read that out loud.

I want to thank everyone who helped me collect and donate over 800 pairs of women's shoes to Second Chance Dress for Success, which helps women in shelters go back to work.

I'm sure the Five Daughters of Zelophehad would have approved of my project. But I'd have to know what size they wore.

Finally, if it weren't for my dad, I could not have done it. I overheard my mom tell him that if medicine doesn't work out for him, he could have a future in the ladies' shoe business.

Thanks, Mom and Dad. I love you!

Shabbat Shalom.

Back at the French Cleaners

It was time for another trip to the French Cleaners in Berkeley to pick up her dry cleaning.

Mrs. Kim pushed the button and the long circular rack started moving before Pearl even had a chance to close the front door.

"Pearl. Rabbi Pearl. Look at you, you are so pregnant. You look so beautiful. How are you feeling?"

"I've felt better since the morning sickness stopped," Pearl replied.

"Morning sickness is good. It means no miscarriage," said Mrs. Kim as she closed her eyes and crossed herself.

"Rabbi, I just said a little prayer for you. That's okay, right?"

"I accept all prayers, Mrs. Kim. Thank you very much."

"Good. Same God."

"But I'm bigger—it's slowing me down. And my ribs feel kind of stretched."

"Yes, I remember. But you do look beautiful. I looked beautiful just like you when I was pregnant with my daughter. Not so beautiful with my son, but that's another story. Let me see ..."

As always, she went through each of the hangers. "Yes, Rabbi Pearl. Two black maternity pants. Two black maternity skirts. One black pants maternity suit. Three white maternity blouses.

"One light blue maternity blouse—good for you, Rabbi Pearl! But even when you are pregnant, they make you dress like this, black clothes every day?"

Pearl laughed. She loved this lady. "You think I should wear a maternity dress at the synagogue?"

"Of course! But not black."

"You don't think I should dress like a undertaker anymore?"

"Well, maybe you would be a very pretty lady undertaker. You would bring in a lot of business. I have a friend from high school, he is an undertaker, makes a lot of money. He is very rich. He tells me there is a lot of money in the undertaking business."

"More than in the dry cleaning business?"

Mrs. Kim laughed her long and unique laugh. "I think so. Also, the customers, they cannot come back and complain, right?"

Now it was Pearl's chance to laugh.

She paid and then lugged the giant bundle of plastic-wrapped black and white (and a little light blue) maternity clothing out to her car.

She promised herself, *One of these days I'm going to wear a red dress to work.*

Turn to Page ...

Pearl sat on the bima of the Lakeshore Temple along with the other clergy, the congregation president, several board officers, and several honored members of the temple. Unlike the others, Rabbi Pearl Ross-Levy was nine months pregnant. Although she was officially on maternity leave, she'd asked Craig if she could attend the service and participate, maybe just a little.

She felt great, she told him. "What am I *supposed* to do on Erev Rosh Hashanah? Sit at home and watch *The Simpsons?* Maybe Krusty the Clown will be leading the service." He couldn't deny her request.

Wearing a somewhat larger than usual white High Holiday clerical gown, Pearl stood and stepped to the podium for a special reading. How special, she was soon to find out.

She smiled, looked at the very large congregation in front of her, and spoke clearly into the microphone.

"We all rise, and turn to page one ... *oh, shit!*"

Three things happened simultaneously:

First, her water broke with what she could only describe as a *whoosh*, the amniotic fluid running down her legs and onto the floor around her feet, creating a small puddle.

Second, there was a collective gasp from the people sitting behind her who'd seen what just happened.

And third, the phrase, *We all rise, and turn to page one-oh-shit* became an instant legend.

Pearl began to observe the world in slow motion as she held onto the podium. She managed to see Jack jump over two rows of pews and then vault onto the bima. Several of the people behind her were now at her side. She realized that Craig and Shelley were gently holding her arms and guiding her away from the podium. Out of the corner of her eye, she saw a woman running up the aisle toward her, yelling into a cell phone. That would her OB/GYN, Dr. Liat Morgenstern, a temple congregant.

Jack helped her walk, half carrying her, backstage. Liat was now with them, still speaking urgently into her cell phone in a manner that was both calm and mildly frantic.

Then Pearl was sitting in a chair and felt a contraction begin.

"I'm okay," she said to no one in particular as she breathed in and out slowly.

"I'm sure you are," Jack replied. "It's the rest of us who are freaking out."

Dr. Morgenstern said, "The ambulance is on its way. We'll have you in Labor and Delivery in ten minutes. Please try not to give birth until then," she said with a tight smile.

"I'll do my best ... *Oy!*" Another contraction. She saw Duke Sniderman trot by with a roll of paper towels.

She could hear Craig speaking to the congregation.

"Thank you all for staying in your seats. To put it another way, *please stay in your seats!*"

The congregation laughed. Craig was good.

"Here's the story," he continued. "Rabbi Ross-Levy, her doctor, and her husband will be off to the hospital very shortly. She's doing fine. She's just into 'sharing,' and wanted you all to have as much fun as she is."

More laughter.

"What I'm thinking is that those of you who weren't able to be in Woodstock for the big concert will now have something to tell your grandchildren."

A few minutes later Pearl watched two attendants wheel in a gurney. They then transferred her from her chair to the gurney, strapped her in, and out they all went through the back door to a waiting ambulance, whose lights were flashing. Then she and the gurney were slid into the back of the vehicle. Both Liat and Jack got in as well, and they were off. The siren was muffled inside the ambulance, but she could hear it.

She looked at Jack. "Sorry to be such a Drama Queen."

He grasped her hand tightly. *"We all rise, and turn to page one-oh-shit'* indeed!"

When asked about it later—as she was, many, many times, she'd simply smile and say, "If you ever wondered if God has a sense of humor, I'm living proof!"

Epilogue

Dr. Liat Morgenstern breathed easier once her patient, Rabbi Pearl Ross-Levy, was in the hospital—gowned, prepped, and hooked up to the appropriate monitoring devices.

Duke Sniderman had dispatched Esther and Rodrigo, the security guard, to Kaiser Hospital, where Esther provided Duke with regular updates on the rabbi's condition. During the remainder of the service, Duke stayed backstage with his cell phone in his hand, relaying these messages to Rabbi Craig Cohen on the bima.

The first update was the most fun, with Craig doing his best TV announcer impersonation.

> *We interrupt this Erev Rosh Hashanah service to bring you this breaking news. Rabbi Ross-Levy has been admitted to Kaiser Labor and Delivery, where she is resting comfortably. We will update you every thirty minutes or as additional details come in from our reporter on the scene. We now return to our regularly scheduled service. Please rise and turn to page ...*

Jack was in the Labor Room with Pearl, ostensibly assisting her in breathing and counting through her contractions, which he timed and entered on a chart he'd created.

Shayna, David, Ruth, and Esther sat together in a nearby waiting area.

After the service ended, Duke and Samantha showed up at the hospital.

Two hours later, Shayna and David decided to go home after being informed by Dr. Morgenstern that the labor might take hours. They decided they would become grandparents whether they sat in the waiting room or not.

Future-Aunts Ruth and Samantha soon left as well for the same reason.

Just after two o'clock on Rosh Hashanah morning, all the major players became either parents, grandparents, or aunts, as a new baby boy announced his arrival with a healthy cry. Altogether, Pearl was in labor for six hours. Not too short, not too long, her doctor informed her. Jack asked a nurse to convey the news to any of their people who might still be in the waiting area.

Esther Robinson was the only one from the Ross-Levy party still present. At midnight she'd gone home to check on her aunt and then returned to the hospital waiting area where she was now dozing in a chair. The nurse gently woke her and gave her the news. As he'd instructed her to do, Esther called Duke at home, waking him, and gave *him* the news. Then she drove home and went to bed.

As *he'd* been instructed to do, Duke called Rabbi Cohen and then Cantor and Mrs. Sanders, waking each with the news. They thanked Duke and then everyone went back to sleep.

As Pearl and the baby rested, Jack phoned his in-laws and his sisters-in-law, as he'd been instructed, waking them all. Everyone was excited for ten minutes and then went back to sleep.

Jack dozed on and off in a chair in Pearl's room. At four o'clock he called his own parents in Florida where it was now seven in the morning. They were awake.

When his mother answered the phone, he asked, "Hello, is this Grandma?"

Shayna Levy gave a little scream, yelled, "Mort, pick up extension!"

Jack gave them the good news. All was well with the baby, whose name would be announced at the bris. His parents promised they would call Josh with the news, and then the airlines to make reservations. Jack told them that since it was four in the morning in California, he was going back to sleep. He did not mention he was sleeping in a chair.

The bris took place on the eighth day of their son's life.

Pearl had called Rebecca Feldenstein, the rebbetzin, who had put in a call to the same mohel who'd circumcised her own four sons.

Colleagues from the temple and the university as well as close friends and neighbors gathered at the home of Shayna and David Ross in Berkeley for the bris. About sixty people in all were present, including Duke and Esther and Mr. and Mrs. Solomon P. Solomon.

Mary Fresa, who'd flown in from Chicago for the special occasion, told Pearl in a private moment, "I'll just assume this isn't 'the extra one' you said you'd have for me."

Pearl had also invited Millie Babson. She wasn't sure why, but it felt right. The Chin family, including Zinnia, was there as well.

Craig and Shelley participated, of course, and the mohel performed the covenantal ritual perfectly, as he'd done thousands of times.

"Trust me. You can trust him," Rebecca Feldenstein had said to Pearl.

Zinnia Chin was one of the few females standing close enough to observe the actual procedure.

"Cool," she said to no one in particular. The Drs. Chin, standing nearby, heard her comment. Once again, they just looked at each other, shook their heads, and smiled.

As Pearl nursed her son, whom she and Jack had named Zachary Seth Levy, the guests started to eat. And drink. And talk. Loudly. And have a good time at what is considered one of the happiest of all simchas.

Zak Levy, after being fed, slept comfortably in his mother's arms.

You look just like your father, Pearl thought.

Four weeks later, Lakeshore Temple congregants received a postcard:

> *Rabbi Pearl Ross-Levy and her husband, Jack, are aware that many of you were present to witness the beginning of the rabbi's labor. If you would like to witness the fruit of that labor, please join us at Shabbat Services on Friday, October 15, or Saturday, October 16, where you'll be able to meet Zachary Seth Levy, born on Rosh Hashanah Day, September 16, 2004, in his first temple appearances. NO GIFTS PLEASE!! If you would like to make a donation in Zachary's name to the Alameda County Community Food Bank, please do so, and we thank you!*

Hundreds of people showed up. Craig noted in his remarks that other than on those occasions when High Holiday services fell on the Sabbath, he'd never seen so many congregants attend Shabbat services.

"You need to have more babies, Rabbi."

"Not for a while," she said as she cradled Zak in her arms. "I have my hands full right now."

October 7, 2005

On Friday night the rabbi and her husband made love, and she conceived.

ACKNOWLEDGMENTS

To Eileen Ostrow Feldman (a.k.a. "Opie"), our wonderful copy editor and friend, we extend our heartfelt thanks for following the life of our rabbi from conception through delivery, catching every misplaced comma along the way.

Rabbi Yoni Regev was the first member of the clergy to review and comment on the manuscript. Noted Catholic writer and friend Alice Camille gave us an early go-ahead, and fellow congregants Lynn Simon, Myra Feiger, Sue Bachman, Trish Elliott, and Kathy Knoll encouraged us and made helpful comments.

Fred Isaac provided valuable suggestions, support, and wisdom over slices of pizza.

Gary M. Sirbu patiently explained the differences between murder, manslaughter, first degree, second degree, voluntary, and involuntary. (I'm glad he's the attorney and not I!)

Friends from many walks of life reviewed the work-in-progress including Toni Littlestone, Will Adams, and (Robert's kindergarten girlfriend) Betty Gleason. Cousin Ed Adler, who loved Millie Babson, gave us an L.A. thumbs-up. Our spouses lived through more than two years of weekly meetings and provided stability and demonstrated endless tolerance.

Mahalo to James and Pamela Au, who gave us our beautiful cover photography and author photos. Jim is a fellow Boglehead and a pretty good guitarist as well!

We know of no greater sources of inspiration than Rabbi Jacqueline Mates-Muchin and Cantor Ilene Keys of Temple Sinai in Oakland, California. Thanks so much to you, and anyone we might have inadvertently omitted.

RS, CdC

ROBERT SCHOEN is the author of the award-winning book, *What I Wish My Christian Friends Knew About Judaism*. He is a musician and has served as Composer-in-Residence at Temple Sinai in Oakland, California. Schoen's book *On God's Radar* chronicles his 2018 coast-to-coast walk in photos, daily blog entries, and essays. He lives in Oakland with his wife, Sharon.

CATHERINE DECUIR is a cantorial soloist, jazz vocalist, and fiction writer whose work has appeared in dozens of publications including *Seventeen* and *The Bellingham Review*. She is currently working on a historical novel based on the lives of her Creole ancestors. She and her husband live in Albany, California.